Montana – wh
and lov

When the fun loving town of Rumor has a special
festival, three sassy waitresses discover the truth
behind the local legend: If you meet a man under
the crazy moon, you're sure to be a bride soon!

MONTANA GROOMS

One Baby To Go, Please by Laurie Paige

'It is always a joy to savour the consistent
excellence of this outstanding author.'
—*Romantic Times*

Marriage on the Menu by Linda Turner

'Ms Turner develops a luscious romance with great
sensitivity, capturing all the wonder of the first
moments of love.'
—*Romantic Times*

Daddy Takes the Cake by Allison Leigh

'Ms Leigh gracefully moves her richly-textured
characters through a plethora of emotions.'
—*Romantic Times*

LAURIE PAIGE

Laurie has been a NASA engineer, a past president of the Romance Writers of America, a mother and a grandmother. She was twice a RITA® Award finalist for Best Traditional Romance and has won awards from *Romantic Times* for Best Silhouette Special Edition and Best Silhouette. Recently resettled in Northern California, Laurie is looking forward to whatever experiences her next novel will send her on.

LINDA TURNER

Linda began reading romances in high school and began writing them one night when she had nothing else to read. She's been writing ever since. Single and living in Texas, she travels every chance she gets, scouting locations for her books.

ALLISON LEIGH

Allison has been a RITA® Award finalist. But the true highlights of her days as a writer are when she receives word from a reader that they laughed, cried or lost a night of sleep while reading one of her books. Born in Southern California, Allison has lived in several different cities in four different states. She currently makes her home in Arizona with her family.

Montana Grooms

LAURIE PAIGE

LINDA TURNER

ALLISON LEIGH

SILHOUETTE®

First published in Great Britain 2004
Silhouette Books, Eton House, 18-24 Paradise Road,
Richmond, Surrey TW9 1SR

MONTANA GROOMS © Harlequin Books S.A. 2002
(Previously titled Montana Mavericks: Under Western Skies)

The publisher acknowledges the copyright holders of the individual works as follows:

One Baby To Go, Please © Harlequin Books S.A. 2002
Marriage on the Menu © Harlequin Books S.A. 2002
Daddy Takes the Cake © Harlequin Books S.A. 2002

Special thanks and acknowledgement are given to Laurie Paige, Linda Turner and Allison Leigh for their contributions to the Montana Mavericks series.

ISBN 0 373 60158 1

009-0604

Printed and bound in Spain
by Litografia Rosés S.A., Barcelona

CONTENTS

ONE BABY TO GO, PLEASE
Laurie Paige

To Logan, the third, but no less loved.
Welcome!

Chapter 1

Jordan Rush was looking for a pregnant woman. Not just any pregnant woman, of course, but the one who carried his child. Illegally.

Following this quest, he turned left off Highway 212 rather than continuing down the road to Whitehorn. The paved country road to the town of Rumor was relatively straight. For a Montana road in the foothills abutting the Beartooth Mountains, that fact was gratifying.

The Beartooth pass to Wyoming was one of the most treacherous highways he'd ever traveled. Tourists coming up from Yellowstone were still talking about it upon arriving in Billings, where his home was located, about an hour east of there.

He gave a grunt of amusement that wasn't in the least funny. He was on a damned treacherous course right now and had no idea where it might end. In court, probably.

Spotting a doe and two fawns grazing in the hilly pasture of a local ranch, he concentrated on the road. A friend of his had rolled a brand-new SUV when a deer had jumped out in front of him. The vehicle had been totaled. Fortunately, his friend had escaped with minor injuries.

One thing Jordan didn't need at the present was more accidents in his life, not that this desire seemed to make much difference to the Fates who controlled people's destiny and laughed at the results.

He rounded the sweeping curve of a hill and saw the town of Rumor nestled in a verdant little valley. With a natural water source, aptly called Cave Springs, tumbling out of a cavern under a limestone cliff, the town was a prosperous community serving ranchers, hunting, fishing and camping enthusiasts and the white-knuckled tourists who braved the winding mountain roads.

A shudder of…dread? fear? apprehension?…ran over him. Anger buried the undefined emotion. He gripped the steering wheel and drove down Main Street, his eyes moving restlessly from store to store and person to person.

A pregnant woman should be easier to spot than the proverbial needle in a haystack. He hoped.

As soon as he got through the three blocks that made up the heart of the town, he signaled a left turn onto Cave Springs Road. A mile farther along, he swung right into a driveway and parked under the carport of a modern cabin with a rustic look.

The rusticity was deceiving. The cabin was less than a year old and belonged to Billings Forestry Products, the company he had founded and nurtured into the largest forestry operation in Montana. The company was a sponsor of the Crazy Moon Festival, a month-long celebration of the lunar eclipse coming up at the end of the summer, designed by the town council to lure in tourist dollars.

The festival suited his real purpose for being there—to find the woman who had been impregnated with his sperm, which the fertility clinic was supposed to have destroyed.

He'd given direct orders to that effect three months ago—as soon as he remembered that little detail—only to find the technician had accidentally transposed two numbers and used his semen instead of that of a sperm donor the previous month.

So now some woman was four months pregnant, carrying *his* child by mistake. The damn clinic was supposed to have been foolproof about things like that; otherwise, he and Nicole wouldn't have gone there.

Stopping on the porch that wrapped around three sides of the cabin, he gripped the support post until the pain of overbearing grief passed. After a moment, he sat on the top step and stared at the mountains with their rows of sharp white jags, exactly like huge teeth protruding from the earth, rising to the west of them.

Nicole. His wife of eight years. Lighthearted and fun-loving. An imp who had loved to tease him about being serious and goal-driven. Not beautiful exactly, but pretty and vivacious and sexy and loving...until the obsession to have a child overtook their lives.

Making love became a matter of ovulation dates and thermometers, of ''fertile days'' and finally of desperation and the fertility clinic and the attempt at in vitro fertilization. He'd sometimes found himself resenting the demand for a child at any cost.

It had been hopeless from the first. The Fates had laughed at their efforts for his wife had never conceived. Instead she died on the first day of May, exactly one year and one month ago, of ovarian cancer.

Nicole, the precious gift in his life. Gone.

Taking a ragged breath, he waited out the grief, knowing it would pass, a cold, cruel wind flowing over the barren plains of his soul. The Bard had been wrong—it wasn't better to have loved, not if a man had to face this kind of bitter loss.

Leaping to his feet, he carried his luggage inside, glad that there were no memories associated with the cabin. After checking the messages in the office next to the master bedroom, he unpacked and tried to plan his next move.

The doctor had let it slip that the woman lived in this tiny town, but had declared the law forbade disclosing the name. It had cost a bundle using the services of a private detective, but the man hadn't been able to pry or bribe the information out of anyone at the clinic.

So here he was, determined to find out on his own just who the woman was. Laughter, harsh and unbidden, welled up in him. How the hell did one find a pregnant woman and ask her how she got that way?

Marisa Stewart fanned herself with the order book. "Is it hot in here or is it just me?" she demanded.

Her friend and boss, Callie Griffin, closed the drawer of the cash register and grinned at her. "It's both, it *is* hot in here *and* you're pregnant."

"Don't remind me," Marisa said, fluffing the

bangs off her forehead. "That had to be a stupid move on my part."

Callie was at once sympathetic. "There's no chance that you'll see the father again?"

Marisa's guilt added to the bloom on her cheeks, apparently a side effect of the pregnancy as was the swollen ankles and enlarged breasts. "Not a chance," she said firmly and mentally squirmed at the lie.

Well, not exactly a lie. There absolutely, positively wasn't a chance that she and the father would get together. In fact, they never had. The baby came from the sperm bank of a fertility clinic in Billings.

For some screwy reason, which she couldn't figure out now, that admission had seemed worse to her than to let her friends think she'd had a weekend fling with a cowboy from the rodeo. At least that had sounded wildly romantic, much more so than the truth.

Callie and Libby, her two best friends, were very sympathetic over her plight and angry with the louse who'd used her and left.

Naturally she'd explained that she'd expected nothing from him and that she wanted the child very much.

Which was certainly true.

Sometimes she did wonder at her mental processes, though. What business did a single woman, nearing thirty, with a one-hundred-and-sixty-acre homestead inherited from her parents and a job as a waitress in the Calico Diner for income, have getting pregnant and thinking she could raise a child alone?

A mere three years ago, she had assumed she would live the American dream of marrying and having a family the usual way. Her fiancé had run off with the manicurist from the Getaway Salon a month before the wedding. A few months ago her mother had died from cancer.

For some odd reason, those events had left her feeling that life owed her something, that she should get what she wanted for a change. She'd wanted a baby.

Now she was having one…and having second thoughts about raising it alone.

The door to the diner—a gutted trailer made over into a diner with a sort of fifties chrome-and-tile decor—opened, letting in another gust of hot air.

Marisa muttered an expletive.

Callie smiled, looking as weary as Marisa felt. It was Saturday night, their busiest time, and already after nine. The diner closed at ten, thank goodness, and had nearly cleared out.

"I'll get him," her boss volunteered. "Why don't you take off? You came in an hour early today."

"No way. He looks like a city dude, which is to say a big tipper. I'll wait on him."

Grabbing a menu and glass of water, she was still smiling drolly when she approached him.

The stranger hooked an arm over the chair back and watched her approach his table. His hair was black. His eyes were blue. He wore boots, faded jeans, a plaid, long-sleeved shirt rolled up on his arms and a black Stetson.

Oh, my, Pierce Brosnan in the role of mountain man. Rugged. Fiercely independent. Handsome as sin, her mother would have said.

Marisa hoped she didn't do something stupid, like faint or drool. Suppressing a rambunctious grin, she handed him the menu. "Good evening. Sorry, but we're out of the special. The chopped steak with mushrooms, onions and gravy is to die for. So is the chicken-fried steak."

"Got any chicken-fried chicken?" he asked.

She wished she had a dime for every time she'd heard that line. "Yep. Comes with country gravy, mashed potatoes and green beans. Homemade buttermilk biscuits or cornbread muffins, both Libby Adler specials made for the diner."

She didn't bother to explain the last phrase to the obviously jaded city dude. Libby supplied the diner with all its breads, pies, cakes and pastries. She was a widow and had the cutest twins, a boy and a girl.

Marisa held her pen over the order pad and waited for the stranger to make up his mind. He looked vaguely familiar, like a face seen in a magazine or something. Hey, maybe he was a celebrity.

Glancing at him, she saw he was studying her instead of the menu. Her T-shirt was a large size and loose, but there was no denying she was pregnant. Her rounded belly stuck out against the soft cotton like a soccer ball tucked into her slacks. She smiled automatically when their eyes met.

He didn't return the smile, but continued to stare at her as if he'd never seen a woman before.

"Uh, your order?" she prodded.

He didn't take his eyes off her as he ordered. "The chopped steak. Baked potato. Salad with ranch dressing on the side. Coffee. Black."

After thanking him and walking away with the menu, she was aware of the intensity of his gaze, focused like a laser beam right between her shoulder blades.

"I think you've made a conquest," Callie murmured as Marisa handed the order slip through the kitchen pass-through.

"Right. Bowled him over with my country girl cheeks and lusciously rounded figure. Bet he's never had a waitress who looked as if she'd swallowed a cantaloupe and was about to swoon wait on him before."

She and Callie smothered laughter at her deadpan quip. Marisa could deliver the most ridiculous news with an absolutely poker face. It confused strangers and delighted her friends. Grinning, she poured the cup of coffee and, glancing at the clock, turned off the coffeemaker. Nearly time to go home.

And not a moment too soon, she mused as she delivered the coffee. Her back hurt, her feet protested each time she took a step and she wondered if she had grease on her nose as the handsome stranger continued to watch her as if unable to tear his eyes away.

Maybe he'd never seen a pregnant woman before? Maybe somebody had recently told him the facts of life and he was fascinated with the evidence of conception before him?

While the food was being prepared, she handled the cash register as the last of the diners departed, then cleaned off the used tables and set them with napkins and place mats for breakfast. That left one lone man in the cozy diner.

Now he was staring out the window at the two couples who'd just left. Both women were pregnant, she realized.

Laughter bubbled up. She choked it back. Seeing three pregnant females in the diner at the same time must have given him a jolt. She thought of telling him it was something in the water and he should be careful, but not everyone appreciated her brand of humor.

After she served the meal to him and refilled the coffee cup, she was busy with clean-up chores. She did like the chrome to sparkle and the glasses to be stacked just so. At ten, the janitors would come in and clean the floors and windows and rest rooms, then they would be ready for another day.

"Go home," Callie ordered.

She glanced over her shoulder at the customer. He rose, looked at the check she'd left earlier, dropped some money on the table and strode out as if he had a hot date. She yawned and nodded to her boss.

While she didn't have to work at the diner on Sunday, the cattle had to be tended and the fences. She smiled ruefully. There truly was no rest for the weary, or the wicked, as the case may be.

Yawning again, she headed out to the pickup that was almost as old as she was. Her father had been so proud when he brought it home. It had been the family's first and only brand-new vehicle.

The mechanic at the service station kept it going for her, and she couldn't bear to part with the ancient truck. Okay, call her sentimental. She admitted it.

Headlights came on behind her. While there were lots of pickups, RVs and cars at the bar on Main

Street, her pickup and the SUV behind her were the only two moving vehicles on the street. For a second she had an eerie sensation that she and the other driver were on their way to some strange destiny that involved only the two of them.

Get real, she chided her imagination.

However as she proceeded, tingles began to creep along her nape. Was the guy following her? They were out of town now, and he was still behind her. Assuming it was a he.

It could be a family going home after...what? The couples from the diner were long gone by now. She hadn't seen anyone leaving the nearby restaurant or bar. No one had been in the public parking lot when she'd left.

If the car stayed behind her when she turned onto her road, she wouldn't go home, but would suddenly do a U-turn at a wide place and head back to town and the sheriff's office.

But what if he blocked her way by pulling across the road? What would she do then?

Heart beating like a piston, she turned onto Two Pines Road. Her house was less than a mile away, a haven so close, yet so far. Gripping the steering wheel, she prepared for the sudden turnaround.

The headlights came around the curve of the main road...the driver was slowing down...he should be turning now.... The headlights swept on by her road, heading north toward Highway 212.

The relief was so great she felt it as a tidal wave through her whole body. A tourist, she realized. On his way to Billings and not sure of the roads.

He, or she, shouldn't be traveling in the hills after dark. Over a hundred deaths from run-ins with deer in the western states had occurred during the past year, the local newspaper had reported recently. Stupid, really stupid.

Feeling righteously indignant, she stepped on the gas and made a dash for home and safety, all the while reprimanding her imagination for putting ridiculous fears into her mind.

Jordan added logs to the fire and sat in the big leather chair, watching the flames devour the wood. To say his mind was in a whirl was putting it lightly.

Three pregnant women in the diner!

He couldn't believe his luck when he first went in and saw the waitress. About five-five, with a curvy figure, curly hair of a deep auburn with blond streaks and smoky green eyes that hinted at interesting thoughts which she was keeping strictly to herself, she'd been a knockout.

She'd also been in the midstages of pregnancy…and she hadn't been wearing a wedding ring.

His thinking processes stalled for a second as he considered something he hadn't previously acknowledged. For the first time in more than a year, his body had reacted to the presence of a beautiful woman.

It was an added complication to an already unbelievable situation. It had shocked him when his libido had reacted immediately upon her coming to the table to take his order. He'd hardly been able to think at all after that.

Frowning, he tried to figure it out, then gave up. He had no time for foolishness. He was here on a mission.

Three pregnant women in Rumor, all at about the right stage of development. Jordan hadn't expected to find them gathered in one place on his first night in town.

However, given that it was the weekend and considering the size of the town with its one main street and four or five side streets forming the entire community, plus the fact that there were only two restaurants in the area, he shouldn't have been surprised.

The Fates were probably laughing their heads off at that clever little ruse. He couldn't help feeling there was some trick being played out, one that he didn't quite get.

Picking up his cell phone, he dialed a number. It was answered almost at once. "Ralph? Jordan Rush. I have a couple of license numbers I need you to check."

"You want names, addresses, arrest records, what?" the private detective asked.

"Names and addresses. I saw all three pregnant women tonight. I'm going to see what I can find out."

"You're in Rumor?"

"Yes. Call me on the cell phone. The phone company is supposed to have the lines to the cabin working tomorrow. I think I gave you the numbers."

"You did. Anything else?"

"No. Thanks for your help."

Ralph chuckled. "How do you find out which one was artificially inseminated?"

Jordan spoke with heavy irony. "With great tact and diplomacy."

"I'll get back to you in the morning as soon as the car tag office opens."

"Thanks."

Jordan stared into the fire after he clicked off the phone, his mind curiously blank. After a while he realized he was studying the colors in the flames—

several shades of gold and red. Like a certain female's hair.

He shook his head as if to dispel the image but it refused to budge. He'd liked the way she cleaned and polished the tables and counters in the diner, as if she wanted to do the best job possible. Her name was Marisa according to the name tag on her T-shirt.

Pregnant. No ring. No man had appeared to see her safely home. She'd turned off on Two Pines Road north of town. He'd been afraid to follow her farther. She might have noticed and been frightened, maybe called the cops.

Now that would have been interesting—him explaining why he followed a pregnant woman to her house because he wondered if she might be carrying his child. Adding another log to the fire, he stayed up long past midnight, trying to think of ways to outwit a very uncertain future.

Chapter 2

Marisa pushed the hair off her forehead and swiped at the perspiration with her sleeve. The temperature was in the high eighties. Returning to her task, she attacked a thistle growing on her mother's grave and yanked it out by the roots. After finishing the chore, she sat on a stone bench and looked over the small country cemetery.

The one-room church had closed years ago as families moved away from ranches that no longer provided a living. The land had reverted to her family who had originally donated the plot for the church and grounds. Thus she mowed and weeded the graveyard herself.

Fanning herself with an old straw cowboy hat, she idly considered the past. Her great-grandparents had buried five children here. She counted the five little gravestones set neatly in a row. Her grandparents had buried three. Her mother and father had buried a son, Josh, killed when he ran into the road in front of a logging truck when he was three. Marisa had been a baby at the time.

A sigh worked its way up from her soul. She wanted so much for her child. A good education, for one thing. She already had money in a fund for that. Most importantly, she wanted him or her to have a full, satisfying life, filled with adventure, a great love and contentment. And children.

She loved the idea of grandchildren and wanted several. At that, she laughed out loud. "One thing at a time," she murmured, laying a hand on her tummy.

Her eyes widened. Pressing harder, she felt the tiny life kick against her palm. She couldn't help but laugh again as she poked along her side. The baby refused to respond a second time, though.

Last night she'd been tired, perhaps a bit discouraged. This morning, all seemed bright and cheerful, and she felt capable of moving mountains. Speaking of which, she had other chores on the ranch to do. Rising briskly, she set the hat on her head and strode toward the truck, then stopped.

An SUV was parked beside the old pickup under the shade of an oak tree near the closed church building. A man stood beside the vehicle. He was watching her.

As she hesitated, he took off his sunglasses and smiled in a friendly fashion. She recognized him as the man from the diner the previous night. That fact didn't relieve her wariness. However she was almost sure she'd seen him before last night.

"Hi," he called. "I'm sort of lost, I think." He looked down the road as if seeking a landmark to guide him.

Marisa crossed the patch of lawn which was rapidly turning brown in the heat and stopped by the gate, keeping the fence between her and the stranger.

"I'm Jordan Rush," he said.

The name registered with her. Billings Forestry Products was the company he'd founded, becoming a millionaire while still in his twenties. He was now thirty-eight and a widower. His wife had died a year or so ago, she recalled, of cancer, like her mother.

"I'm looking for a track of state land we're supposed to start logging. Section 19N-104W," he continued.

"It's another mile down the road. Turn right onto a dirt track. There should be a sign where the section starts. Are you going to clear-cut?"

The answer was important to her. Clear-cutting resulted in soil runoff that silted up the creeks. The mud would be carried into the stream that provided water for her cattle.

"No, thin cutting. We'll use a helicopter to get the big timber out." He smiled at her, his teeth flashing white and even in the hot sun.

Her heart actually fluttered. "Good," was all she said and waited for him to leave. He came over and opened the gate.

Marisa had to step back when he entered. She carefully moved to the side, keeping a good ten feet between them.

"These your folks?" He stopped by the stone bench and studied the names on the stones.

"Yes."

"Stewart? Is that your name? Marisa Stewart?"

"Yes."

"I noticed your name tag last night," he said. "Don't be afraid. I won't hurt you."

Relaxing, she gave him one of her deadpan stares. "That's what all serial killers say to their victims."

To her surprise, he laughed. "I haven't started on that career yet. It's all I can do to keep up with my present one."

"As owner of Billings Forestry Products?"

"Yes. Don't you believe I'm Jordan Rush? Here, I'll show you my driver's license."

"That's not necessary. I saw your picture in the paper Thursday. The article said you were sponsoring several of the special events at the festival."

"Right. We do a lot of business around here." He gestured toward the mountains and the trees that covered them. "It seemed like a good idea to get to know the town. Several of my loggers live in this area."

"You have a place on Cave Springs Road."

He nodded. "It's closer to the logging operations. It's also cooler here during the summer than in Billings. At least, I thought it was."

"This heat is unusual. By the time the eclipse happens, we'll probably have several people go mad and shoot up the place. The city council might be sorry for thinking up the Crazy Moon Festival."

"Maybe."

She couldn't tell if that was agreement or not. He opened the gate, stepped through and held it for her. She dug the keys out of her pocket and headed for the truck. He made sure the gate was securely closed before following. She liked this evidence of respect for those buried here.

His SUV was new and shiny, she noted as they approached the parking area. Her truck, coated with dust, looked as if it had hit the road once too often.

The vehicles formed a solid contrast between her lifestyle and his.

When he held the door of the old pickup open for her, she smiled her thanks, her heart doing another shiver as he stared at her as if unable to tear his gaze away. She started the truck. He closed the door and stepped aside.

With a wave, she drove off, back to her house. She was aware that he was still in the old churchyard when she pulled into her driveway. He seemed…interested, for lack of a better word…in her.

Glancing at her rounded abdomen, she wondered why.

"Marisa, are you sure you feel up to this?" Callie asked, looking her friend over.

"I'm fine. Quit worrying. Besides, when word gets out that Libby is supplying the booth, we'll be sold out long before noon."

Libby Adler laughed. "Maybe I'd better go home and get to baking. Oops, I promised the twins we'd go to the park if they were very good this morning while I got everything ready for the booth." She glanced out the window. "Did you ever see so much activity? Everyone is really bustling."

The Crazy Moon Festival was officially open.

The dedication had been given by the mayor Sunday morning. Booths were set up on three sides of the block surrounding the city park and there were lots of things to see.

Marisa had already noticed that Billings Forestry Products had a booth demonstrating all the items derived from wood that it made. It was only three booths down from the diner's location. "I'd better get over there."

Callie and Libby waved goodbye. Marisa strode down the street, pulling a little red wagon behind her. On it was a coffee urn and several more boxes of muffins and goodies.

Once on site, she covered the four tiny tables with red-checked oilcloths and tacked them in place, giving the Calico Diner booth the air of a French sidewalk café. She would be serving gourmet coffee and pastries until she ran out, then she'd return to the diner, hopefully in time for the noon rush.

Callie's brother, Daniel, co-owner of the diner, was going to help during lunch, too. He was the local vet and a peach of a guy. Marisa wondered why she hadn't fallen for him long ago.

She grinned as she pulled the wagon nearer to the counter. Close to her age, her best friend's big brother had been a classmate. Daniel was simply too familiar, more like her own brother than a pos-

sible husband. But he'd grown up into a very nice
person and she did love him….

"Here, let me do that," a masculine voice interrupted. Jordan Rush lifted the heavy coffee urn and
peered at the full counter space in the booth.
"Where do you want it?"

"On the wagon." She pointed to the spot where
it had been sitting.

He replaced it, then straightened and looked her
over the way Mrs. Stinson in the sixth grade used
to when she suspected a student was cheating.
"You shouldn't be lifting heavy things."

"I wasn't," Marisa felt compelled to mention.

His eyes met hers. They grinned, then laughed.

"Sorry," he said. "I'm not used to…"

Words obviously failed him as he gestured
vaguely toward her and her rounded tummy. "Pregnant women?" she asked politely.

"Uh, yeah. Are you supposed to be on your feet
so much? You may be working too hard."

At this declaration, Marisa's mouth actually
dropped open. She closed it before he noticed.
Never had a man, outside of family, seemed so worried about her.

Her heart fluttered so hard she had to put a hand
to her breast to calm it. "Thank you for your concern. Sit down and I'll treat you to one of Libby's
famous wild walnut and blueberry muffins."

"Libby?" He took a seat at a table, his muscular frame looking too big for the wrought-iron chair.

"One of my best friends, the other being Callie who owns the diner." She looked a question at him. "You saw Callie Saturday night when you stopped in. She was doing the cooking."

"I remember." He looked pensive.

A ping echoed through Marisa. Her friend was twenty-five, a natural blonde, tall and long-legged, the kind of woman that men fell for. Not that she was jealous or anything.

Forcing those thoughts aside, she poured him a cup of coffee and heated the muffin in the microwave oven with a generous portion of butter. After seeing that he had a fork and napkin, she stood in the booth and fanned herself with an old-fashioned cardboard fan mounted on a stick, given out by the Whitehorn Funeral Home.

Nine o'clock and the heat was already oppressive.

A group of tourists stopped and after much debating, ordered several pastries and bottles of chocolate milk. By the time they left, Jordan had finished the muffin.

"That was the best thing I've ever eaten. Who did you say made it?"

"Libby Adler."

"Does she have a shop here?"

"No. She does her baking from home, so she can care for her twins, a boy and a girl," Marisa added.

"She should open a bakery."

"You could go into business with her," Marisa said in a perfectly serious tone to match his. "Maybe you'd find a new use for wood products, like adding fiber to pastries to make them healthier."

He studied her for a moment while she maintained an angelic expression. He chuckled. "You're a laugh a minute."

Another group came up, a ranching family she knew. They chatted while placing their order.

"I just heard the news about you at church yesterday, Marisa. Beatrice Stinson said two of the girls from the Getaway Salon were discussing it at the library. Until Harriet Martel came over and told them to be quiet," the wife said, grinning. When Ms. Martel, the town librarian, spoke, others listened. "When is your baby due?"

"In November. The tenth."

Marisa saw Jordan Rush listening intently as she disclosed the information. He frowned, saw her watching him and glanced away.

A sinking feeling attacked her insides. A man like him would never be interested her anyway, even if she weren't four months pregnant. She mentally shrugged aside the idea even as a tiny hope sprang to life in her.

Really, she couldn't be seriously thinking…no, it was just too ridiculous, too insane…too…too stupid to be contemplated.

With that notion firmly disposed of, she concentrated on her job as a steady line of customers bought the delicious muffins and pastries. As she'd predicted, the food was sold out before noon.

Pulling the wagon with the empty urn, she started back to the diner. Three booths down, Jordan was demonstrating how a debarker machine removed the bark from trees. She paused while he explained the various products made from the bark. His knowledge and enthusiasm for his subject were contagious. He had quite a crowd of locals listening to every word as well as tourists.

Business at the diner was brisk when she arrived. Callie was trying to wait tables and handle the cash register. Daniel was in the kitchen. A high school girl was busing tables and handing out menus and glasses of water.

"Thank goodness you're here," Callie called out. "We need help. See if you can find Libby at the park. Tell her I'll baby-sit the twins for a week if she'll come in."

Marisa hurried to the playground in the park. She had to dodge around dozens of people who sat on the grass eating their lunches and chatting. She found Libby on a bench talking with another mother and explained the problem.

"I'll take the twins home with me this afternoon," she volunteered, "if you can stay during dinner."

"Will do," Libby said and called the twins to her.

"Aunt Marisa," shouted Bobby when he spotted her with his mom. "Look what I found." He held out an arrowhead made of black obsidian.

"That's a good one," Marisa praised the artifact.

Patty, his six-year-old twin, flung her arms around Marisa and pressed an ear to her tummy. "I'm listening to the baby," she told everyone within three city blocks who cared to listen. "He's gurgling."

Several friends in the vicinity chuckled as Marisa willed herself not to blush.

"Voices down," Libby reminded the children. "Can you entertain yourselves quietly while I help Aunt Callie at the diner?"

"Yes," the twins chorused and rushed ahead of the two women. "Can we have a milk shake when we get there?"

"If you're really good, you can have it on the way to Aunt Marisa's home," Libby told them.

Marisa looked up into a pair of deep blue eyes.

She realized Jordan had been watching the tableau with the children. Heat ran up her neck. He seemed to take in everything that happened around her. It was unnerving.

And exciting? some part of her coyly inquired.

Yes, that too, she had to admit. She suddenly wished he hadn't come to town...or that she hadn't gone to the fertility clinic.

No. That wasn't true. She already loved the child growing inside her. Not even for a handsome rogue like Jordan Rush would she give up her baby.

At two, when she went off duty, she and the twins piled into her pickup and merged with the traffic heading down Main Street. Everyone in Red Lodge, Whitehorn and the surrounding territory had apparently heard of the Crazy Moon Festival and wanted to be in on the first events of the celebration. It augured well for the entire month.

If the heat would only let up, she added, turning on the air-conditioning full blast.

"I get to ride Blaze," Patty said as they turned into the ranch drive.

"No, I do!" Bobby shouted.

"You both do," Marisa intervened. "Patty gets to hold the reins first, then you can," she said to Bobby.

As if the gentle old horse even needed guidance. The mare would walk up and down the road and around the house as long as the kids were on her, then stop by the hitching post when Marisa signaled her with a whistle.

"Let's ride bareback," Bobby said in as near a normal voice as he could muster. He wanted to be a cowboy and loved riding and having adventures. He could walk across the grass to the barn and come back with a fascinating tale of all he'd seen on the way.

"Okay," Patty said.

Marisa put the bareback pad on Blaze and let Patty lead the mare out of the barn. Both children mounted from an old tree stump that was handy.

The mare ambled along the lane with Bobby shouting for her to "Git-up!" every other breath. Patty, in front and holding the reins, was smiling happily.

Marisa's insides compressed into a ball of longing. How wonderful it was to have two kids like Bobby and Patty. Libby was so lucky.

Recalling Terrence Adler's death at an environmental demonstration that had turned violent, Marisa reassessed her opinion. Raising two kids alone wasn't easy, but Libby had done it. Her husband had died a month before the twins were born, leaving Libby to face the birth alone.

Just as she would be when her child was born.

Marisa inhaled slowly, carefully. Never had she

felt so vulnerable as she did at this moment. An image of blue eyes watching her every move came to her.

What was it about Jordan Rush that caused this sudden uncertainty to plague her?

Chapter 3

"Okay, time for a rest," Marisa told the twins after they'd fought off stagecoach robbers and other villains while riding Blaze up and down the driveway.

She let them remove the bareback pad and reins, then turned the gentle old mare into the pasture with a bucket of oats for a treat. Back in the ranch house kitchen, they packed up cookies and chocolate milk, then headed for Stewart Creek which ran behind the stock barn.

"This is the same creek that runs behind our house," Bobby informed them when they arrived at a shady nook beside the little stream. The creek was shallow at this spot and had a natural sandy bed with few rocks to stumble over.

Patty picked a boulder to sit on. "We know that. It's nice here. We can wade."

"Who's that?" Bobby wanted to know, staring upstream.

Marisa squinted against the late afternoon sun and spied a fisherman angling toward them, fly rod in hand. She recognized the man even from a distance and with the sun in her eyes. "Jordan Rush," she told the children.

"Hello," he called as he crossed the sandy cove and stopped beside the threesome.

"Hi. Did you get any fish?" Bobby asked.

"Not a one. Got two bites, though." He rubbed his neck and grinned. "Mosquitoes, I think." His gaze swung to Marisa. "I thought I'd ask for first aid."

She shook her head. "I didn't bring the kit. If you're going to die, would you do it on someone else's property?"

The twins thought this was hilarious. Bobby gleefully demonstrated how Jordan might have a choking fit and fell to the ground in a tortured finale while Jordan watched with a bemused expression.

"Are all kids this delighted at the idea of someone dying?" he asked when Bobby finally expired.

"I'm not," Patty declared with a disgusted glance at her brother. "Boys are really stupid."

Bobby returned from the dead. "I am not!"

"Are, too!"

"We'd better eat before the ants arrive," Marisa said, opening the knapsack. She gave each of the twins a packet of cookies and a sports bottle of milk. "I'll share," she told Jordan and handed him half her treat.

"Thanks." He sat on a boulder next to hers. After she took a drink of the chocolate milk, he did the same. "While I've sometimes evidenced foot-in-mouth disease, I don't have anything worse," he said with a grin.

"Foot-in-mouth," Bobby repeated and demonstrated by pulling one foot close to his mouth and opening wide. He and his sister giggled.

Marisa smiled, too. So did Jordan. As their gazes locked, sensation poured over her, and hunger filled her with restless needs she'd long ignored. She saw Jordan swallow as if the cookie had stuck in his throat. She offered him the bottle of milk. He took a big drink, handed it back, then looked into her eyes again, all simple, mundane acts, yet filled with significance...

No, she was being fanciful.

Gazing at the dark green of the mountains in the distance, she wished she'd met this man months, or years, ago, back in a time when she'd still believed in dreams and happily ever after. She sighed unconsciously.

"Tired?" he asked.

She realized she was. "Some."

"You need to rest more." His eyes went to the rounded swell of her tummy. He turned to the twins. "You two know how to fish?"

"Sure," Bobby said. "We've done it lots of times."

"We have not." Patty gave her brother a stern glare for lying.

"Living here in the mountains, you have to learn to fish for trout. It's required. Come on, I'll show you."

Marisa watched as Jordan entertained the kids for an hour. Then he accompanied them to the house. The next thing Marisa knew, he was grilling the hamburgers she'd prepared for supper and exchanging stories with the twins about their funniest adventures. The four ate outside at the picnic table as the sun dipped behind the far hills.

At seven, the phone rang. It was Libby. "I'm on my way home. I'll swing by for the kids in about fifteen minutes. I need to stop at the Minimart first."

"Tell her I'll drop the twins off when we finish our meal," Jordan said.

"Good idea," Bobby agreed. "We haven't had dessert yet."

Marisa explained what was happening to Libby. "Take your time. I'll see that the twins get home okay."

After she and her friend hung up, she served ice cream with strawberries. Jordan ate a big serving, declaring it the best dessert he'd ever eaten, this in addition to two hamburgers crammed with all the fixings and a large helping of chips and dip.

Marisa realized it had been over three years since she'd had a man at her home for a meal. Her dad had died when she was a teenager. Her fiancé had preferred to dine out. Brad also hadn't liked being around children.

It came to her that she'd been lucky he took off with another woman. He'd have made a terrible husband and father, at least for her. They hadn't wanted the same things at all.

After wiping the stickiness from little hands and mouths, Marisa got her keys. "Let's go, guys."

"My truck is near here. I'll drive."

Marisa considered, then shook her head. "Libby would worry if a stranger showed up with the twins."

He gave her an amused glance. "I assumed you would ride with us."

"It's out of your way—"

"Hush," he said quite gently.

She hushed. Riding in his SUV, the kids strapped safely in the rear seat, she fought a sense of depression that had no cause. They dropped the twins off at their house, said hello to Libby and returned to the ranch, the entire round trip taking less than twenty minutes.

"You were very good with the twins," she said when he stopped at her house. She opened the door and paused before getting out. "Thanks for helping."

"My pleasure." He swung down from the vehicle and came around to her side, falling into step as she headed for her house.

A tingle started someplace in her middle and radiated out to the extremities. "Uh, would you like some coffee?"

"That would be nice."

She realized she really hadn't expected him to agree. In fact, she'd thought he would be anxious to be gone after spending the afternoon and evening with a pregnant woman and two adorable but talkative kids.

He settled in a rocking chair on the old-fashioned porch while she made the coffee. After she brought out two mugs, she, too, sat and observed the changing hues of the sky as twilight deepened into dusk.

Frogs and crickets sang in unison down by the

creek. A red-tailed hawk soared toward a roost in the pine forest to the west of them. Marisa tried to think of something interesting to say, but came up blank.

"It's peaceful here," he murmured. "I didn't realize how much I needed the quiet."

"Ah, the life of a busy logging tycoon," she teased but softly as the quiet filled her, too.

His smile flashed, then was gone. He lazily turned his head in her direction...and took her breath right away.

The intensity of his gaze was like that Saturday night when he came to the diner, as if he sought answers to a riddle that only he knew. She saw interest in those azure depths. Inside, some part of her wanted to respond to that interest. She looked away, worried about this desire to throw caution to the wind.

A thump, then a bulge, called attention to her tummy. The baby had bunched up against her right side in a noticeable knot. She laid a hand over the spot, embarrassed by her so evident condition and angry with herself for it.

She'd chosen this route, knowing there would be some raised eyebrows. She could live with Jordan's quizzical glances, too.

To her surprise, he reached over, then paused a few inches before touching her. She realized he wanted to feel the baby, a reaction that seemed natural to a lot of people and other mothers had warned her about.

"It's okay," she said in a husky near-whisper. "You can touch, if you want."

"I do. Very much."

She sat very still as he laid his big, warm hand on her abdomen. The baby relaxed and the bulge disappeared. Jordan rubbed his hand over the hard mound the size of a small melon, his face serious, introspective.

"Why?" he said.

She thought she knew what he was asking, but wasn't prepared with an answer. "Why what?"

"Why are you alone?" He lifted his gaze from her body to her eyes. "Where is the man involved in all this?"

"He...he isn't around."

Eyes narrowed in anger, he demanded, "He left you alone to have a child?"

"Well, actually, I didn't tell him. I didn't want him to stay out of obligation or anything."

"Such noble sentiment."

Marisa squirmed against the hard wooden slats of the rocker at his sardonic quip. "Not really. I thought it was a fair exchange. He wanted a good time with no strings. I wanted a baby and, uh, also no strings."

"What did you do, kick the guy out as soon as you knew you were pregnant? Didn't you think he deserved to know he'd fathered a child?"

"I...it really isn't any of your business."

A second of taut silence greeted her statement. She felt too vulnerable to tell him about the sperm bank and she certainly wasn't going to spin him a tale of unbridled passion in Billings for a weekend. He would think she was the biggest fool around.

"No, I guess it isn't," he agreed in an odd tone.

With that, he strode to his SUV and left, becoming a moving shadow among the other shadows of the night.

A long time passed before the tension ebbed from Marisa. As the night closed in, with only the creak of the rocker to keep her company, Marisa felt the emptiness reach out to her. It was a different kind of loneliness than she'd ever experienced before.

Odd that she hadn't felt this way when her fiancé had run off with the manicurist. She smiled, glad that she hadn't married him. He was definitely the wrong man....

So who was the right one?

Jordan stopped at the intersection of Two Pines Road and Main Street. Instead of turning right, he swung into a U-turn and headed back to Marisa's house. His headlights picked her out, still sitting on the porch, when he arrived.

"I'm sorry," he said when he stood on the sidewalk in front of the steps.

"That's okay."

He sighed, disgusted with himself. "No, it isn't. You have a right to make choices for your own life. Without advice from others."

She laughed. "I've had plenty of that the past four months."

"All well-meaning, of course," he said, sympathy as well as amusement in his tone.

"Of course."

He sat on the porch and leaned his back against the post. The moon had come up. It bathed the landscape in an iridescent glow. The deep sense of peace returned as they sat there in a silence that was comfortable.

Yet he was aware of her, and he knew she was aware of him, knew it bone-deep, in the throb of hot blood through his body, in the hum of sexual tension that vibrated along every nerve, in the threads that drew him to her, her to him, binding them....

"You fascinate me," he finally admitted.

"W-why?"

He smiled at the startled question. "Damned if I

know.'' Standing, he moved to her and held out his hand.

After a pause that lasted an eternity, she put her hand in his and let him pull her to her feet. Now they stood an inch apart, their eyes searching for answers in each other's faces.

''Maybe there aren't any answers,'' he muttered. ''Maybe there's just this.''

He hadn't meant to kiss her, hadn't meant to act upon the attraction, hadn't even thought of it, not really.

That was a lie.

Perhaps it was her audible little sigh that did him in, but he stopped resisting and pulled her into his arms. He had to bend to her a little, until she rose on tiptoe, then she fit his six-one frame perfectly.

With a groan, he found her mouth and took the kiss he'd been wanting for hours. Her mouth was as sweet as he'd known it would be. When he took the kiss deeper, she responded with a delicate shiver that he felt all through his body.

She laid her hands on his waist, not embracing him as he did her, but holding on, as if she needed his strength.

Heat raged through him, the hunger demanding immediate satisfaction. He forced the primal urge to obey his command, knowing instinctively that she needed gentleness from him.

He could give her that. For now. For this moment, the kiss was enough.

Their tongues touched tentatively, then with more confidence as the passion bloomed like a perfumed flower between them. Running his hands into her hair, he held the kiss until they were both breathless with longing.

Slowly her hands moved to his arms, then upward and finally around his shoulders, curving her body just so until there were no spaces between them. His heart beat like a pagan drum, its rhythm stirring and compelling.

"This is insane," she said, panting when they finally came up for air.

"Sweet insanity," he agreed, unable to quit exploring her with his mouth. He kissed along her jaw and the neckline of her shirt until he found the pulse beating heavily in her throat. He lingered there, liking the fact that she was as affected by their embrace as he was.

"Jordan…"

"Marisa," he said, not letting her voice the question he could hear in her tone.

She leaned her head back so she could look into his eyes. "What are we doing?"

A lightness of spirit engulfed him. He chuckled. "It's called making out, I think."

She surprised him by smiling. "Yes, but why?"

"It feels good." He nibbled on her ear and felt her shiver again.

He liked the feel of her breasts against his chest. He could also feel the hard swell of her abdomen and found it didn't bother him at all. This tiny bit of life nestled inside her could be his child.

It was a staggering thought, one he hadn't come to grips with although he'd known from the moment he saw her that it was possible. However, the reality of it was much greater than the philosophical possibility.

Taking a deep breath, he settled in the rocker and urged her into his lap. Holding her tucked against him, her head on his shoulder, he rocked them while fragments of thoughts raced through his mind.

Did he believe her story about how she became pregnant? It sounded plausible enough, except that he knew someone in this town had gone to the fertility clinic. Laying a hand on her tummy, he wondered if this baby was his.

Was that possibility affecting his judgment and the attraction he felt for her?

With a finger under her chin, he tilted her head so he could study her face. The moon was new, but its light was enough to see her expression and the uncertainty in her eyes. When she smiled, he realized it was a cover for emotions she didn't want to disclose.

Then his gaze locked on her delectable mouth. Her eyes seemed to darken, becoming defiant and challenging in ways he couldn't yet fathom. Unable to resist, he slowly bent his head until he found her mouth again.

Marisa knew this wasn't wise, that an involvement between her and Jordan was impossible. If they started seeing each other, her friends would conclude that he was the mysterious man in her life and the father of her child.

They would expect her to marry him and live happily ever after. What would she tell everyone when *she* didn't understand what was happening?

The wind took on the chill of nighttime. Holding on to his shirt, she trembled as doubts rushed through her. He held her closer, his lips demanding a response, one that she couldn't withhold or hide from him.

For long moments, she let herself drift in a half dream of contentment, excitement and fantasy. The sweep of headlights along the road brought her out of it.

"Shh," he said. "It's just a car passing."

She pushed herself upright, her palms flat against his chest. "A neighbor. They'll wonder who's here."

"What will you tell them?"

Her answer seemed important to him. She rose and stood a few feet away, wrapping her arms across her chest for warmth. "Nothing. It's none of their business."

"Your stock answer." He stood and leaned his palms against the porch railing. "Is that what you'll tell the child when he asks about his father?"

Shock reverberated through her at the stark question. "No. I'll tell him, or her, the truth." She pressed her lips together, not at all sure about this. But could she spin the yarn about a casual weekend fling to a youngster who needed roots and a sense of being wanted?

"Will you?" Jordan challenged.

She cringed from his harsh stare, sensing his disapproval and feeling that he knew more than he was telling. How could he? No one knew the truth about her pregnancy but the doctor and the technician at the clinic. They were sworn to secrecy by the law. At least, she thought they were.

Assuming her deadpan expression, she told him, "Actually I thought I'd go with the stork theory of acquiring babies. Or perhaps the one about finding the little one under a cabbage leaf."

When he clenched his fists, she realized she'd only added fuel to his anger.

"I'm sorry," she said. "I didn't mean to be flippant. It's just that I haven't thought that far ahead."

"Did you think at all before you got in this fix?"

"Yes," she said coolly. "I considered the pros and cons carefully and discussed them with the doctor—" Horrified at nearly giving herself away, she quickly added, "When I went to confirm my condition."

Jordan's eyes moved restlessly over her face as if trying to detect truth from lies. She held his gaze until at last he heaved a breath and nodded. He strode down the steps, then turned and looked at her.

"I want to see you again," he said on a softer note.

"Why?"

"Because."

She was torn between wisdom and desire. At last she nodded. "I'm sure we'll see each other frequently during the festival. Our booths are only a few feet apart."

"That isn't what I meant."

He wasn't going to back off, she realized. Bolts of electricity buzzed through her. "We've only just met. I think we should wait until we know each other better."

"How long? A week? A month?" His eyes raked over her. "Until after the baby?"

"I don't know," she admitted. "I'm not ready to see anyone right now."

He frowned as if he was going to argue, then he smiled. "I'll be around," he told her, then flicked her a jaunty salute and left.

Long after his SUV had disappeared into the night, she stood in the moonlight, her mind whirling with thoughts that were full of insanely cheerful hopes and equally strong fears.

"Really, this is all too much," she finally muttered and went inside to try to sleep before she had to go to work the next day.

Chapter 4

At ten the next morning, Jordan straddled a stool at the counter of the diner. He knew Marisa was safely out of the way, working at the food booth. The diner was busy but not rushed as at lunch and dinner.

The owner, Callie Griffin, brought him a glass of water and a thick ceramic mug. "Coffee?"

He nodded.

"You need to see a menu?"

"No, coffee is all I want. And some information."

She poured the coffee, then set the pot behind her on the hot plate. "What kind of information?"

Jordan recognized the flicker of suspicion that went through her eyes. People in small towns didn't open up easily about one of their own to strangers.

"I'm Jordan Rush. I have a cabin—"

"I know who you are. Is Marisa the topic of the information you want?"

He hesitated at her bluntness, then nodded.

"So what do you want to know?"

"Everything." He realized that was true.

Callie grinned wryly. "I'll be back." She went off to take care of the cash register, then walked through the diner with the coffeepot before returning. "Now," she said, studying him with candid blue eyes. She tucked a flyaway strand of hair into her ponytail. "Marisa."

"Yes."

"She's twenty-nine, Rumor-born and bred. Her roots go back several generations and she owns the original family ranch. Her father died some years ago. Her mother died last year of cancer."

Jordan couldn't stop the pain that speared through him, this time for Marisa. She, too, had suffered a major loss and from the same illness.

"Yeah, it was tough," Callie said as if reading his mind. "Is that all?"

He shook his head. "What about men?"

"As, in her life?"

"Yeah." He held her piercing gaze until she relaxed.

"None at present," the diner owner assured him, her eyes sparkling with impish humor—at his expense, he figured.

"But in the past?"

Callie sobered. "Her fiancé took off with a bleached blonde from the Getaway Salon three years ago." She gave her own natural blond tresses an indignant toss.

"What kind of person was he?"

"Besides being a scumbag, he was a salesman for an equipment company—tractors, combines, riding mowers, that kind of thing. He was ambitious. Really good-looking, though. And a smooth talker."

Jordan didn't like anything about the man. "The guy was a jerk."

"Yes, but I'm glad he was one before they married rather than her finding out afterward."

Jordan waited but nothing more was forthcoming. He smiled. "Okay, I'm curious. She's pregnant. She told me the father didn't know about the child."

"Is your interest serious?"

He thought of the other two women in the area who were also pregnant. Since meeting Marisa, he'd almost forgotten about them. Visions of the previous night and hot, sweet kisses warmed his blood. "Yes."

"No matter that she's four months pregnant?"

He nodded and held her probing gaze.

Callie huffed out a breath as if she'd been really worried about his answer. "Okay then. The guy, uh, the father, was a rodeo cowboy she met in Billings one weekend. Marisa insists she knew it was a weekend fling and expected nothing from him, but you'd think...well, as far as I know, he's never bothered to contact her at all."

Jordan was surprised at how relieved he felt. "Good. She's free to date anyone she pleases."

"And does that please you, Mr. City Tycoon?" Callie challenged, tilting her head to one side to study him.

"It does, Ms. Small Town Entrepreneur." He grinned at Marisa's protective friend, who grinned, too.

"She's leery, but I think she may be interested," Callie leaned forward to confide. "Be careful with her."

He finished up the last of the coffee. "I will." It was a promise he meant to keep.

Marisa had the afternoon off, then went back in to help during the dinner rush. From the town park, she could hear the blast of a rock 'n' roll band entertaining the visitors to the festival. The diner booth was serving hot corned beef sandwiches with all the fixings tonight, plus a selection of Libby's cookies, brownies and muffins. Even from this distance, she could see a line in front of it.

After parking, she locked her car, a thing she rarely bothered to do. With so many strangers in town, she should be careful, though. Jordan Rush came immediately to mind.

Glancing at the rising moon, she had to smile. She'd come to terms with the attraction between them during the sleepless hours of the previous night. It had been three years since she'd dated. According to the newspaper article, he'd been alone for more than a year. An interest between them was a normal thing, one born of mutual loneliness.

They just weren't going to act upon it. She'd decided that in the wee hours of the night, too. With a child to plan for, she had no time for a real fling with the handsome logging tycoon.

But he did make her heart beat faster.

It was the coming lunar eclipse or the heat or something in the air, she told herself as she went to the booth. Jordan was the first person she saw, sitting at one of the little tables, the special before him.

"Hi," he said while she stashed her purse under the counter and pinned on the name tag.

"Hi." She hadn't realized the morning after—the evening after, she corrected—would be so awkward.

He gave her a lazy perusal, as if he liked what he saw, then smiled at her, knowledge in his gaze. She wished she hadn't responded quite so enthusiastically to his kisses.

Flustered, she took over from the high school senior who'd worked the afternoon shift. When the customers were served and dispersed, only Jordan was left at the table.

"More coffee?" she asked and filled his cup without waiting for a reply. Her hand shook slightly, and she felt the familiar glow on her cheeks.

"Thanks," he said.

The booth had a rush for the next two hours. She hardly noticed when Jordan left. She ran out of food and closed the booth shortly before nine. Jordan strolled over from his booth. Her heart did its clumsy flutter.

"Any coffee left?"

She shook her head, then continued the cleaning chores. He watched silently while she finished. When she grabbed her purse and headed for the diner with the cash box, Jordan strolled with her.

"I'll walk you to your car." He placed a hand in the middle of her back.

It felt warm and protective. Nice. "I have to stop by the diner." She speeded up, but he easily kept pace. At the diner, he went inside while she turned the money over to Callie.

Her boss cast a significant glance at Jordan, who stood by the door, then gave her a big grin and a thumbs-up.

Marisa shook her head slightly, but smiled at the ridiculous situation. Callie and Libby had been trying to find someone for her for three years. Saying good-night, she hurried out, Jordan staying with her.

"Callie says you met a cowboy in Billings and had a weekend fling. Is that true?" he asked.

Marisa gasped at the broadside. "Really, that's none of your—"

"Business," he finished for her. "I know."

"Did you talk to Callie about me?"

"Yes." His tone dared her to make something of it.

"Well, really."

"Yes, really. I want to know the truth." He stopped her in the shadows under an old oak tree near where she was parked with hands on her shoulders. "It's important."

She ducked her head as she told the lie. "Yes, it's true."

He sucked in a harsh breath. "Did you plan it in advance?"

"Yes. I'd been wanting a family for some time. I realized that I'd be thirty this fall, so..." Her throat closed up and she shrugged.

"So you lured some sucker in to be your stud," Jordan concluded, anger evident in every line of his muscular body.

"He didn't object."

"I'll bet. Hell, why couldn't I have been the one you met? Or were you looking for specific characteristics?"

She lifted her chin and refused to answer as embarrassment flushed her face. The truth was she had chosen the sperm donor based on the description given to her at the clinic: blue eyes, dark hair, a bit over six feet, highly intelligent and enterprising.

Jordan snorted as if disgusted with the whole argument and stalked off. Marisa stood there for a minute, then went to her car.

Pausing, she watched the people milling around the carnival-type amusement rides or simply sitting on the grass listening to the band. Young people danced on a wooden pavilion, their carefree laughter reminding her of days long ago.

She'd never felt so lonely.

Instead of going home, she crossed the street and entered the park, winding her way through the crowd to a bench near the dance floor. A mother holding a sleeping baby sat on one end. She took the other.

For a while she was content to watch, but after a bit she gazed around the crowd. When she realized who she was looking for, she was annoyed with herself.

Spying an old friend from high school, she automatically smiled. He came over.

"Hi, how ya' doing?" he said.

"Fine, Butch. How about yourself?"

"Fine." He nodded toward the pavilion. "You wanna dance?"

She realized that she did. Anything seemed better than going home to emptiness. Somewhat self-conscious, she let her former classmate take her to the makeshift floor. The music had a fast beat and they swung easily into the rhythm.

"You're good," she told him at one point. She didn't recall that from their high school days.

"Took some lessons down in Billings. Thought it might make me more interesting to girls."

"Did it work?"

"Nah. Can't think of anything to say when we're not dancing."

At his wry grin, she laughed. Butch swung her around him, then out and back. Marisa stared into blue eyes observing her every move. Her breath caught in her throat. Fortunately the music ended just then.

"That was lovely. Thanks. I've got to run." She rushed for her truck as if being pursued by demons. It didn't work.

"Not so fast," Jordan said, clasping her wrist and bringing her flight to a halt.

"Jordan," she said, half in protest.

His smile was hard-edged. "How about a dance with me?"

She shook her head. "I don't think so."

"Why not?"

Her own temper rose to meet his. "I don't have to explain myself to you."

So why did she feel guilty about dancing with Butch? She couldn't explain that to herself. She most certainly didn't have to account to Jordan.

"Is there a problem here?" a masculine voice asked.

Holt Tanner, a deputy with the sheriff's department, stepped between them. His narrowed gaze went from her to Jordan.

"Ask the lady," Jordan suggested coolly, dropping his hold on her.

Holt swung back to her.

"No. No, there's no problem," she quickly assured the lawman. "We were just arguing about…about one more dance before I leave."

The deputy's eyebrows rose skeptically, but he moved on. "Take care," he said with a sharp glance at her, then at Jordan.

"Right," Jordan muttered, his eyes on her. He held out his hand.

Not sure what she was doing, Marisa laid her hand in his. They went to the wooden floor and squeezed in among the closely packed couples while a slow love song wailed into the night. They danced in one small spot.

Her mind blank, she followed his steps automatically until, at last, the music and the rhythm took her. She relaxed against him.

"That's better," he murmured. "Maybe the deputy will quit watching us now. Yeah, there he goes, off to stop another crime in the making."

"Will you hush?" she whispered, catching the amused glance of a nearby couple.

"Yes, ma'am."

Unable to resist, she nestled in his arms and laid her head on his chest as he drew her closer. Tension hummed between them, bringing its own compelling beat. She wished they were alone. She wished she'd met him long ago when they both were young and unhurt by life. She wished...

"I've stayed away from women," he said softly, for her hearing only. "For over a year. Longer. All the time my wife was ill. I avoided even the most casual touch. I didn't want the desire.''

She heard the despair in his voice and understood the rage as he waited out the months, knowing the illness was winning and there was nothing he could do. Some people would have welcomed a few hours of forgetfulness and taken them without regret.

"I hated the helplessness," she said.

He nodded. "All the treatments, the pain, all for nothing in the end."

"I know. I'd read to my mother for hours until she could no longer stand the pain. Then I'd give her another pill and she'd sleep...."

"That was the worst, watching her sleep, knowing there was only more pain when she woke."

She stretched up on her toes and wrapped her arms around him in silent grief.

"I don't want pity," he murmured gruffly.

"It's not for you alone."

His chest lifted against hers, then he let the breath out in a long sigh and held her close. The music echoed the loneliness that surrounded them, binding them in ways she couldn't name. It was scary and wonderful....

He gazed into her eyes. "Come with me."

A whirl of emotion filled her, robbing her of wisdom or a sense of self-preservation. She nodded.

He expertly moved them to the edge of the dance

floor, then joining hands, they hurried across the grass and away from the crowd. Her heart was beating heavily now, not fast but with a deep, solemn throb that seemed to shake her whole being.

In his SUV, buckled in and staring into the night as they drove down Main Street, she said, "Sometimes I wish things could have been different."

"We all do."

His voice was quiet, reminding her of the whisper of the wind on the lake at times, of the soft loneliness of rain on a window, of life as she'd once dreamed it would be.

At his place, her gaze took in the rustic elegance of the log house, built on the massive lines of a lodge. Inside she stood at the threshold while he flicked a switch, filling the soaring great room with the soft light from two lamps. He laid an arm over her shoulders and looked deeply into her eyes.

"Will you stay?" he asked on that same quiet, heart-stirring note.

"Yes. For tonight."

She didn't know why she felt compelled to add the last two words. Perhaps to assure herself she knew what she was doing and that there were no promises between them.

Taking her hand, he led her to the master bedroom. Closing the door behind them, he turned to her, his gaze dark and questioning, as if he thought she might break and run at any moment.

She shook her head, denying the possibility. The need was too great. For both of them.

Sensing more than hunger in him, she kissed him deeply, tenderly, knowing there were things between them that neither might want to acknowledge. "This could be dangerous," she warned as they stopped beside the bed.

"It already is. It was the moment I walked into the diner and saw you."

A shiver played delicately down her spine. He rubbed her arms, then slowly worked on the buttons of the shirt she wore. She stroked along his chest and torso, found the hem of his polo shirt and tugged it up and out of the way.

His flesh was solid and warm beneath her seeking fingers, the pleasure of touching him so sharp it was painful. Inside, a golden coil curled tighter and tighter until she thought she would explode from the force of wanting, needing him.

"Tonight is mine," she said fiercely, not understanding the words at all.

"Yes. Tonight."

But his eyes promised eternity, and his kisses spoke of forever.

Chapter 5

Jordan woke at dawn with streams of sunlight flickering through the trees and over his face. Marisa lay curled against his side, her backside touching his hip. He had absolutely no desire to move.

"Hi," she said, also not stirring.

He found himself smiling for no reason. "Good morning." Without realizing what he intended, he leaned over and kissed her ear, then the side of her face.

"What time is it?"

"Not quite six."

"I have to get home. The mare is in the barn. She needs to be put out to pasture."

"Let's go do it, then we can have breakfast in town." He swung out of bed. The chilly air served to invigorate him, but he laughed when Marisa groaned. She shivered as she grabbed her clothes and pulled them on.

Jordan thought of inviting her to shower with him, but knew by her averted face that she would refuse. He noted the slight trembling in her fingers as she dressed. Ah, the morning-after syndrome, he mused, warmed by the fact that their night together wasn't just a passing episode for her.

Nor for him.

A flush of desire spread over him as he thought of the hours they'd spent exploring and touching and tasting....

"The coffee should be ready," he told her, averting the direction of his thoughts to the more practical. "I'll be with you in a moment."

He headed for the shower, washed and shaved in record time and walked into the kitchen twelve minutes later.

Marisa stood at the counter, coffee mug in hand. She glanced his way, gave him a brief but distant smile and picked up her purse. "Ready?" she said in a perky manner.

The smile reappeared on his face. She might think they were done with each other, but he had other ideas. He would make that clear.

"Let me grab a cup," he said and poured himself a mug of the steaming coffee. He realized he was hungry this morning and looked forward to waffles and sausage or something equally decadent for breakfast.

The phone rang before they got out the door. He answered on the second ring.

"Jordan, Ralph here," the detective said. "I have some information for you. Fred Benson is a retired police detective living near Rumor. He checked out the car registrations for me. I think we can safely rule out one couple. They married two months ago. Fred said it was a shotgun wedding. The bride was two months pregnant and her father was furious with the guy, who worked for him. I don't think she was artificially inseminated."

The P.I. chuckled at this last quip. Jordan glanced at Marisa, waiting now by the door like a deer ready to bolt at the first opportunity. "What about the other one?" he asked, careful not to mention a couple or ask about names.

"Yeah, they're the Calaveras. Fred says they've been married almost ten years, no kids. They would certainly qualify for help by the clinic's standards. You want him to check further?"

"Yes. ASAP."

"Got ya," the detective said cheerfully. "I'll get back." He hung up.

Jordan experienced an emotion he could only describe as disappointment. It came to him that he *wanted* Marisa to be the one...the woman carrying his child....

"Is everything all right?" she asked, giving him a concerned perusal.

He nodded with a lot more confidence that he felt. If it was another woman, one married and with a stable family life, what should he do? Leave them alone? Seek partial custody of the child? It was one hell of dilemma: whether to honor their right to privacy—after all, they had dealt in good faith with the clinic—and ignore his own flesh and blood, or to go to them and explain what had happened, maybe become a sort of honorary uncle to his child....

"Are you sure everything is okay?"

He liked the sincere worry in her eyes. She wasn't as distant as she tried to pretend. "A minor business snafu."

Shrugging as if the phone conversation hadn't been important, he studied the woman who had spent the night in his arms and given him the most complete sense of peace and contentment that he'd ever known.

Tenderness and other emotions whirled within. Needing to touch her, he took her arm and opened the door. At the SUV, he helped her inside then paused before starting the engine. "Last night was good. I don't intend for it to be the last between us."

A weight seemed to roll off him. No matter what happened about the child and the mix-up at the clinic, he knew there were things between him and this woman that needed to be explored and sorted out. They had to find out if there was a future for them.

It came to him that this was the first time in months that he'd thought of a future, a personal one, for himself.

Marisa insisted that Jordan take her to her truck, left in town the previous night. She refused his invitation to breakfast, provoking a frown then a lazy grin from him. "It isn't over between us," he'd told her as she prepared to drive off. "Don't think *I'm* going to be a one-night stand."

Little bolts of electricity ran over her each time she thought of his statement and the look in his eyes when she'd left him. Refusing to think of the future, she devoted her attention to the ranch chores, then to her work when she returned to town and the diner.

When she finally got a break midafternoon, she sat down to lunch at a back table in the diner. Fred Benson, a retired cop, came in, saw her and ambled

over. She'd known him all her life. Mr. Benson and
her dad had been poker-playing buddies since before she was born.

"How are you doing, girl?" he asked, taking a
seat after telling the teenage waitress to bring him
a coffee.

"Fine. How about yourself?"

"Can't complain." He was silent when the coffee arrived and watched, his gaze still sharp, until
the waitress was out of hearing range. "Need to ask
you a few questions."

Her nerves went on red alert. "Yes?"

"I'm going to level with you, but this is strictly
confidential. You understand?"

She nodded.

"There was a mix-up at a fertility clinic over in
Billings about four months back," he said in a low
voice. "A woman was, uh, given the wrong, ah…"

Her insides clenched as the retired detective
searched for the proper words. "Medication?" she
suggested.

"Well, they used the wrong sperm donor," he
finally said. "Another couple had tried that in vitro
fertilization method, but it hadn't worked. There
was an error when another female came in to be
fertilized." He paused, then added, "Damn, I feel
like we're talking about cows."

She would have laughed if the topic hadn't been

so serious. "The woman was given the couple's, uh, samples, and now they want to know who is having their baby by mistake?"

"It's worse than that," he told her. "The wife died. Turns out she had cancer. That's why she couldn't have a child. When the man called to have the last vial destroyed, he found out it had been accidentally used."

"I see." Marisa let out a ragged sigh, knowing what was coming as she put two and two together. The facts could add up to only one terrible conclusion.

"I don't suppose that female could be you?"

She gazed into his kindly old face and hesitated on the brink of telling him the truth. She needed to confide in someone, to discuss what should be done, but not yet. She had to come to grips with the shock first.

She was positive the man was Jordan and the woman who hadn't been able to conceive had been his deceased wife.

Grief and concern for him overwhelmed her. She couldn't imagine the shock he must have felt upon learning he was to become a parent along with some unknown woman.

"Marisa?" the former lawman prompted.

"No," she denied. "It wasn't me. I'm sorry. I can't help you. Or him. I have to get back to work."

She took her plate of half-eaten food to the kitchen and returned to duty, preparing the diner for the evening dinner rush. The traffic through town had slowed down as it always did during the middle of the week, but they were busy enough that she didn't have to think for the next few hours.

At five before nine, just as she flipped the Open sign over so that it read Closed, Jordan came in. A tremor shook her like an earthquake rumbling through the mountains.

"Hi, gorgeous," he murmured to her, his smile sexy, his gaze warm. "Got any coffee left?"

She poured him a cup, then quickly finished refilling the last of the sugar containers. At nine, she was ready to go, but she managed to find little things to keep her occupied. While Jordan looked out the window as a car of teenagers zoomed by, radio blasting a bass beat over the town, she grabbed her purse and dashed into the kitchen, intent on escaping from the back door.

"What's happening?" Callie wanted to know, glancing into the dining room where Jordan sat at the counter.

"Uh, I'm finished. I'll see you tomorrow."

Callie held up a hand like a cop at a street corner. "Wait. What about Jordan Rush?"

"What about him?" Marisa tried to look nonchalant and uninterested in the timber tycoon.

Callie studied her. "Libby got a haircut today at the Getaway. She said Tyne Calaveras was there, telling some story about Fred Benson asking about her baby."

Marisa's legs grew weak. She leaned against a counter for support. Things seemed to be escalating out of control.

"Fred wanted to know if Tyne's pregnancy was normal or if maybe she'd gone to the fertility clinic in Billings."

Marisa saw black spots before her eyes. She was pretty sure that meant she was going to faint. She dropped her purse and bent over to pick it up. When she came upright, dizziness washed over her like a cold spring rain.

"Are you okay?" Callie asked.

"Yes. Just came up too fast." She saw Jordan turn back toward the kitchen and realized she'd missed her chance to get away before he knew she was gone. "So, did Tyne go to the clinic?"

"No. She said they had waited until they got their old ranch house remodeled and some money ahead before they started their family. According to her, everything was planned and is right on schedule."

"I see," Marisa said weakly.

Jordan slid off the stool and strode toward the

kitchen door. "About done?" he asked, opening the swinging door and peering at the two women.

"We are," Callie said, giving Marisa a quick grin. "By the way, Libby said there was a rumor floating around about your pickup staying in town last night, but you were nowhere to be found. Until you showed up this morning. Harriet Martel said she saw you when she opened the library and that you looked fine to her."

Marisa groaned as the telltale rush of blood lodged in her cheeks.

Jordan spoke up. "She was safe."

"With you?" Callie challenged, her eyebrows raised.

"Yes."

Feeling like a schoolgirl caught in a compromising position by an angry parent, Marisa thought she was going to melt on the spot as Jordan returned her boss's stare, daring further comment from her.

However, Callie merely smiled. "Good," she said.

Marisa interrupted the ridiculous scene by rushing toward the door. "I've got to go home."

Jordan took her arm and guided her outside. "My place or yours?" His gaze was gentle as he turned it on her.

She tried to think, which was difficult with all the wild ideas that were going on in her brain, plus

the caressing motions his fingers were making on
the inside of her elbow. "I'm tired," she said
lamely.

He nodded. "I'm not surprised. You put in over
ten hours today at the diner. Do you still have
chores to do at the ranch?"

"No, I'm through for the day."

"Good. You need to rest." His smile flashed in
the moonlight. "We didn't get much sleep last
night."

"Jordan," she began, then stopped, not sure exactly what she wanted to say. Nothing, she decided.
She needed to think first. "I think I'd rather be
alone tonight. I'm not playing coy or anything,"
she hastened to add at his fierce expression. "This
has happened so fast. I need to think about...about
things."

He cupped her face between his warm palms.
"Okay, I can live with that. Call me when you get
home. I want to know you arrived safely. Okay?"

She nodded. He stayed with her until she was
buckled and locked securely in the pickup, then
watched her drive off. Numbly she followed the
road to the ranch, one refrain beating over and over
in her brain.

Was Jordan the father of the baby she carried?

Chapter 6

"Jordan, glad to catch up with you," Nick Sullivan, President of the local Chamber of Commerce, called out. Nick was coordinating the festival for the town, so he and Jordan had consulted many times over the preceding months since the forestry company was footing the bill for most of the special events.

Jordan nodded a greeting when the man came over and joined him at the table at the back of the booth where Jordan had been doing business on the cell phone.

Nick scanned a page in the notebook that rarely left his hand these days. "The Chamber council thinks the logging demonstration would be a big draw for the weekends, so we want to move it from Thursday to Saturday. We're thinking of having a Paul Bunyan contest each Saturday, then a grand champion finale of the Saturday winners the last Saturday of the month, just before the eclipse. We'll open the contest to anyone who wants to try the events, of course, but can you supply several men for it?''

Jordan forced himself to concentrate as his attention wandered three booths down where Marisa worked. She'd had a steady stream of customers since eight that morning. It was now past two in the afternoon, and he was worried about her being on her feet so long in ninety-degree heat.

''Sure. How about Saturday afternoons around three? That would work for my crew.''

''Great. Could you also provide a purse? I was thinking of something for each Saturday event winner and then maybe a thousand dollars for the grand champion?'' Nick grinned as he asked for more money.

Jordan had to smile. He knew the Chamber and city councils thought Billings Forestry Products was their personal cash cow. He considered his sponsorship a goodwill gesture for the company and an added bonus for his personal reasons for being there.

"A hundred dollars for each weekly event," he told Nick. "If we do five events, that's five hundred a week, then three hundred for the champion of each event the last Saturday, and a thousand to the grand champion. We'll have to use judges and a point system. It's unlikely any one guy can win all five events. You'll have to supply the judges."

Nick's grin broadened. "Can do. Let's see, log-rolling, broad-ax cutting, chain-saw slicing… What else?"

"Topping."

"Oh, yeah. That means climbing up a tree with a safety belt, then cutting the top off, right?"

"Right. How about a team event using a cross-cut saw?"

Nick was busy scribbling in the notebook. He snapped it closed and rammed it in his shirt pocket. "That's good. Great, Jordan. I knew you'd think of something." With a two-finger salute, he was on his way.

Looking for the next victim, Jordan surmised with a wry smile. Actually he liked the man. In fact, he liked the whole town. The three women associated with the Calico Diner—Marisa, Callie and Libby—were interesting women. The three friends were industrious, caring individuals who had won his admiration during the five days he'd been in town.

Funny, but it seemed longer. However, he'd learned during his wife's illness that a few days could be a lifetime and that forever could be compressed into the sixty minutes of a single hour.

The old pain and loneliness hit him, but not as hard as in the past. He knew that life went on after a tragedy, but now he realized he could welcome the sunrise once more and that each day wasn't simply a drudgery to be gotten through.

Marisa.

The name pinged through him, an echo of pleasure and joy he'd never thought to experience again. If the baby she carried was his… His insides leaped at the thought.

The town was aptly named, he thought with sardonic amusement. Rumors were flying in Rumor.

Every citizen was avidly wondering about the man who'd hired Fred Benson to find the pregnant woman who'd gone to the fertility clinic.

Jordan had overheard snippets of conversation all day, here at the forestry booth, on the streets, in the diner where he'd gone for coffee that morning and at the booth where he'd had lunch at noon. He figured he'd better tell Marisa before the news got out that he was the man.

Tonight, he decided. He'd tell her tonight. Then he'd wring a confession out of her about her pregnancy.

He realized he wanted to be the father of her child and that he was jealous of the cowboy she'd been with, if such a person existed. Which he very much doubted.

However, there were a couple of other pregnant women who lived in the county that Benson was checking out. The man was supposed to report in that afternoon.

Marisa came by the booth.

"Hey," he called and sprang to his feet. He fell into step with her. "Done for the day?"

She avoided looking him in the eye. "I don't know. I have to check with Callie in case she needs help at the diner during dinner."

"I want to see you tonight," he told her, determined not to be put off.

"Well, I might be late—"

"I'll wait however long it takes."

Marisa was quiet, knowing there was no use arguing with him. Jordan could be a very determined man. If he was the accidental sperm donor, she had no doubt that he would find out who the woman was. What would he want?

Could he take the child from her, get joint custody, or what? She didn't know the law.

Perhaps she should see him and carry on their affair. Maybe they would fall in love and marry. They would have the child as a bond... A sharp sigh escaped her as longing rolled over her in a tidal wave. Dream on.

"What?" he asked, holding her arm tighter. "Are you in pain? Is it the baby?"

Looking into his worried eyes, she wanted to weep, to wail at fate. Somehow she felt she'd been tricked into this farce they played. Rumors were flying fast and thick in the town and many furtive glances had come her way during the day from people she'd known all her life.

"No, I'm fine. It's just..." She couldn't think of a reason for her sigh. "Here we are," she said brightly and dashed into the diner. "Hi, Callie, how's it going?"

Her boss's gaze darted from her to Jordan and back. "Fine. I'm glad you're here. Can you help for a couple of hours? Kelly and Brenda will be here at four," she said, mentioning the two high school girls who worked part-time.

"Sure." Marisa went behind the counter and stashed her purse. "I have to work," she told Jordan.

His lips thin with anger, he nodded. "I'll see you tonight." It was a promise.

And a threat, she realized with a tremor of dread. She would have to tell him the truth. Then what?

For the next two hours, she worked steadily as tourists, lured by the festival, filled the town. They came in to escape the heat and ordered tons of sodas, ice cream, banana splits and other cold snacks. When the teenagers arrived for their shift, she was glad to let them take over.

"Wait up," Callie requested. "I saved three of the lunch specials for us. Libby is coming over with fresh pies and will join us."

Marisa's heart dropped to her toes, as the saying went. She now understood exactly what that old cliché meant. Well, there was nothing to do but get it over with, she decided fatalistically. Besides, she needed to talk to her friends before she faced Jordan that evening.

After Callie helped Libby unload her stock of pies and treats, both women joined Marisa at a table in the back corner which was relatively private. Marisa smiled as a pair of blue eyes and a pair of brown ones gazed at her.

"I see I must confess all," she said in a low voice.

Her friends leaned closer. "I think you'd better," Libby agreed, also speaking softly.

Marisa studied their worried expressions, then, looking down at the table, she admitted there had never been a handsome cowboy, there had never been a romantic weekend in Billings, there had never been unbridled passion that resulted in the baby she'd wanted.

"A fertility clinic," Callie murmured. "You went to a fertility clinic?"

"Yes."

"And got Jordan's...uh...Jordan's..."

Marisa smiled at her friend's hesitation. "His semen sample by mistake. The lab technician got the vial mixed in with those of the voluntary sperm donors apparently."

"Oh, no." Callie pressed her hands against her breast as she stared at Marisa.

"Oh, yes," Marisa said glumly.

"What are you going to do?" Libby asked.

Marisa shook her head and shrugged helplessly.

Callie spoke up. "He was with you when you came in. Does he know or suspect?"

"I'm afraid so. He's coming over tonight. What should I do?"

"You have to tell him," Callie said. Her eyes suddenly sparkled. "He'll surely want to marry you."

Marisa sighed shakily. Callie was a romantic. She'd been in love with Nick Sullivan for years, but he seemed to think of her only as the younger sister of his good friend, Daniel. Libby's husband had been more interested in his crusades and demonstrations than his family. Jordan wanted his child, which was why he'd come to town. He was inter-

ested in her because of that. The passion was just
an added complication between them.

Were the three friends forever destined to love
the wrong men? she wondered.

"He wants the baby, not me," she corrected
gently.

Libby laid a comforting hand on her arm. "Are
you sure? Perhaps you'd better give him the chance
to say what's on his mind. And I agree with Callie—you have to tell him."

"I know. It's just so difficult to admit the truth
after telling all those lies." She smiled, a miserable
effort but a sincere one. "Thanks for listening. I
will confess all when he comes over tonight. It's
the only fair thing to do. Then...then we'll see."

In the meantime, she had ranch chores to do. As
she rose and bid her two best friends farewell, she
realized how very tired she was. Her legs were
trembling with fatigue as she climbed into the old
truck and headed north on Main Street. At the edge
of town, she slowed and turned left onto Two Pines
Road. Almost home. She yawned and speeded up.

A shadow burst from the brush beside the road,
then another and another. Marisa realized a family
of deer were cutting across the road. Her reaction
was instinctive. She swerved the wheel sharply to
avoid the doe and her two babies. They leaped the

opposite ditch and raced into the pasture, getting safely away.

Marisa tried to pull the truck back onto the road, but the loose gravel spun from the grip of the tires. She bounced over the drainage ditch, hit the fence, went through and dropped into a shallow arroyo about six feet deep.

When the truck hit bottom, her head snapped forward. The seat belt caught, but not in time to stop her forehead from cracking against the steering wheel. She saw spots of colored lights spiraling away from her like the special effects from some movie about outer space, then she fell into a void that was dark and cold and very, very lonely.

Weeping, she covered the baby with both hands to protect the innocent life within, then she simply blacked out....

Jordan made the turn onto Two Pines Road, then muttered a curse as something sharp and metallic-sounding scraped the SUV. From the periphery of his vision, he saw a flash of reflected light and stopped to check it out.

Leaving the lights on, he climbed out of the truck and walked down the road with a flashlight. He found a gaping hole in the fence, with one post ripped out of the ground.

A piece of barbed wire had recoiled when the

strand broke and stuck out in the road. He carefully rolled and secured it on a fence post so no one else would run over it and perhaps puncture a tire.

A voice called out in the night. "Hello?"

The hair on his neck stood up. He walked forward over the rough ground riddled with gopher holes, bunch grass and rocks of varying sizes from pea gravel to boulders.

"Who's there?" he called.

"Jordan? It's Marisa. I'm in the dry creek."

Running forward, stumbling twice, he found the arroyo. He played his light over her truck.

"My door is stuck," she told him when he flashed the light in her face. She shielded her eyes with one hand.

"Are you hurt?" he demanded, fear crawling up his spine like a troop of millipedes.

"I'm not sure. I'm having odd pains...."

He wrenched at the door but couldn't get it to budge. "It's jammed. There's a dent in the bottom. You must have hit a boulder. I'll try the other one."

The door on the passenger side opened okay. He climbed inside and unbuckled her seat belt when she fumbled with it.

"What happened?" he asked.

"The doe and her two little ones ran across the road in front of me. I was distracted—" She stopped and laid a hand on her abdomen. "Ohh," she whispered.

"Pains?"

"Yes," she said on a gasp.

"Let's get you to the hospital." He helped her out of the truck and up the steep bank as gently as he could.

"I can walk." She pushed his hands away when he would have lifted her into his arms.

Suppressing his own rabid worry, he guided her to the SUV and tucked her in the back seat. She lay down on her side and curled her knees toward her chest.

"Hurry," she said.

As fast and as cautiously as possible, he turned around, then headed for Whitehorn and the modern hospital located there. He dialed 9-1-1 on the cell phone and alerted the emergency crew of their arrival. They were ready when he pulled under the portico.

Before he got the engine turned off, they had Marisa on a stretcher. She was still curled into the fetal position, her hands on her tummy, when they wheeled her away. He was told to move the truck.

Grimly, he parked nearby and went inside. There he was detained by the emergency room clerk. He gave Marisa's name and address and telephone number. He had no idea about her insurance. He handed the woman his business card. "I'll take care of the bill," he said, his eyes scanning the swinging doors where the medics had taken Marisa.

Leaving the young woman protesting, he went through the doors. The first cubicle was empty. The second held a man with a bandaged hand. The third contained Marisa. The emergency room doctor was questioning her.

Jordan stepped up to the side of the bed and took her hand. When she glanced at him, he gave her a quick once-over. She had a red lump on her forehead. Both eyes were swollen and already beginning to blacken.

"Are you her husband?" the doctor asked.

"No." Jordan hesitated. "Her fiancé."

"You'll have to step aside. We're taking her in for a sonogram."

"Would it be okay if Jordan came with me?" Marisa asked, clasping his hand tightly.

Jordan sent the doctor a challenging stare. The man shrugged and nodded. "We'll use a gurney," he said to the nurse who stood on the other side of the examining table.

In a few minutes, they were in another room with a technician. Jordan had to wait outside while she was put into a hospital gown. The nurse told him to come in.

He watched silently while they ran the wand over

Marisa's abdomen. Then on the computer monitor a surreal scene flashed into view. He swallowed hard as he recognized the shape of the four-month-old fetus floating in her womb. He could easily identify the eyes, the spine, fingers and toes, a tiny heart.

"Heart's strong," the doctor said.

Relief swept over Jordan. A hand sought his. He closed his fingers around Marisa's as they both stared intently at the monitor.

"No placenta detachment. Everything looks good," the doctor assured them. "Are you hurting anywhere? Other than your head," he added with an amused smile at her lump. "Let's get an ice pack on that," he said to the nurse.

"My lower back is achy," Marissa said. "It feels as if a band tightens across it every little bit."

The doctor nodded and made some notes on a chart. "We'll keep you overnight for observation. I think the contractions are reactionary but not anything serious." He patted Marisa on the shoulder. "The baby is well protected in his snug nest. I didn't see any problems there."

Marisa's grip tightened on Jordan's hand. "His?"

The doctor grinned. "Well, I could be wrong, but it looked like a boy to me."

Jordan's knees felt weak. A boy. The baby was

possibly a boy. It all suddenly seemed very real to him—the baby, Marisa, his part in the conception of this child, which he was sure was his.

A mistake? Or a miracle?

He leaned close to Marisa. "Our baby is fine," he whispered. "He'll be a big, fine boy."

She looked at him solemnly, her eyes dark and troubled, questions in the mossy green depths. He was shooed out by the nurse while Marisa was transferred to a room in the maternity wing. When he was at last allowed to see her again, she was hooked up to an IV—to keep her hydrated, the nurse told him, and ease the contractions.

He stood beside the bed, studying her while she slept. An ice pack covered her forehead and eyes. Her auburn hair gleamed like banked embers against the pillow. He lifted a strand and curled it around his finger, then kissed it and laid it back in place.

Marisa didn't stir.

His heart contracted in a painful squeeze, then beat hard. He was afraid, he realized, afraid for this woman…that she would die….

It was too terrible to contemplate.

Chapter 7

"I'm fine," Marisa insisted.

"Good," Jordan said without cracking a smile.

She gave up on protesting. He was taking his duties as her Good Samaritan very seriously. Helping her out of the wheelchair, which the nurse had insisted on using, Jordan half lifted her into his truck.

"My pickup—"

"I called the garage. They promised to haul it in this morning and check it out."

Since he had everything under control, there was nothing to say. "Thank you," she murmured.

He looked worried about using the seat belt. "It

should be okay,'' the nurse told him. Nodding, he
buckled her in, then got in the driver's side and
headed for Rumor.

Marisa leaned her head on the seat and watched
the countryside roll swiftly by. They arrived at the
ranch thirty minutes later. The light was flashing on
the answering machine when they entered the
kitchen.

"Don't you ever lock your doors?" Jordan demanded, following her inside.

"I forget sometimes."

He looked grim.

Ignoring him, she listened to the recorded messages. *Beep. Friday, 8:00 a.m.* "Come in at nine in
the morning," Callie said. "You can leave at two.
Libby and I think you need more rest."

"A wise decision," Jordan murmured.

Beep. Friday, 8:50 a.m. "Uh, hey, Marisa. This
is Jack, down at the garage. I've got some bad
news. The pickup is beyond fixing. The hood, ra-
diator, both fenders and both doors need replacing.
You got some bent rods. The drive shaft is twisted.
I, uh, talked to the insurance office. They said to
write it off as totaled."

"No," Marisa said. "I want it fixed."

Beep. Friday, 9:15 a.m. "Marisa, I just heard
about your wreck. Are you okay? Call me as soon
as possible, you hear? Oh, this is Libby. Callie and

I are worried sick since Jack came in a minute ago and reported the news.''

Beep. Friday, 9:20 a.m. "Marisa, this is Callie. Libby and I are on our way to your place. Jack said Jordan was bringing you home this morning. Stay in bed. Don't worry about food or anything.''

Beep. End of messages.

Jordan grimaced. ''Looks like we're going to have company.''

Marisa hit the erase button. She put on a pot of coffee in preparation for guests.

''What are you doing?'' he demanded.

''Making coffee. Libby will bring boxes of muffins and pastries. I'm hungry. Are you?''

''No. Yes. Who cares? You're getting in bed. Now.''

She finished measuring out coffee grounds and added water, then started the coffeemaker. ''I think I will rest for a while. On the sofa,'' she added so he wouldn't rush her off to bed before she could stop him.

''All right.'' He led her to the sofa as if she might break if he didn't keep a hold on her.

Marisa let him arrange a pillow behind her and cover her legs with an afghan although the temperature was already in the low eighties. She felt an odd sort of grief as she thought of the old truck. ''I hate to leave the truck in a junkyard," she said softly. "It's like abandoning a friend."

"I'll get it," Jordan promised. "My first pickup was one I rebuilt, practically from scratch and using mostly junkyard parts."

She smiled her thanks.

"We need to talk before your friends arrive," he said, his expression determined. He paced about the small living room. "You've heard the rumors in town, I'm sure."

She didn't pretend ignorance. "Fred Benson was my father's friend. He asked me about the baby. He said there had been a mix-up at a fertility clinic in Billings and that the man didn't intend to be a sperm donor." Stopping, she looked him directly in the eyes. "Are you that man?"

A muscle clenched in his jaw. The silence grew...and grew. At last he nodded. "I intended to tell you last night. When we had some privacy. I was afraid you'd figure out it was me, especially if you were the woman who..."

Marisa inhaled carefully as he stopped and stared at her, his eyes demanding the truth. Her body felt like glass that would shatter at the slightest movement. She gently laid a hand on her abdomen where the baby rested peacefully.

My child, she thought. And Jordan's.

"Is the baby mine?" he asked, putting into words the confrontation she'd dreaded.

Blood rushed to her head. She clutched the arm of the sofa, afraid she was going to pass out. "Please," she whispered.

He must have sensed her desperation and realized it was real. Heaving a sigh, he walked out. She heard water running, then his footsteps. He returned with a damp cloth which he laid on her forehead. "Aren't you supposed to keep an ice bag on your bruises?"

She nodded. "Twenty minutes on, twenty off."

He went into the kitchen and returned with a plastic bag filled with ice cubes and water. She slipped down until she could lay her head on the sofa arm and covered her face with the washcloth and laid the ice bag on top.

"Did you go to the clinic?" he asked.

"I told you I met someone…" She stopped, unable to continue the lie. Pushing the ice pack aside so she could observe his face, she asked, "What will you do when you find the mother?"

"That depends on who the woman is." He paused in his pacing and studied her through narrowed eyes. "If she's married and has a stable home, then I'll either drop it or I'll talk to them about being included in their lives, a sort of honorary uncle position, the way Libby's twins claim you and Callie as aunts.''

Marisa nodded. ''And…and if she's not m-married?'' She could hardly get the word out.

He dropped to his haunches beside her and took her hand. ''Tell me the truth, Marisa, before I go out of my mind wondering if *this* is ours.'' He laid his big, warm hand on her rounded tummy. ''Was there a cowboy in Billings?''

''Please,'' she whispered, pulling her hand free and pressing it to her temple. ''I need to think.'' Numbed by fear, she could barely speak.

Grim-faced, he shook his head. ''It's past time for thinking. You have to tell me the truth.'' He clasped her shoulders and pulled her upright, his expression haunted and determined. ''Are you going to answer my question, or do we go with DNA testing when the baby is born?'' he demanded, lowering her to the sofa again.

She shook her head. ''I went to the clinic in February for the fertilization.'' She sent him a pleading glance for understanding. ''I'm going to be thirty my next birthday. I have some money saved. And insurance from my parents. I can afford to raise a child. In a town like this, there are plenty of friends to help. Libby. Callie and her brother, Daniel. Nick Sullivan is a good friend.''

''So, you are the woman,'' he concluded.

"Yes."

"Why the story about a cowboy and a wild weekend in Billings?"

She wanted to touch him, but his face was so grim, she was afraid he would reject any sympathy from her. "It seemed so…so unromantic to admit to going to a clinic. So sterile and old-maidish, as if I couldn't get a man."

"My God," he said, his jaw clenched.

"I know. It was silly, but I guess I wanted to pretend my baby was the result of passion and perhaps some feeling between the parents rather than what it actually was—a procedure in a doctor's office."

He nodded stiffly. "Did you suspect the baby might be mine before you spent the night with me?"

She searched her memory of the past week. "No. I didn't know it was you until Fred Benson questioned me. He said the clinic had made a mistake and that the sperm donor was a man whose wife couldn't conceive so they'd tried in vitro fertilization, but then she'd died of cancer. That's when I knew the man had to be you."

Holding her gaze, he nodded.

Her spirit dropped to her toes. "So you were interested because of the baby. You came to town looking for a pregnant woman, one who carried your child.''

He sat on the sofa, his hip pressed against her thigh. ''At first, but my reasons changed after I met you. That's why I asked the detective to take over the search. I wanted to be with you. The attraction was real from the moment I laid eyes on you.''

She nodded, wishing she could believe that. ''Because of the baby,'' she said softly. ''You want the child.''

''Both,'' he corrected. ''I want you and the baby.''

Before she could reply, a car pulled up and stopped in front of the house. Callie and Libby rushed in, carrying several boxes. ''Wait, there's more,'' Callie said when they'd been invited inside and had placed the boxes on the dining table. They brought in four quart jars of soup, homemade rolls, a blueberry pie, roasted chicken and two covered platters filled with meat loaf, mashed potatoes, green beans and fried apples.

''For lunch,'' Callie explained, putting a gallon of sun-made tea on the counter. ''We have to get back. Kelly and Brenda are there alone and the town is filled with locals and tourists. Lunch will be busy. Uh, any news you two want to share?''

''I know about the baby,'' Jordan said.

Her friends looked from one to the other. Marisa

managed a smile for them. "We were just discussing what we should do when you arrived."

"Aren't you going to get married?" Callie demanded.

"Yes," Jordan said.

"No," Marisa spoke at the same moment.

"Yes," he quietly insisted.

"We'll see you two later." Libby grabbed Callie's arm and tugged her outside.

From the window, Marisa could see her friends talking a mile a minute as they drove off. "I don't expect marriage, Jordan. What happened was a terrible mistake. I'm so sorry."

"Sorry that the baby's mine?"

She nodded. "It must hurt, knowing it was supposed to be your wife who had the child." She twisted her hands together, afraid to look at him, knowing he would see the pity she couldn't hide and hate it. As he must hate her.

"Yes," he said quietly. "It hurts. It hurt when she was ill. It hurt when she died. For a while it hurt like hell knowing some other woman was going to have the child we had so desperately wanted. Then curiosity took over. Maybe it was morbid, but I wanted to know about the woman and why she had to go to a clinic to have a child. Then I wanted to make sure the baby had a good home. Finally I realized I wanted to know if I could be a part of its life.''

"I'll share," she promised. "I would never keep you away from your son."

"I know that. But what about us, Marisa? What's our future going to be?"

His eyes bored holes through her soul. She felt they played parts in a great tragic farce whose final curtain loomed in the shadows, waiting to fall.

Was the last act to be one of tragedy or happiness? It depended on the answer to one question: did he want her, or did he want the child and felt he had to take her as part of the bargain?

"I don't know," she said to him and to the questions inside herself.

"I'm not going to disappear from your life," he told her. "I intend to stay around and help our son grow into manhood. Make up your mind to that."

With that, he walked out, leaving her to ponder the future that whirled through her mind in a whirlwind of emotion and fragments of thought.

He couldn't possibly love her, the pragmatic part of her reasoned; they had only known each other a week. But so much had happened during that time.

"Love," she whispered. Love had happened. It knew no boundaries of time or place.

What of him? She was sure he still grieved for his wife, deeply and sincerely. She could never take the place of his first love, and she didn't want to. What she wanted was her own space in his heart. Was that possible?

If he wanted her only for the child, could she conceal her love and accept a marriage for the baby's sake?

Jordan walked along the creek behind his house. It was midafternoon and he was vaguely aware of being hungry. One thought dominated his mind: the baby was his.

His and Marisa's.

The past swept through his inner vision like an old movie played over and over.

"Tonight, darling," Nicole would say, holding the thermometer out so he could see. She was so excited and full of hope...of expectations that never panned out.

They tried everything anybody told them—medical advice, old wives' tales, folklore, anything and everything. Pausing by an old oak, he beat the heel of his fist against the rough bark as remembered frustration hit him. He thought he'd somehow failed Nicole when, month after month, she didn't conceive the child she so desperately craved.

He'd wanted to give up as desperation changed to blame and their marriage grew shaky, but she'd grown more and more determined. It came to a point where he no longer wanted to make love with the wife he'd adored.

Then the awful truth had been discovered. Ovarian cancer. That had been the source of the faint pain she often experienced in her side. The desperation then focused on saving a life rather than making one.

"Nicole."

The name echoed along the rocky banks of the creek and was borne away upon the rushing murmur of the water. It carried the loneliness of his soul in the word. He realized he'd spoken it aloud.

A cool wind passed over him. Glancing at the sky, he saw the clouds had built into a massive thunderhead, promising rain and lightning that afternoon. He was in a prominent strike zone, standing under a tall oak next to the water. Time to get back to the house.

Yet he remained even as thunder rumbled.

Nicole. Clinging to him as the last moments closed in, both of them afraid, unable to discuss a future that ended only in death.

Lightning flashed from cloud to cloud, then closer as a bolt hit a rocky promontory less than a mile from him.

As if the flash cleared his mind, he knew he was a coward. He was still afraid of facing the future. He'd only been going through the motions of living for the past thirteen months, but in his heart, he'd felt his life ended on a cold, misty day in May.

Then had come the mix-up and the child. And Marisa. Alone but taking a chance on life. Grabbing the future with both hands as she planned for the baby.

The lightning again traced a branching zigzag across the sky. *Marisa.* His heart seemed to expand until it filled his entire chest. *Marisa.*

A laugh suddenly burst out as he thought of her tale of a wild and romantic weekend to explain the baby. There was only one man she was going to have such a weekend with, and that was *him.*

As the thunder cracked like the sound of doom over his head, he raced across the fields for home. Jumping into the SUV, he spun the tires as he headed back for the one place he had to be—with the woman he loved.

Marisa jerked awake at the sound of an engine and tires sliding to a stop on the gravel drive. Frowning, she glanced outside and saw Jordan swing down from his shiny truck and dash across the yard, leaping over a flower bed instead of using the sidewalk.

He entered the house without knocking. "It's me," he said.

She pressed a hand to her chest at the look in his

eyes. "So I see. Are the stagecoach robbers after you?" she asked with a straight face.

He grinned, took a deep breath, then leaned against the door facing, hands jammed into his pockets while he looked at her...and looked at her.

She rubbed a hand over her face and smoothed her hair back. "What? Do I have spots on my face or something?"

"Or something," he told her, his smile deceptively lazy while the expression in his eyes grew more heated.

"Jordan, what is it?" she finally demanded, not sure whether to be alarmed or fascinated by this change.

"You," he said softly. He came to her, dropped to his haunches beside the sofa and gathered both her hands between his, his expression so serious it was frightening. "Just listen, okay?"

She hesitated, then nodded.

"A year ago, I was a mess. I hated everything and everybody. I resented families I saw in restaurants or shopping malls or at the gas station. It make me angry that they had what Nicole and I had tried so hard to achieve. They took their happiness for granted. To preserve my sanity, I withdrew from emotion, even from friends I'd known all my life."

Marisa stared into his eyes and didn't interrupt. She knew the anger and despair he spoke of.

"I got rid of everything that reminded me of Nicole—clothes, furniture, the house. Finally I cleaned out my desk at work. An old receipt reminded me there was one more thing to take care of."

"The fertility clinic," she murmured.

"Yes. I called, but it was too late."

When he fell silent, she waited, not sure what was coming. His eyes searched hers, and she saw the sadness in the blue depths. It reached out to her, too.

She wished she could comfort him. She could give him her love, the forgetful bliss of their bodies, but peace was something that could come only from his own heart.

"Fate," he murmured when the silence became unbearable. "I thought it laughed at me, mocked the pain and loneliness. Now I realize it had other things in store. You. And this."

Marisa watched as he laid a hand on her. She felt the baby kick at the slight pressure, then relax as if he realized it was his father.

Jordan inhaled deeply, then continued. "The accidental fertilization was my second chance, although I didn't realize it at the time. I was furious. It seemed to be just another way of laughing at me, of hurting me."

She couldn't keep from touching him then. She

removed a hand from his clasp and caressed his cheek. "Oh, Jordan, I'm so sorry. If I'd never gone there—"

"No," he said sharply. "If you hadn't gone, we wouldn't have the baby. Without the baby, I might never have met you. That would have been the worst fate." He cupped her face with both hands. "I know that now."

The bleakness of his eyes lessened, and his smile appeared, so sweet and sad and filled with other emotions she couldn't read, it broke her heart.

"Because if I'd never met you, I'd have never known the love I feel in my heart right now."

She stared at him, not sure she was hearing right.

"Love for you," he added softly.

"Jordan…" The one word was all she could get out.

"I've fallen hard for you. I know it's only been a week, but some things don't take a lot of time. I want you to give us a chance, Marisa."

"Jordan—"

"There's an attraction between us. It was there from the start. I know you feel it, too. I want a chance to make it grow."

"Jor—"

"I won't push for marriage," he said, not letting her speak. "Not yet. But that's what I want. Marriage and you and the baby. In other words, a life."

She waited, but he was silent now, looking at her solemnly, waiting for her decision, his eyes dark.

Like her, he didn't dare hope, she realized. That might be a challenge to the Fates. She sighed as happiness bloomed within her like a giant red rose.

"So do I, my love," she said, leaning close to she could gaze into his beautiful eyes and let him see the truth in hers. "I want a life with you and our son and maybe other children, if we're so lucky. Whatever we get, I'll cherish forever. I promise you that."

His breath caught, then he let it out with a gusty sigh. "You mean it?"

She nodded. "I love you. I realized it ages ago, but it was so soon…and then there was the complication of the baby. When I realized it was yours, I thought you might hate me because I had the child that should have been yours and…and…"

"Nicole's," he finished for her. "I've never hated you. That didn't enter into it. But I was confused about the attraction. Then there was the need to make sure the baby would be all right in its home. Finding out there was no man in your life, I realized I wanted to be that man. Today I realized why. I love you, Marisa." He gave her a fierce look. "Marry me or face the consequences."

"What consequences?" she asked in surprise, little thrills running helter-skelter over her nerves.

He touched his nose to hers. "I'll haunt your every second until you do."

Marisa only had to move a tiny bit and their mouths would touch. She wanted that very much. Very, very much. "In that case, I accept your humble proposal."

Laughter filled the room, his and hers, as he swept her into his arms, gently, of course, then proceeded to kiss her until they both were breathless.

The phone rang while they kissed and talked and kissed and made plans and kissed. They let the machine pick it up.

"Marisa, this is Libby. There had better be a wedding in your future. I've got the cake nearly made and Callie thinks we should have the reception in the park. The twins want to help decorate with wild flowers. Daniel says he's the logical choice to give you away. Fred Benson says he is. You'll have to decide. We're here at the diner if you'd like to call and let your friends know what's going on."

Marisa studied Jordan's face, which gave nothing away. "It's a small town," she began.

He smiled. "And a great place to get married. And to raise kids. To grow old together. I can think of worse fates."

He kissed her so gently, so sweetly she thought she might faint from the bliss of it.

"The worst thing would have been never meeting you," he added. "I can handle anything else."

Looking into his eyes, she knew they both could. Life could be hard. It was unpredictable. It could also be wonderful...

* * * * *

MARRIAGE ON THE MENU
Linda Turner

Chapter 1

"Hey, Callie, this chicken enchilada is fantastic! Can you give my wife the recipe?"

"Sorry, Dave," Callie Griffin told the town sheriff with a grin as she quickly cleaned the table next to his. "It's a secret."

"Forget the enchiladas," Carter Jones retorted from a booth at the far end of the diner. "I want the Louisiana catfish recipe. This stuff melts in your mouth!"

Delighted with her customers' response to the new specials she had added to the menu that very day, Callie could have danced on a tabletop. Yes! When the Rumor town council and Chamber of

Commerce had decided to hold a monthlong festival to celebrate a lunar eclipse, the town bigwigs had seen the Crazy Moon Festival as a way to drum up tourism and raise money. The second she'd heard about it, however, Callie had heard opportunity knocking.

A year ago she'd taken over the running of the diner after her father's heart attack had convinced her parents to retire. Ever since, she'd wanted to spice things up, turn up the heat and make the Calico Diner one of the most popular eateries in Montana. She'd never expected to have help from the city council. The minute she had heard about the festival, she'd immediately gone to work with her cook, Ben Walters, on revamping the menu and developing new specials.

She liked to think both she and Ben were excellent cooks. Still, she'd been more than a little nervous when she'd run an ad in the morning paper, announcing her Crazy Moon specials, simply because she hadn't known what to expect. Her customers were loyal—but set in their ways. They loved the old, familiar comfort foods that had been on the menu for years. She'd been afraid they wouldn't welcome change, but she needn't have worried. From the moment she'd opened the front door that morning, there'd been a steady stream of customers—old and new—and she hadn't had a moment to sit down all morning. Thrilled, she couldn't have been happier.

Reminding herself to send thank-you cards to each member of the town council and Chamber of Commerce for their imagination and farsightedness, she sailed into the kitchen with a huge grin on her face. "We're a hit," she said, giving him a high five. "Now if we can just keep up with the demand."

"No problem," Ben assured her, his crooked grin cocky. "I've got everything under control." Tall and bald, with the grace of a dancer and the patience of Job, he seldom, if ever, got ruffled. "You going to check on Marisa?" he asked as she headed for the back door.

"I want to make sure she's not overdoing it."

"I'll hold down the fort," he promised as he dished up an order of chicken and dumplings. "Tell her I've got another mess of catfish and fries ready if she needs them."

Hurrying out to the food booth that was constructed a short way down Main Street from the diner, she couldn't get over the number of people in town to celebrate the crazy moon. Main Street had been turned into a street fair, and antique dealers, jewelry makers and arts-and-craft specialists lined the thoroughfare, selling their wares. Interspersed among them were food booths offering everything from hot dogs and smoked turkey legs to cotton candy and candied apples. The smells of cooking food floated down the street on a summer breeze, and Callie closed her eyes and drew it in with smile. Just that easily, she was transported back to childhood.

There was nothing she loved more than a fair, and given the chance, she would have liked to wander up and down the street and check out all the booths. But that wasn't going to happen today. It was the first day of the festival and things were too crazy. Some of the customers who hadn't wanted to wait in line for a seat at the diner had drifted outside to her food booth, and the line was now halfway down the block. Pleased—and worried that her waitress and friend, Marisa Stewart, who was handling the booth, might be in over her head—she rushed over to help her. She needn't have worried, however. Marisa was handling the crowd with ease while she carried on a running conversation with Libby Adler, a friend and single mom who did much of the baking for the diner to help earn money to support her twins.

"You should have called me," Callie scolded Marisa as she stepped inside the booth to help her. "You're supposed to be taking it easy."

"I told her the same thing," Libby said, "but

she wouldn't listen. You know how she is when she thinks she can do something on her own.''

Callie did, indeed, know that. Four months ago, sure that Mr. Right was never going to come to Rumor, Montana, Marisa decided she didn't want to wait any longer to have children. So she went to a sperm bank in Billings, and took care of the matter. It wasn't the ideal way to have a baby, but luckily, the story had a happy ending when Marisa met and fell in love with Jordan Rush, the sperm donor and father of her baby.

''Will you two stop it!'' Marisa laughed as she served jambalaya to the next customer. ''Look at me! Do I look like I'm suffering?''

Callie had to admit she didn't. With her red hair curling about her shoulders, her green eyes dancing and her curvy figure beginning to plump with pregnancy, she was the picture of health. ''I just don't want anything to happen to you or the baby,'' she told her. ''Jordan would kill me.''

''Did I hear someone mention my name?'' Jordan Rush said with a grin as he stepped up to the booth.

''Jordan!'' Love lighting her eyes at the sight of her fiancé, Marisa leaned across the counter to give him a quick kiss. ''What are you doing here? I thought you had a meeting.''

''I did,'' he replied, ''but it was canceled at the

last minute, so I thought I'd drop by to see you and make sure you weren't working too hard.'' Glancing at Callie and Libby, he arched a dark brow. ''She is, isn't she?''

They didn't have to say anything—their expressions gave them away. Chuckling, Jordan said, ''I figured as much. That's why I took the rest of the day off. I plan to make sure she takes plenty of breaks.''

''Hello?'' Marisa said, waving her hand. ''Do I have any say in this?''

''Not a bit,'' Callie told her with a grin. ''I'm leaving you in good hands.''

''We should be so lucky,'' Libby added wistfully.

Callie had to agree. Every time she saw Marisa and Jordan together, she sighed in envy. Jordan was obviously crazy in love and so protective—Callie would have loved to have found someone so wonderful, but she wasn't holding her breath. The man she had secretly loved for years didn't know she was alive, and even if she'd wanted to find someone else, there was no time. She'd been preparing for the fair for months, and now that it was here, she didn't have time to turn around, let alone find a man. The diner and her food booth would keep her busy all day, and she'd signed up for a food booth at the carnival every evening, as well. By the time the festival was over, she'd be so tired, she'd be lucky if she remembered her own name.

And Libby's situation wasn't any better. As a single mom with twins to raise, whatever spare time she had was devoted to the baking business she ran out of her home. It would take a special man to take on a ready-made family.

Callie didn't doubt for a minute that that man existed, just as her own Mr. Right was out there somewhere under the crazy moon. But who had the time to look for him?

Resigned to being alone, at least for now, she told Marisa, "Ben has another batch of catfish ready if you need it. Jordan, take good care of her. If you need me for anything, just holler. I've got to get back to the diner. Martha probably needs some help."

Martha Charles had worked for Callie's parents for years as a waitress, but she'd had to quit to take care of her sick husband. He'd died recently, however, and when Martha had asked her if she could have her old job back, Callie had been thrilled. She needed the help. Unfortunately, it had been quite awhile since Martha had waited tables, and she couldn't have chosen a busier day to return to work. Not wanting her to get overwhelmed, Callie was handling the counter and more than half the tables.

"Sorry, Martha," she said breathlessly as she

hurried back inside and found the older woman
frantically taking an order at Callie's station. "I had
to check the booth. Why don't you take a break for
a while? I can take care of things here."

Grateful, Martha wilted in relief. "Thanks," she
said, pushing a wisp of gray hair out of her eyes.
"I didn't realize how out of practice I was. I'm
pooped!"

"Go put your feet up," Callie said with a grin.
"You've earned it."

She didn't have to tell Martha twice. Retreating
to the kitchen for her own lunch, she left Callie to
deal with the unending stream of customers that
flowed through the front door. Another woman
might have groaned at the thought of taking on the
hungry crowd alone, but Callie was in her element.
She'd grown up helping her parents at the diner and
her customers were like family. Greeting the new-
comers with smiles, she chatted with them about
their kids and grandkids, found them tables and delivered hot, steaming food to them in record time.

Her father had always told her that if she treated
her customers like they were guests in her home,
they would keep coming back for more, and it was
true. She had customers who came in every day,
and today was no different. As she laughed at
something Ben said as he served up yet another
batch of catfish, she turned to see who was next in

line for a table. And there, right in front of her, was her brother Daniel and his best friend, Nick Sullivan...the man she loved.

Callie took one look at Nick and felt her heart trip at the sight of him. Lordy, lordy, he was something! With his dark blond wavy hair that just brushed his collar, hazel eyes and square cut face, he looked like a young Nick Nolte. For as long as she could remember, she'd been trailing after him like a lovesick schoolgirl, but all he saw when he looked at her was Daniel's little sister. It was incredibly frustrating.

Still, she couldn't hold back a smile when her eyes met his. "Be still my heart," she teased. "If it's not my big brother and the president."

Nick might have been president of the Chamber of Commerce, but he was still the boy who had spent more time at the Griffin home than he had his own, and he was well used to her teasing. Giving as good as he got, he said, "We saw the line out front and thought you must have put a sign in the window that the president eats here. So where is it, Alley Cat? I'll send a photographer over to take a picture of it for my scrapbook."

Callie grinned at the irritating nickname he'd called her for as long as she could remember, and retorted, "I've got the printer working on it right now. I told him to make two—I thought you might

want to put one in your living room window. Just
so people will know where our very own president
lives,'' she added, flashing her dimples at him.
''Think of what it'll do to real estate values in your
neighborhood.''

Her brother chuckled. ''All right, you two, that's
enough. We've got some serious celebrating to do.
The festival's barely started and Main Street is
packed. Can you believe it? Rumor's on the map!''

And Nick was largely responsible for that. He
was the one who'd pushed the town council to work
with the Chamber on a festival to celebrate the
eclipse. He'd worked day and night to make it happen and had every right to be happy with the results. Even though it was early yet, it was evident
that the festival was going to be an incredible success. Hotel rooms for miles around, including those
in nearby Whitehorn, were booked solid for the rest
of the month, and people were coming from as far
away as Colorado and Washington to celebrate the
crazy moon.

''We've always been on the map,'' Callie said.
''No one knew it but us.'' Grinning, she glanced at
Nick again. ''Maybe we should have put up a
sign.''

''Cute,'' he laughed. ''Real cute, Alley Cat.''

''One can only try,'' she tossed back saucily, and
led them to their table at the very rear of the long

mobile home her parents had transformed into a diner before she or Daniel had been born. Not bothering to hand either of them a menu, she pulled out her order pad and looked at them over the top of it. "It's a special day, so you've got to try the specials. So what's it going to be? Catfish, jambalaya or chicken enchilada?"

"Catfish," Nick said promptly.

"I'll take the enchiladas."

Her pencil still poised over her order pad, Callie lifted a delicately arched brow at Nick and said, deadpan, "Will there be any to-go orders with this?"

Another man might have thought she was serious, but Nick knew her too well. A blind man couldn't have missed the glint of mischief in her blue eyes. The corner of his mouth curling into a smile of anticipation, he leaned back in the booth and perused her in amusement. "Since I'm eating lunch here, why would I need something to go?"

"Why, for your groupies, of course," she said innocently. "From what I've heard, you're quite the catch, Mr. President. Every woman in town is throwing herself at you. So where are they? Waiting outside for you? You should send something out to them. Chasing a man is hard work. I'm sure they've worked up quite an appetite."

Seated across the table from him and in the pro-

cess of taking a drink of water, Daniel choked, but
Nick just grinned. No one was more amused than
he by the way the women of Rumor had reacted to
his job and title. They acted like he was some kind
of rock star or something…all of them, that is, but
Callie.

"So when are you going to join the band-
wagon?" he tossed back. "I keep waiting for you
to call and ask me out, but the phone never rings."

"Damn," she swore teasingly. "Don't you hate
it when that happens? Maybe *you* should try calling.
You might be surprised with the answer you get."

"Maybe I will. What'd you say your number
was?"

"I didn't."

She didn't have to. He knew her number as well
as she did, though she knew better than to expect
him to call. He might flirt with her, but she didn't
dare read anything into that. She was just Daniel's
little sister to him, and it was driving her crazy. She
was twenty-five years old, for heaven's sake! If he
didn't notice soon that she was all grown-up, she
was going to grab him and lay a kiss on him that
would knock his socks off. Until she could work
up the nerve to do that, however, all she could do
was flirt right back and hope that something she
said opened his eyes.

"You're a resourceful guy," she told him, giving

him a wink. "You know where to find me." Leaving him thinking about that, she turned to greet the next customer waiting for a table. "Hey, Mac, come on in. I've got a table right next to the window for you."

Chapter 2

Watching Callie laugh and chat with her customers as she waited tables, Nick couldn't take his eyes off of her, and that surprised the hell out of him. What was the matter with him? He'd known Callie all his life—she was practically family. As a little girl, she'd trailed after him and Daniel and made a general pest of herself, and he and Daniel had loved teasing her. They'd grown up together, sharing birthdays and holidays and family crises, and she, along with the rest of her family, had been there to tell him goodbye when he'd left for college. And through all of that, he'd always thought of her as just a kid.

When had she grown up?

Stunned, he couldn't stop his eyes from roaming over her. God, she was beautiful! Why had it taken him so long to notice? As a kid, she'd been tall for her age and thin, and she was still slim and long-legged. But somewhere along the way, she'd developed curves. And grace! She moved up and down the diner with an ease that he couldn't help but admire, cleaning tables, carrying trays of food, welcoming each new customer with a smile that was open and friendly and pretty as a picture.

His gaze lingering on her mouth, Nick felt something stir inside him and couldn't look away. With her long blond hair pulled back in a ponytail, her cheeks pink with a natural blush and her blue eyes dancing with amusement as she responded to something one of her regulars said to her, she drew the gaze of every single man in the place. And she didn't even notice.

Seated across from him, Daniel arched a brow at him. "You look like you've just been hit over the head with a two-by-four. What's going on?"

"I have," he admitted, his eyes still on Callie. "Tell me something. Why didn't Callie marry that guy she fell for in college? What was his name? Bernard or something like that? You remember— the geeky guy she brought home for Christmas one year."

"Of course I remember," Daniel retorted. "How could I forget? From the moment Callie walked in the door with him, he started preaching about how much sugar everybody ate at the holidays and how bad it was for you, then he ate *four* pieces of pecan pie after Christmas dinner! And one of them was mine! Bozo. I didn't like him at all. What the devil *was* his name?"

"Baxter," Nick said, suddenly remembering. "Baxter Smythe. He was from New York and walked around with his nose in the air—except when he looked at Callie. He was crazy about her. Why didn't they ever get married?"

Surprised by the question, Daniel frowned. "I don't know. That was her first year of college, wasn't it? She'd never been away from home before. Maybe she was just lonely. Who knows? I never did think she was as nuts about him as he was her. Why? Why are you bringing that up now? That was years ago."

"I don't know," Nick said with a shrug. "I was just wondering. Who's she seeing now?"

"No one that I know of." Giving Nick a hard look, he growled, "Okay, what's going on? Why the sudden interest in Callie? Is there something going on that I don't know about? You're acting like you've never seen her before."

Nick felt like he hadn't. "I don't know. I was

just sitting here watching her work, and I realized that she's all grown up. And I don't even know when it happened. When did she get to be so beautiful?''

If Nick had been talking about anyone else but his sister, Daniel wouldn't have thought a thing about it. Nick was a free agent, and he'd never had any trouble getting a date—especially since he'd become president of the Chamber of Commerce. He had women coming out the wazoo, the lucky dog, and although he was smart enough not to let all the attention go to his head, there was no question that he was thoroughly enjoying himself.

So why was he suddenly looking at Callie?

Troubled—dammit, what had gotten into Nick?—Daniel sat back in his seat and said dryly, ''I didn't notice—she's my sister. So why have you? You're not getting ideas about her, are you?''

''And if I am?''

Daniel had to give his old friend credit. He could have denied any interest in Callie, and Daniel would have believed him. But Nick was nothing if not honest, which was one of the reasons he was so popular with the ladies. He didn't lead them on or pretend an interest that wasn't there. And now he'd turned his attention to Callie.

Frowning, Daniel didn't mind admitting to himself that he was worried. He'd known for years that

Callie was in love with Nick, but he'd never said a word about it to her or Nick. There were just some places a brother and a best friend didn't go, and pushing his nose into how his two favorite people in the world felt about one another was one of them. So he kept his opinion to himself and waited for the day when Callie either gave up on Nick or he finally realized that one of the best women in the world was right under his nose. Daniel had just about given up hope that either of those things would ever come to pass. Now that the latter had happened, he had to wonder if the lunar eclipse had something to do with it. After all this time, that seemed to be the only explanation.

"Well?" Nick prodded him when he didn't immediately answer. "How would you feel about me asking her out?"

Not quite sure, Daniel hesitated. He and Nick had been friends forever. He loved him like a brother and would have liked nothing more than to welcome him into the family as his brother-in-law. But Nick wasn't interested in marriage—at least he never had been before—and Daniel was sure that in the long run, his sister would settle for nothing less. She never talked about it, but she was the kind of woman who would want a husband and children and a dog or two to take care of and love. That's why she loved the diner so much. She got a lot of pleasure out of making her customers happy and comfortable. How could she and Nick possibly be compatible when they wanted two different things out of life?

"Just be careful," he said gruffly. "Don't hurt her. I don't want to have to take your head off or anything—then we couldn't be friends. You'd be mad at me, and I'd be furious with you and Callie would be livid with both of us for acting like Neanderthals. And we both know how Callie is when she gets angry. You don't want that and neither do I."

He was serious and teasing and warning his old friend at the same time. Another man might have been offended, but Nick was like family and he was as protective of Callie as Daniel. His expression solemn, he said, "She'll be safe with me. You have my word."

The catfish was delicious, just as Nick had known it would be. Callie was a fantastic cook, which was one of the reasons why he had lunch at the diner every day. Ben handled most of the cooking for her, but he could taste Callie's touch in every dish. Then there was Callie, herself. He loved watching her work.

You were honest with Daniel, a voice growled in

his head. Be honest with yourself. You love watching her.

He couldn't deny it. Lately, it seemed like every time he walked into the diner, he found himself watching her more and more. And he didn't know why. It wasn't as if she had had a fancy makeover or something at the Getaway, an exclusive inn and beauty spa that had opened in town a few years back. She still wore her long blond hair pulled back in a ponytail, and she'd never been one to lather on a lot of makeup, thank God. She looked just as she always did, fresh-faced and pretty. And suddenly, all he wanted to do was touch her.

Confused, needing some time to himself, Nick didn't linger after lunch to tease Callie, as he usually did. Using the excuse that he had to attend a Chamber of Commerce meeting in five minutes, he made a quick escape as soon as he finished his meal, surprising not only Daniel, but Callie, as well. He usually always flirted with her when he paid his bill at the cash register, but not today. Leaving his payment and tip on the table while she was busy at the far end of the diner, he waved at her, then quickly hurried out the door.

He'd scheduled the monthly meeting to correspond with the opening day of the festival so that any unexpected problems that cropped up could be dealt with immediately, but as he listened to Rumor's businessmen rave about the success of the festival so far, his thoughts kept drifting back to the Calico Diner...and Callie. She was just so cute! And when he flirted with her, there was always a sparkle in her eyes that made him grin. Would she go out with him? He liked to think she would, but what if she turned him down? Would it change their relationship? Would she be uncomfortable around him? He was only just now beginning to realize how much he enjoyed her company, and the last thing he wanted to do was risk losing her friendship.

But he wanted to date her, dammit! And kiss her. Just once.

"What about the fireworks extravaganza, Nick?" the mayor asked. "Have you heard back from that company in Minneapolis your cousin works for? We need that bid as soon as possible. Nick?"

Abruptly dragging his attention back to the meeting, Nick looked up to find Pierce Dalton and every prominent business owner in Rumor watching him in amusement. For the first time in years, he blushed. "Sorry about that. I haven't been able to concentrate all morning."

"It must be all those women you've got chasing you," John Crew, the owner of the local auto shop, said with a smirk. "It tires a man out."

John would know, Nick thought wryly. The

women of Rumor had been sighing over him for years. "Actually," he told John, "it's a family situation."

Callie was like family, he reasoned, though he suddenly didn't like thinking of her that way at all. That, however, was something he intended to keep to himself. Everyone at the meeting might have been among the elite of Rumor's movers and shakers, but they liked to talk, just like everyone else, and his feelings for Callie were private.

"The bid on the fireworks will come in this afternoon," he told the mayor. "I've been assured that it'll be well within our budget. What about the street dance? Have we got a band lined up yet?"

Donna Mason, the owner of the Getaway, was in charge of organizing the dance that would be held the night of the lunar eclipse, and she immediately launched into the problems she was having booking a band. Thankful he was no longer the center of interest, Nick sat back with a quiet sigh of relief and forced himself to focus on the meeting. It wasn't easy. If he let his attention drift the slightest bit, he found himself thinking about Callie.

And that was really starting to worry him. The last woman he'd mooned over was Belinda Clark. He'd been sixteen at the time and he'd flunked math because all he did in class was daydream about her in her cute little cheerleading outfit. It had taken him months to get over her.

Silently groaning at the memory and the comparison, he told himself he was working too hard. He'd been so involved with organizing the Crazy Moon Festival that he hadn't gone fishing in months. Maybe he'd take Friday off and drive up to Moose Lake for the weekend. He'd rent a cabin and just get away by himself for a while. He could use the break.

But even as he planned the minivacation, he knew he wasn't going anywhere. He had responsibilities with the festival—he couldn't walk out on those just because he couldn't get Callie out of his head. He'd have to wait until next month to go fishing.

Stuck, he was wondering how he was going to get through the month without doing something stupid—like grabbing Callie and kissing her senseless—when Wayne Barrett, a member of the town council, joined him after the meeting. "Hey, Nick, I know you've been busy—everything's pretty hectic with the festival and all—but I was hoping you'd have a chance to call my niece. Shelly? Remember? I told you about her last week."

Swearing silently, Nick forced a smile. Wayne had dropped by his office last week to tell him about his niece, Shelly, a teacher who was off for the summer and visiting him and his wife, Janice. She didn't know anyone but family in the area, and Wayne was hoping to make her stay more enjoyable by introducing her to some people around town. The first person he'd called was Nick.

Wayne had claimed he was only trying to help Shelly make friends, but Nick knew when he was being set up. Wayne wanted him to date his niece. And while Nick appreciated the vote of confidence, he really hated blind dates. They were uncomfortable and awkward, which was why he hadn't agreed to one in years. He was sure Shelly was a nice woman, but alarm bells went off at the mere thought of taking her out.

He couldn't, however, tell Wayne, "Thanks, but no thanks." He was on the town council, and Nick worked with him and other members of the council on a regular basis. The last thing he wanted to do was offend him. Especially when he was asking such a simple thing. He wasn't suggesting that he marry her or anything, just be nice to her and take her to dinner. He could do that for an evening.

And in the process, he just might be able to put Callie out of his mind for a while.

"I'm sorry," he apologized. "I meant to call, but everything's been so hectic with the start of the festival that it just slipped my mind. Why don't I call her in a couple of days? Things should be calmer by then and maybe we can go to dinner. Is she home during the day? What's the best time to call?''

Pleased, Wayne said, ''She and Janice have been antiquing the last few days, but as far as I know, they don't have any plans for the rest of the week. Call whenever you have a free moment. Or stop by the house after work one day,'' he added. ''We could barbecue or something.''

''I'll call,'' Nick promised. ''Janice might not like it if I just showed up at the house for dinner without warning. And Shelly would probably like a little advance warning, too.''

Wayne obviously hadn't thought of that. ''Oh, of course. I guess that would be awkward, wouldn't it? Thanks, Nick. You don't know how I appreciate this. I want Shelly to have a good time, but she's not going to meet anyone hanging out with me and Janice. This'll be great.''

Nick didn't know about that—all he wanted was someone to help take his mind off of Callie. At this point, he didn't think Cameron Diaz could do that, let alone a first grade teacher from Denver.

Chapter 3

In a town the size of Rumor, Montana, there just wasn't that much to do, so the Crazy Moon Festival was like the Olympics, the Fourth of July and Christmas all rolled into one. Main Street was teaming with people all day long, and as evening approached, it seemed as if everyone in the state turned out for the opening night of the carnival. The local high school band played the national anthem, the mayor officially welcomed everyone to the Crazy Moon Festival and the festivities began. The lights on all the rides sprang on, children rushed through the gates to buy tickets and get in line for rides and the scent of funnel cakes and cotton candy drifted on the evening breeze.

The excitement in the air was electric, and watching the smiles on the faces of the townspeople and tourists alike, Nick should have been pleased. Even though it was only the first day of the festival and it might be too early to tell, he felt sure he and the town council had a hit on their hands. By the end of the month, the town coffers would be overflowing with funds, and everyone would be slapping each other on the back for a job well done.

Later, he was sure he would appreciate that. For now, however, all he could think of was Callie. As he walked through the festive crowd, he found himself looking for her in the face of every person he passed. And all the while, she was in her food booth over by the Ferris wheel.

"Don't go there," he muttered to himself. "You saw her at lunch. That's enough."

He'd had all afternoon to think about her, and he'd decided that maybe it would be wise to keep his distance. They'd been friends for a long time and he didn't want to risk losing that. Just because he was interested in her didn't mean she felt the same way about him. Sure, she flirted with him, but lots of women flirted. That might not have meant anything except that she trusted him enough to practice her feminine wiles on him. With one wrong word, he could destroy that trust forever.

There's no need to rush into anything, he told

himself. She's not going anywhere and neither are you. Give yourself some time to consider all the pros and cons before you do anything.

He should have listened to his common sense. It would have been the wise thing to do. But even as he acknowledged that, he found himself heading for the far side of the carnival grounds...and Callie.

He heard the calliope music of the Ferris wheel long before he reached it. Its lilting melody floated on the evening air like a balloon dancing on a breeze, calling to the child in everyone. Just at the sound of it, a smile curled the corners of Nick's mouth. He was still smiling when the crowd parted in front of him and he found himself right in front of Callie's food booth.

Not surprisingly, there was a line of customers in front of the booth that was ten people deep, but there could have been a thousand first graders there, all clamoring for a hot dog, and Nick never would have noticed. The second his eyes landed on Callie, he saw nothing but her.

In all the years he'd known her, he'd seen her with her hair down only a handful of times. Even then, he'd never seen her like this. She'd changed from the waitress uniform she'd worn at lunch to a bright pink spaghetti strap tank top and white capris, then let down her ponytail so that her hair flowed in a cascade of golden waves down her back. Nick took one look at her and immediately felt his mouth go dry.

She was so beautiful, he thought with a groan. Why had it taken him so long to see that? How could he have been so blind when she was right there under his nose? He'd eaten at the diner every day for years, and not once in all that time had he really looked at Callie. Until now. There was a freshness to her, an innocent girlishness, that made him ache to reach for her. All he could do, however, was get in line.

Later, he couldn't say how long it took him to get served. His eyes on Callie, he waited patiently and never noticed when the line got shorter. Suddenly, he was standing right in front of her and there was nothing between them but the half wall of the booth. Given the chance, he would have been happy to just stand there until the carnival closed for the evening. Was it his imagination or did her eyes light up just at the sight of him?

"Well, if it isn't the heartthrob of Rumor," she teased.

"You're full of sass this evening," he retorted with a quick grin. "You think you're pretty cute, don't you?"

"What else can I think?" she tossed back, playfully batting her lashes at him. "Every time I turn around, you show up on my doorstep. What's a girl supposed to think except that you're smitten with her?''

He knew she was teasing, but she didn't have a clue how close to the mark she was. ''Well, I don't know,'' he drawled. ''Every time I come into the diner, Ed Guthrie's sitting at the counter eating a piece of apple pie. Does that mean he's smitten with you, too?''

Ed was old enough to be her father and shaped like a bowling pin. Callie burst out laughing at the very idea that he might be taken with her. ''Ed never had eyes for anyone but Mabel Tucker and you know it. There goes my theory on adding one plus one and getting two. I guess that means you're not interested, either. Darn!''

Tempted to tell her just how interested he was, he only grinned. ''You know, I'd love to stand here and discuss that with you, but I'm holding up the line and the natives are getting restless. How about a glass of lemonade, Miss Sass? It's a good night for something tart.''

''Then maybe you'd better go hunt down Jennifer Fields,'' she said with a wicked twinkle in her eye as she handed him his lemonade and took the dollar he handed her. ''From what I've heard, she's the only tart in town.''

''Maybe I should go look her up,'' he retorted with a chuckle, and stepped aside so the next customer in line could place his order. Not even glancing at the man, Nick was tempted to hunt down Jennifer just to see what Callie would do, but he never got the chance. He'd hardly stepped away from Callie's booth when he heard her say stiffly, "What are you doing back here? I told you to leave me alone."

"Aw, sweetheart, don't be so cold. I like you. I thought we'd go take a ride on the Ferris wheel when you take a break. C'mon. It'll be fun."

"No! I'm not interested. Now if you'll excuse me, I've got other customers to wait on."

As Nick watched, she glanced past the man who was harassing her to the group of high school girls waiting in line behind him, but Callie's admirer had no intention of being dismissed so easily. Standing his ground, he reached into the booth, grabbed her wrist, and growled, "I'm not going anywhere until you promise to ride the Ferris wheel."

Outraged, Nick couldn't believe the man's audacity. He didn't know who he was—since he'd never seen him before, he assumed he was a drunk tourist, in town for the festival—but he didn't give a damn. He had no right to put his hands on Callie.

Furious, he strode quickly back to the booth. "Let go of her," he growled. "Now!"

"Yeah, right, buddy," the tourist sneered. "So you can make time with her yourself? I don't think

so. I saw you flirting with her. You had your
chance, and you struck out. Now it's my turn. Get
lost.''

Nick liked to think he was an even-tempered
man, but seeing another man's hands on Callie was
all it took for him to lose his cool. How dare he
manhandle her! Steaming, he wanted nothing more
than to bury his fist in the drunk's pudgy stomach.
Before he could stop himself, he took another step
toward him.

Thankfully, his common sense reminded him that
as much as he wanted to, he couldn't do something
that stupid. He was the president of the Chamber
of Commerce and was expected to act civilly, if
possible. He couldn't hit the jerk unless he swung
first, but he sure as hell could make him think he
would.

His hazel eyes narrowing dangerously, he glared
at him, nose to nose. ''If you don't let her go right
this minute, I'm going to make you wish you'd
never been born. And if you don't think I can, try
me. I've got a black belt in karate and can break
every bone in your body if I want to. So what's it
going to be? Are you going to remember the manners your momma taught you and let the lady go,
or should I have Ms. Griffin call for an ambulance?
If you don't release her this instant, you're going
to need one.''

For a second, Nick thought the jackass was going to call his bluff. His fingers tightened around Callie's wrist, and he just stood there, considering his options. Something the idiot saw in Nick's eyes, however, must have convinced him that Nick meant business. Grudgingly, he released Callie, then forced a weak laugh. "Man, you don't have to get so bent out of shape! I was just kidding."

"Then there's no harm done," Nick retorted. "Get your food, then get the hell out of here. You're holding up the line."

Hurriedly turning back to Callie, who had watched the exchange wide-eyed, the man said, "I'll just take a lemonade, please. I'm not very hungry." And with his face partially turned away from Nick, he shot Callie a quick wink.

Her heart beating crazily, Callie made sure her lips didn't so much as hint at a smile, but it wasn't easy. She'd met Tim Frost several hours ago when he'd stopped by for an order of catfish and fries. The carnival had just opened, he was the only one at her booth, and when he teasingly asked her why her boyfriend wasn't helping her work the carnival, she'd told him that the man she was crazy about didn't know she was alive. His eyes twinkling with mischief, Tim had immediately volunteered to help her open his eyes and had concocted a plan to make Nick jealous.

Amused, Callie had sincerely doubted that Nick would fall for such an obvious setup, but she hadn't been able to resist giving it a try. Even when she flirted outrageously with him, he still didn't take her seriously! What was a woman to do except play the helpless female in need of rescuing?

And it worked. Better than she'd ever imagined! Elated, she almost laughed aloud, but she didn't dare. As she handed Tim his lemonade and change, Nick watched the exchange with a scowl, just daring the other man to so much as look at her wrong. His lowered eyes dancing with laughter, Tim turned away and beat a hasty retreat.

"Are you all right?" Nick asked quietly.

All right? she thought wildly. She felt wonderful! But she could hardly tell him that. "I don't know what got into the guy," she said huskily. "One second he was fine, and the next, he was coming onto me like there was no tomorrow."

"Forget him," he said roughly. "He's a jackass."

"A very persistent one," she agreed. "Thanks for coming to my rescue."

"My pleasure." Looking around at the crowd of people who walked the midway, he frowned. "I thought Daniel was helping you with the booth tonight."

"He is," she said, and glanced at her watch. "He

was supposed to be here at nine. And here he is,'' she added with a smile as her brother hurried around the side of the booth. ''Running late, as usual.''

''Only ten minutes,'' he huffed. ''C'mon, give a guy a break. I had a chance to ride the tilt-a-whirl with Tiffany Stevens, and I wasn't about to pass that up. She fell right into my arms.''

''Please,'' Callie said with a grimace. ''Spare us the details. All that peroxide's pickled Tiffany's brain.''

''Sisters just don't understand,'' he told Nick. ''Hey, what are you doing here? If you're going to help Callie run the booth, I'll go hunt down Tiffany again.''

''Not a chance,'' Nick retorted. ''I'm taking Callie for a walk. She needs a break.''

Surprised, Callie never even saw her brother frown. Her heart pounding, she was suddenly bursting with happiness. A walk, she thought, dazed. He wanted to take her for a walk! It wasn't a date, but it was the next best thing, and there was nothing she wanted to do more than go with him.

But should she? Heady with success, she hesitated. It was one of those warm summer nights when people did crazy things. The music and laughter of the carnival-goers floated on the air, and anything seemed possible. With no effort whatsoever, she could let herself believe that he could fall in love with her tonight if she just gave him the chance.

Which was why, a voice in her head said, you've got no business going anywhere with him. You're too attracted to him.

She couldn't deny it. But neither could she resist him. Not when he seemed to be finally looking at her as a woman. She'd waited too long for this night. "I could use a break," she told Daniel. "It's been really hectic."

"But—"

"We won't be gone long," she promised. "If you get overwhelmed, call Libby on your cell phone. She said she could lend a hand this evening if we needed her. Okay? I'll be back in a little while." And not giving him time to object further, she quickly turned to Nick with a smile and said, "Let's go."

Within seconds, they had disappeared into the crowd, leaving Daniel staring after them in frustration. He only had to see the glow of his sister's smile to know that she was as happy as a clam at high tide. He should have been happy for her. He was. But Nick was his friend, dammit! How the hell had this happened? What was going on? It had to be the crazy moon.

Chapter 4

Callie had had her share of dates in high school and college, so she wasn't a novice when it came to men. She liked them, enjoyed their company, and seldom had any trouble talking to them. But as she and Nick slowly made their way down the midway, she'd never been more nervous in her life. Idiot! she told herself silently. What are you so nervous about? This is Nick, for heaven's sake! You knew him when he was just a kid, when he had braces and made a fool of himself over Belinda Clark when he was sixteen. There's nothing to be nervous about.

Logically, she knew that. But logic had nothing

to do with what her heart was feeling at that moment. She didn't know how she knew it, but she
knew that whatever happened tonight between her
and Nick would forever change the rest of her life.
And that shook her to the core of her being. It
seemed like she'd wanted him forever. But now that
she had his attention, was she ready for it?

"You're awfully quiet. Is something wrong?"

Jerked out of her musings by his quiet murmur,
she looked up to find him watching her with hazel
eyes that saw far too much. A blush stinging her
cheeks, she laughed shakily. "No. I was just remembering how long we've known each other. Do
you remember the time when we were kids and you
and Daniel built a tree house in our backyard?"

A crooked grin curled the edges of his mouth.
"Yeah. We spent the night up there one night when
a thunderstorm blew in. We were so scared, we
were afraid to climb down, and your dad had to
come up and get us."

"And the time I made my first cake and forgot
to put the eggs in? It was awful."

"But the icing was great. You changed your
mom's recipe, and after she found out how good it
was, she started using it on the cakes at the diner."

Amazed, Callie blinked. "You remember that?"

"Of course. I didn't care that the cake didn't hold

together. That icing was the best thing I'd ever tasted.''

Touched, Callie could have hugged him for that. She loved to cook, and there was nothing she appreciated more than compliments on her cooking. "If I remember correctly, you and Daniel scraped the icing off the cake and ate every bite of it,'' she said with a chuckle. "You didn't even save me a taste.''

"You're damn straight,'' he retorted, grinning. "You had a whole bowl set aside in the refrigerator that we weren't supposed to know about, you little pig. We knew what you were up to.''

Denying nothing, she laughed gaily and had no idea how the sound of her laughter enchanted him. Did she know how pretty she was? Her blue eyes danced, and her whole face lit up when she smiled. With no effort whatsoever, she drew the eye of every man they passed.

Suddenly wanting, needing, her to himself, Nick took her hand. "C'mon,'' he said when she looked at him in surprise, "let's get out of here for a while. I can hardly hear you.''

The music *was* loud, and on the nearby roller coaster, the delighted screams of the riders carried easily on the night air. All around them, people were laughing and talking and you had to practically shout to be heard. Her heart skipping at the

thought of being alone with him, Callie cautioned
herself against jumping to conclusions. Just because
he was holding her hand and wanted to get away
from the crowd didn't necessarily mean he was in
a romantic mood. He might just want some peace
and quiet so they could talk.

Yeah, right, her common sense drawled. And if
you believe that, you need a keeper. Don't be so
naive. The man's interested in you.

She wasn't quite so sure she believed that, but
she couldn't resist the temptation to find out if it
was true. "All right," she said huskily, and let him
lead her away from the lights and people and into
the woods on the north side of town.

Lost in the wonder of holding hands with him,
she didn't notice how far they'd walked until they
came to the barn at the old Sutton place. Surprised,
she stopped in her tracks. "Daniel must be having
a fit wondering where I am. I've got to get back."

"Are you kidding?" he chuckled. "He's probably got every single woman in town offering to help
him. If we rush back now, we'll spoil all his fun."
Tugging at her hand, he grinned. "C'mon, let's
check the place out. I bet you haven't been in the
barn since that time we jumped from the hayloft
and old man Sutton caught us and threatened to call
the sheriff."

"You're absolutely right," she laughed. "If my

dad had found out about that, Daniel and I would have been confined to our rooms until we were thirty-five.''

"We weren't hurting anything—just checking out the hayloft. Let's do it again," he coaxed. "Your dad'll never know. Nobody ever comes around now that old man Sutton's in a nursing home and the place has been leased to the Murphys. And it's not as if we're doing anything illegal. We're just reliving the past.''

She shouldn't have. She was playing with fire. But when he grinned at her like a little boy, his hazel eyes full of mischief and daring, then squeezed her hand, she was helpless to resist him. "Just for a few minutes," she agreed. "Then I really do have to get back to the booth.''

"Ten minutes," he promised her, and led her into the barn.

The Murphys used the old barn to store hay, and as Callie followed Nick inside, the scent of childhood memories tugged at her heart. A fond smile of remembrance curled the edges of her mouth. "It didn't take much to entertain us back then, did it?''

"I like to think it still doesn't," he replied with a grin. "I don't know about you, but I could spend the rest of the evening right here.''

"Doing what? Jumping off the hayloft? I don't think so.''

''No, doing this,'' he rasped, and pulled her into his arms for a kiss.

It seemed like Callie had waited her entire life for just this moment. She'd dreamed about it, ached for it, longed for it with every fiber of her being. Nothing she'd imagined, however, had ever come close to the wonder of being in his arms. Magic. There was no other way to describe it. Her heart singing with joy, she melted against him and kissed him back, wanting the moment to go on forever.

Stunned by the desire she stirred in him so effortlessly, Nick groaned. He was a man who'd had his share of women—he'd thought he'd known what to expect. He hadn't had a clue. Sweet. Dear heaven, she was sweet! She moved against him, wrapping her arms around his neck, and just that easily, she drove him crazy. Need tearing at him, he gathered her closer and took the kiss deeper.

Lost in the taste and feel and wonder of her, he assured himself he would find the strength to let her go soon. In a minute, he promised himself. He just needed to hold her, kiss her, a little longer.

But one kiss led to another, then another, and desire turned to sweet, wonderful madness. Alone together in the musty darkness of the barn, they seemed to be the only two people in the world. Wanting, needing, more, he swept her off her feet and into his arms, only to lay her down in soft bed of hay in one of the stalls.

"Nick…"

She reached for him, drawing him down to her, and that was nearly his undoing. Straining to hold on to his control, he couldn't stop himself from sinking down into the hay with her even as he warned, "We've got to stop, sweetheart. You're driving me out of my mind."

"Not yet," she whispered, kissing him again. "Just a little longer."

Wrapped in each other's arms, her body soft and inviting under his, Nick couldn't find the strength to resist her. Not when she held him and kissed him with a tenderness and passion that seemed to come straight from her heart. Alarm bells clanged in his head, but all he heard was Callie's soft sighs and moans as he ran his hands over her hips and breasts, learning the feel of her, the softness of her, the wonder of her.

When his control actually shattered, he couldn't have said. He needed to touch her, to feel her skin against him. Somehow, clothes melted away, and suddenly, she was as eager to touch him as he was her. They caressed each other with slow hands and lingering kisses, and just that easily, their hearts beat together in time to a rhythm only they could hear. And Nick forgot all about stopping, all about

the carnival, all about the fact that Daniel was waiting for them to return. All he could think of was
Callie. Holding her. Kissing her. Loving her.

Later, he never remembered moving over her,
parting her legs. Desperate for more of her, his only
thought to claim her completely, he surged into
her...only to freeze when she stiffened in pain.
"Nick!"

Shocked, he looked down at her in the dark shadows of the barn and blurted out, "You're a virgin!"

Tears pooling in her eyes, Callie nodded miser-
ably. "I was afraid you'd stop if I told you," she
choked. "I didn't want you to stop."

She said it so simply—and didn't have a clue
what she did to him with her admission. How could
he stop when he needed her more than his next
breath? he wondered. Even now, he should have
been pulling out, backing off, stopping...but he
couldn't. It was too late for that. It had been, he
realized, from the moment he first kissed her.

"I wouldn't have stopped," he said huskily,
leaning down to kiss her with an aching tenderness
that tugged at his heart. "I would have taken more
care with you." Brushing her lips with his, he murmured, "Like this."

He moved over her, seducing her with soft
words, soft kisses and caresses that were softer than
air, and in seconds, Callie had forgotten the pain.

Her senses swimming, she moaned and moved under him, seeking something she couldn't put a name to. "Nick…please…"

His smile tender in the darkness, he said, "That's right, sweetheart. You're so pretty. I love touching you, kissing you…"

With quiet words and slow hands, he slowly built back up the flames of passion, until Callie was lost to everything but Nick. His touch, the heated passion of his kiss, his scent, the hard length of his body. Deep inside, need tightened like a fist, then clawed at her, and her mind blurred. Gasping, her heart thundering, she lifted her hips to his, once, then twice, then again and again. Emotions pulled at her, her breath tore through her lungs. Then, just when she thought she knew what to expect, she shattered, liquid stardust bursting through her body. Dazed, she cried out in delight. "Nick!"

If he lived to be a hundred, Nick didn't think he would ever forget the sound of his name on her lips when she came apart under him. That alone triggered his own release, and afterward, he wanted to do nothing but hold her. She was a virgin! Why hadn't she told him? They needed to talk, but somewhere in the distance, they heard a man call his dog, and they both realized that their private hideaway wasn't quite as private as they'd thought.

"We need to get dressed," he said quietly.

"And I have to get back to the booth," she said huskily, not quite meeting his eye as she hurriedly grabbed her clothes. "Daniel will be wondering where I am."

Don't! Nick wanted to say. Don't turn away from me. Not after what we just shared! But the intimacy between them had been shattered, and too late, Nick realized that he'd rushed them both into making love when they'd only just now found each other. Because of that, their friendship was irrevocably changed, and it was all his fault.

Outside, the man chasing his dog whistled for him, and this time, he was much closer than before. Swearing silently, Nick jerked on his clothes in record time. "We need to talk," he told Callie quietly as they left the barn and hurried back to the carnival.

"I can't right now," she said as they approached her food booth. "Daniel looks like he's got his hands full."

Her brother was, in fact, swamped with customers, and, thankfully, too busy to notice the blush that stung her cheeks. "Thank God!" he said in relief when he looked up to find her and Nick hurrying toward the booth. "Where have you been? I ran out of catfish, and Marisa hasn't answered her cell phone, and I'm going crazy. We need more fries and ice—"

"I'll call Ben," Callie said, reaching for her cell phone. "He can bring everything we need from the diner."

"I'll get it," Nick volunteered. "My truck's just around the corner, and I can be there and back before you can even track him down."

He had a point. Digging out her keys to the diner, Callie tossed them to him. "Everything's labeled and stored in the freezer. Bring four bags of everything, and we should do fine."

He was gone in a flash, leaving Callie alone with Daniel to handle the hungry crowd lined up in front of the booth. Facing her customers with a rueful smile, she said, "It looks like we underestimated how well our food would go over. We've sent Nick for supplies, but it'll be at least ten minutes before we can start cooking. For those of you who want to wait, I've got free chocolate cookies."

A cheer went up from the crowd. Grinning, Callie quickly handed out cookies, and just that easily soothed her customer's hunger. Watching her, Daniel could only shake his head. "I don't know why I didn't think of that. Thanks, sis. I was about to pull my hair out. Where were you?"

"We just went for a walk," she said with a shrug. "I didn't mean to be gone so long, but we were talking and I lost track of time."

"No problem," he replied easily. "You looked a little frazzled when you left. Did the break help?"

Her emotions still in a whirl, Callie didn't have an answer for that. Not when she felt like her whole world had just turned upside down. Nick had made love to her. She'd loved every moment of it, but how did he feel about her? He'd never said.

"Callie? Hello? Where'd you go? Are you okay?"

Snapping back to her surroundings to find her brother frowning at her worriedly, she swallowed a shaky laugh. No, she wasn't all right! She was confused, elated, worried if the loving they'd shared had meant anything to Nick. But that was hardly something she could say to Daniel.

Forcing a smile, she said, "Sure. Why wouldn't I be? The new specials are a hit and we're selling everything in sight. If this keeps up, we'll both be driving new Mercedes by the end of the month."

She sounded like she was on top of the world, but Daniel knew her better than most, and she half expected him to tell her to knock off the bull. But she met his gaze unflinchingly, and something in her eyes must have convinced him that she was fine. His frown easing, he grinned. "You can keep the Mercedes. I'd rather have a new SUV."

"An SUV it is," she retorted, and sighed in relief. If she could fool him, maybe she'd be able to act like her old self the next time she saw Nick. Until she knew how he felt about her, she had no intention of letting him know she'd lost her heart to him.

Chapter 5

Nick had never considered himself a coward, but after he delivered the supplies Callie needed to her booth, he made a quick excuse and headed home. He told himself he just needed some time to himself, but all he could think about was Callie. With no effort whatsoever, he could remember ever touch, every kiss, every sigh he'd pulled from her. And just that easily, he wanted her again.

Dear God, what had he done?

She'd been a virgin, an innocent, he thought as he reached his apartment. And he'd taken her like a man possessed. In a barn, no less! He must have been out of his mind. There was no other explanation. She was the sister of his best friend. He'd known her all his life, but he hadn't thought of any of that when he'd kissed her. With nothing more than a kiss, a touch, his common sense had flown right out the barn door.

Cringing at the thought, he restlessly prowled the confines of his living room and wondered how he could have been so irresponsible. He'd never even considered that she might be a virgin...or thought to use protection.

Did she hate him now? He wouldn't blame her if she did. She might have been a mature woman who successfully ran her own business, but in her heart, she was a girl...an innocent girl who'd no doubt dreamed of the day she gave herself to a man for the first time. Nick seriously doubted any of those dreams took place in a barn in a pile of smelly old hay.

Swearing, he was thoroughly disappointed in himself. He didn't treat women this way. Especially one he'd known practically all his life! He respected and liked her and damn sure should have shown her a hell of a lot more caring than he had. At the very least, she deserved that. She should have had romance and flowers and happily ever after. Instead, he'd given her hay.

He'd treated her like some woman he'd picked up on a street corner and that ate at his gut. He was better than that. He had to apologize, had to find a way to make this up to her. Grabbing his keys, he headed for the door. He had to talk to her right now!

But even as he opened the front door of his apartment and started to step outside, he knew there was nothing he could do tonight. Callie had her hands full at the carnival and couldn't leave Daniel to handle things so she could go off with him again. He'd have to wait until tomorrow.

Resigned, he had no choice but to call it a night and go to bed. But he didn't sleep. Every time he closed his eyes, all he could think of was Callie...the shape and feel and taste of her. It was, he realized with a groan, going to be a long night.

The next morning was just like any other at the diner. The breakfast crowd started arriving at six-thirty, and by seven, the place was packed. When she wasn't seating customers or taking orders, Callie was whisking through the tables, refilling coffee cups while Elvis sang ''All Shook Up'' on the jukebox. Ben had the kitchen well in hand, Libby had delivered fresh-baked pastries at dawn, Marisa was taking it easy handling the regulars at the counter. Life couldn't have been more normal.

But as she chatted with a tourist from Cheyenne who was in town for the festival, Callie had never felt less like herself. All night long, the images of her and Nick making love had played in her head, haunting her dreams. She'd woke this morning aching for him, reaching for him.

"Callie? Yoo-hoo? Are you going to just carry that coffee around or share it with the rest of us?"

Blinking, she snapped back to attention to find Gladys Perkins, one of her mother's best friends, grinning at her. Gladys was like family and one of the biggest teases in town. Callie could always count on Gladys to make her laugh, and that was something she sorely needed today. Anything to distract her from the memories of last night.

"My mind's a jillion places this morning," she told Gladys with a grin as she stepped over to her table to top off her coffee. "I was thinking about lunch."

"And here I thought you were daydreaming about a new beau," she teased. "I could have sworn I saw you on the Ferris wheel last night with Jason King."

Callie burst out laughing. Jason was a mama's boy who was sixty if he was a day, and his favorite topic of conversation was bugs—spiders, roaches, ants and anything else that crawled. "You must have forgotten your glasses again," she retorted, chuckling. "You know you're blind as a bat without them."

"I'm not that bad," Gladys protested, her green

eyes twinkling. "Even without my glasses, I know a good-looking man when I see one." Nodding toward the diner entrance, she grinned. "There's one right there."

Glancing up, Callie felt her smile slip as her eyes locked with Nick's. Gladys made another teasing remark, but she didn't even hear her. All her attention was focused on Nick. She'd been waiting for him to show up all morning, and she hadn't realized it until now. Her heart started to pound at the mere sight of him. Without thinking, she took a step toward him. All she wanted to do was walk into his arms and feel him hold her again.

Some of the biggest gossips in town were sitting at the tables that ran the length of her diner, however, and she could just hear them now if she treated Nick as anything other than a friend. The news would spread like wildfire, and people would have them dating and engaged by lunchtime.

Cringing at the thought, she stopped in her tracks. No, she told herself. After last night, everything had changed between her and Nick, but that was no one's business but their own. So she gave him an easy smile and greeted him just as she always did—with a smart remark. Placing her hand over her heart, she said, "Somebody call the paramedics. I think I'm going to swoon."

Normally, Nick would have grinned and held his

own with her, but not today. Only a faint smile curled the corners of his mouth as he said gruffly, "I need to talk to you. I know you're busy, but this is important."

In all the years that she'd known him, Callie had seldom seen him so somber. Alarmed, she said, "Yes, of course." Motioning for Marisa to take over for her, she followed him into her office and quickly shut the door behind her so they could talk in private. "What's wrong?" she immediately demanded. "It's not Daniel, is it? Or my parents? Oh, God, Nick, tell me it's not Dad! He hasn't been feeling well lately, but Mom couldn't talk him into going to the doctor. If something happened to him—"

"It's not your dad," he cut in quietly. "Or your mom or Daniel. Nothing's wrong."

Surprised, she frowned. "Then what did you want to talk about? You look so serious."

"I know you're busy and this isn't the best time to do this, but I've been thinking about you all night. I thought you needed to know that I'm going to marry you."

Whatever Callie had been expecting, it wasn't that. Sure she must have misunderstood him, she sank into the chair behind her desk. "I beg your pardon?"

A slight smile curled one corner of his mouth. "You heard me. I'm going to marry you."

Over the years, Callie had lost count of the number of times she'd fantasized about marrying Nick. In her dreams, she had the entire wedding planned. It would be a candlelight service, and there would be flowers everywhere. Her dress would be lace and satin, and she'd look like a princess as she walked down the aisle on her father's arm to marry the man she loved.

How many times had she seen his face in those fantasies? Every time, it was filled with love. But now, as he told her he was going to marry her, she searched his eyes for signs of his feelings, and all she saw was determination. Just that easily, her dreams crumbled.

She didn't, however, cry. Tears would come later. Instead, she studied him curiously. "Why do you want to marry me, Nick?"

"You could be pregnant," he said stiffly, "and it's all my fault. You were a virgin. And I was so caught up in the moment, I didn't think to use protection. I never should have been so careless. I know better."

"So you want to marry me to make up for that?"

He nodded somberly. "I thought about it all night, and it seems like the only logical thing to do. You know how gossip is in this town. If you're pregnant, people will talk, and I want to protect you from that. If we get married, then everyone finds out you're pregnant, no one will say a thing.''

Callie supposed she should have been touched. He was willing to take extraordinary steps to protect her reputation. But as much as she loved him, she knew she'd rather spend the rest of her life alone rather than marry him because he felt some twisted sense of obligation.

''I appreciate the offer,'' she said quietly, ''but I'm afraid the answer is no.''

He couldn't have looked more stunned if she'd slapped him. ''What? What do you mean...*no?* Dammit, Callie, I'm trying to protect you!''

''I know,'' she said with a sad smile. ''And it's very noble of you. But I can't.''

She would have said more, but Marisa knocked on the office door just then and stuck her head in. ''Sorry to interrupt, Cal, but Todd's here with the milk delivery and he swears you ordered enough cottage cheese to feed an army.''

Her timing couldn't have been better. The conversation was over as far as Callie was concerned— she just needed an excuse to end it. Rising quickly to her feet, she said, ''I'm sorry, Nick, but I've got to get back to work.''

Not giving him time to say a word, she hurried out like the hounds of hell were nipping at her heels, and Nick didn't know whether to be relieved or hurt. He'd just asked her to marry him, dammit, and all she'd said was *I can't* before she ran off to deal with cottage cheese! Didn't she realize this decision he'd come to hadn't been any easy one? He'd never asked a woman to marry him in his life. It wasn't something he'd done lightly, and she hadn't even given a reason for turning him down flat. The least she could have done was think about it for a few days.

Quit your crying, his common sense growled. If you had any brains, you'd be counting your lucky stars. If you married her, you'd fall in love with her, and then where would you be? In deep trouble!

He couldn't argue with that. Last night, she'd touched something in him no woman ever had, and it scared him. The last thing he wanted to do was fall in love with her. Oh, he knew her parents had a great marriage and he'd always envied them that, but he didn't want to love anyone that much. His parents had had that same type of closeness, and when his mother had died, his father had fallen apart. That was five years ago, and his dad still grieved. He would for the rest of his life. Watching him, feeling his pain, Nick had decided that he wanted nothing to do with that kind of love.

Knowing that, he should have thanked God that Callie had had the good sense to turn him down, then found a way to forget that he'd ever made love to her. But he was hurt, dammit! When a man proposed to a woman, the least she could do was take more than two minutes to consider it. That was just common courtesy!

Irritated, his appetite nonexistent, he was tempted to skip breakfast and leave through the diner's back door, but his pride wouldn't let him slip away like a thief in the night. He'd done the honorable thing and proposed, and just because she'd turned him down didn't mean things had to change between them. He didn't want to lose her as a friend. So he returned to the dining room and tried to act as if nothing had happened.

It wasn't easy. Even though he took a seat at the counter and Marisa waited on him, he couldn't take his eyes off Callie. She laughed and chatted with her customers, and all he could think about was last night and making love with her in the hay. He wanted her again, and it was driving him crazy. He had to get out of there.

"Hey, what's wrong?" Marisa asked when he didn't touch the coffee and doughnut he'd ordered. "Are you sick?"

"No, I just remembered some paperwork I left at home," he fibbed. "I don't have time for breakfast, after all."

"No problem," she assured him, quickly bagging the doughnut for him and pouring him fresh coffee in a foam cup. "You can take it with you. Are we going to see you at lunch? The special today is lasagna, and it's fantastic."

Nick didn't doubt it. But he was never going to be able to get Callie out of his head if he didn't put some space between them. "It sounds great," he replied, "but I don't think I'm going to be able to make it."

Leaving her a generous tip, he wished her a good day, waved at Callie and headed for his office. But work offered little distraction. His concentration was shot to hell, and every time he dropped his guard, he could feel Callie's touch, taste her kiss. Disgusted with himself, he knew there was only one way he was going to forget her. With another woman.

Then he remembered Shelly Barrett. Wayne had been urging him to give her a call. Maybe this was a good time. Flipping through his Rolodex, he found Wayne's home number and quickly dialed it before he could have second thoughts. A split second later, he had Shelly on the line.

"Hi," he said. "This is Nick Sullivan. Your uncle told me you were visiting from Denver, and I was wondering if you'd like to go out to dinner."

Chapter 6

What had she done?

All morning, the question ate at Callie, and too late, she realized she may have made a terrible mistake. She couldn't remember how long she'd loved Nick—it seemed like forever. Because of him, she'd been convinced that happily ever after truly did exist, and all she'd ever wanted was for him give her a chance to share it with him. Miraculously, he finally had. And what had she done? Turned him down flat. She must have been out of her mind.

But he didn't propose out of love, she reminded herself. Only out of guilt, and a marriage based on that didn't have a prayer of working.

The logical part of her brain knew that and accepted it, but her heart disagreed. Okay, so maybe he didn't love her now. But he was attracted to her—last night had proven that, if nothing else. She'd read once that men had to have sex with a woman before they could really fall in love. So what if he was already falling in love with her and didn't know it? If she just gave him time, maybe they could find happiness together. Wasn't love worth the risk?

Torn, unable to think of anything but wedding bells and Nick, she inadvertently served an omelet to Sally Hawkins, instead of the pancakes she'd ordered. "Whoa," the older woman gasped, shrinking back in her seat with a comical grimace. "You know I don't eat anything that comes out of the wrong end of a chicken. Get those nasty things away from me."

Too late, Callie realized her mistake. "Oops! Sorry about that," she said, quickly whisking the omelet away. "You ordered pancakes, didn't you? What did I do with them?"

"You gave them to Tom Bishop," Marisa said with a grin as she joined her and delivered Sally's pancakes to her. "Tom ordered biscuits and gravy. The omelet goes to Joyce Stevens. I'll take that to Joyce while you take a break."

"I'm fine—"

"You're on another planet, dear," Sally said with a grin. "Take a break. You look like you could use one."

"She's right," Marisa said. "You haven't sat down all morning. Go relax and let Ben heat up a cinnamon roll on the grill the way you like. I can handle things for now. The breakfast crowd is thinning out—if you want to put your feet up, you'd better do it now. In another hour and a half, the lunch crowd will hit and you're going to be running back and forth between here and the food booth like a chicken with its head cut off."

Hesitating, Callie told herself she shouldn't. If she sat down now, all she'd do was stew over Nick. Work at least gave her something else to think about...well, most of the time, she added ruefully. But Marisa was right. She had been going nonstop all morning, and once the lunch crowd started straggling in, the pace would pick up and she wouldn't have a moment to herself for the rest of the afternoon. Normally, she thrived on that, but she hadn't slept much last night and her mornings didn't normally start with a marriage proposal. Maybe she did need a break.

"All right," she sighed. "But just for a few minutes. Then it's your turn."

Breakfast was just about over; everyone had been served. Marisa would only have to refill coffee cups and give people their checks, so Callie left her in charge and retreated behind the counter to the kitchen, where Ben was already working on lunch. "Need some help?" she asked.

"Not on your life," he retorted. "You're supposed to be taking a break."

Not surprised that he'd heard—after all, the kitchen was just on the other side of the counter from the dining area, she wrinkled her nose in a grimace. "Okay, so I'm a little distracted this morning. I can still cook."

"I don't think so," he said dryly. "You've been mixing up orders all morning. The next thing you'll mix up is sugar and salt, and we'll all be in trouble."

"I'm not that bad," she grumbled, but she knew she was. Sighing, she dropped onto a stool. "Okay, I'm taking a break. Is everybody happy?"

Chuckling, Marisa took a seat on the opposite side of the counter. "I am. How about you, Ben?"

A grin split his rough-hewn face. "Couldn't be better."

"Well, that takes care of us," Marisa said. Arching a brow at Callie, she pinned her to her chair with sharp green eyes that saw far too much. "What about you? Are you happy?"

Put on the spot, she tried not to squirm. "Of course. Why wouldn't I be? The specials have been a big hit and the festival's just started. We're making money hand over fist. If this keeps up the rest of the month, I just might be able to put some money down on that land I've been wanting to buy on Stony Creek. What more could I want?''

She smiled easily enough, but Marisa wasn't fooled. ''What's going on?'' she asked quietly. ''And don't shrug and tell me nothing,'' she warned before Callie could do just that. ''I know you have a lot on your plate right now and you're distracted with trying to run the diner and the food booths for the carnival and festival. If I had the responsibility of all that on my shoulders, I'd be lucky to have any hair left. But you thrive on that kind of thing. So what's wrong?''

''Nothing,'' she insisted, lying through her teeth. ''Really. I'm fine.''

Fighting to keep her gaze steady, Callie should have known better than to think she could pull a fast one on Marisa—they knew each other too well. They'd worked double shifts and early mornings together more times than either of them could remember, and through thick and thin, they'd always been fast friends. They knew when the other was worried or hurting or on top of the world, and there were seldom secrets between them.

But even though Callie knew she could trust Marisa with her life, she couldn't tell her about last night. Every dream she'd ever had had come heart-stoppingly close to coming true in Nick's arms, then he'd ruined everything this morning when he'd proposed just because he thought she was pregnant. As much as she cared about Marisa, that wasn't something she could share with her or anyone else. It was just too private.

So she met her gaze head-on and prayed that the pain she was feeling wasn't reflected in her eyes. She needn't have bothered. Marisa frowned in concern, but she didn't, thankfully, push her. ''When you want to talk about it, I'm here for you,'' she said quietly, and leaving it at that, she returned to work.

Blatantly listening to the entire conversation, Ben plopped a heated cinnamon roll on the counter in front of her. ''Here,'' he said gruffly. ''Eat. It'll make you feel better.''

Sudden tears welling in her eyes, Callie gave him a watery smile. ''Thanks,'' she said huskily. What would she do without friends? She hoped she never had to find out.

The next two days were the busiest—and the loneliest—of Callie's life. Whether she worked the diner or her two food booths, she found herself continually looking for Nick, but he was nowhere to be found. He didn't even come in for lunch as he usually did, and she couldn't help but be concerned. Was he sick? Worried, she almost asked her brother if he'd heard from him, but she hadn't forgotten how surprised he'd been when Nick had insisted on taking her for a walk the night they'd made love. If she showed too much interest in Nick's whereabouts, she'd be opening the door to questions she wasn't prepared to answer.

So she kept her worries to herself and contemplated calling Nick herself. But he knew where she was and from all appearances, he seemed to be avoiding her. And that hurt. Was he ending their friendship because she wouldn't marry him? Was that what his silence was all about? Or did he regret making love to her and this was his way of telling her he wanted nothing more to do with her?

Pain squeezing her heart, that thought haunted her sleep. Miserable, needing answers even if they weren't the ones she wanted to hear, she made a decision to call him the first chance she got the following day. That was Saturday, however, and everyone in the state of Montana seemed to be visiting Rumor. People started coming in for breakfast right after she opened the front door at six-thirty, and by eight o'clock, the line was out the door. It didn't let up all day.

Too busy to even take a break for her own breakfast, Callie sent up a silent prayer of thanks that

she'd had the foresight to call everyone into work
that morning. She'd even hired a couple of high
school kids to help with the weekend rush, and they
still were snowed under with customers. Normally,
she would have loved the hustle and bustle, but all
she wanted to do was call Nick. As breakfast gave
way to lunch, she told herself the pace was bound
to let up soon. Then she'd have some time to call
him.

But the lunch hour stretched out to two, then
three and four, and there still wasn't an empty seat
in the house. And outside, Main Street was just as
crowded as people enjoyed the street fair and
waited for the carnival to open as evening
approached.

"Man, this is something, isn't it?" Marisa said
as she hurried behind the counter to fill glasses with
iced tea for table six. "Where are all these people
coming from?"

"Wyoming, Idaho, the Dakotas." Grinning, Callie reeled off the neighboring states. "The city
council and Chamber of Commerce really did their
jobs, didn't they? Now maybe the council will have
enough to build that youth center they've been talking about for years."

"Speaking of the Chamber," Marisa said, suddenly remembering, "you're never going to believe
what I just heard. Nick's seeing Wayne Barrett's

niece. She's visiting from Denver for the whole month. You must have seen her around…she's tall, pretty, brunette. I think her name's Shelly…."

Shocked, Callie hardly heard the rest of Marisa's description. No! she wanted to cry. She hadn't seen her and didn't want to because she wasn't dating Nick. She couldn't be. He wasn't the type of man who jumped from woman to woman. Especially when he'd just made love to her a few days ago. He'd asked her to marry him, for heaven's sake! Granted, she'd turned him down, but he still wouldn't turn around and immediately date someone else. Marisa must have misunderstood.

But even as she tried to take comfort in that, the bell over the diner's front door rang merrily, and she glanced up to see Nick walk in. And at his side was a tall, beautiful woman with jet-black hair.

Later, Callie would have sworn her heart stopped dead in her chest. Nick's eyes met hers, and for a moment, neither of them moved. Then he seemed to remember the woman at his side. "Callie, this is Shelly Barrett," he said stiffly. "You know… Wayne's niece."

For the life of her, Callie couldn't summon more than a curt nod, even when silence stretched into awkwardness. Uncomfortable color stinging Nick's cheeks, he hurried to add, "I was telling Shelly how good your strawberry shortcake is, so we thought we'd come in for dinner and dessert. It looks like you've got a full house, though. Maybe we should come back another time.''

Standing as if turned to stone, Callie just looked at him. He'd brought another woman to her diner just two days after they'd made love. Did he really think she cared if he brought her back another time? Talk about insensitive! She loved him, dammit! How could he do this to her?

Without warning, sudden tears stung her eyes, horrifying her. No! she thought furiously. She wouldn't cry. Not in front of him and this... woman! She wouldn't let either one of them know she cared so much. She'd smile and be nice and after their meal, give them each a serving of strawberry shortcake big enough to choke a horse.

So she blinked back the tears, squared her shoulders and somehow found the strength to face Shelly. That was as far as she got. Suddenly, without warning, nausea rolled in her stomach and rose in her throat. ''Excuse me,'' she gasped, horrified. Clapping a hand over her mouth, she ran for the rest room.

She reached it just in time. Five seconds later, the little bit of food she'd had time to eat that day was history. Spent, she leaned weakly against the rest room vanity and winced at her image in the mirror. She looked like death warmed over. If she could just lie down for a moment...

But even as she toyed with the idea of resting for a few moments on the small love seat in her office, she knew she couldn't. The diner was packed...and Nick and Shelly were waiting for dinner and dessert.

Tears welled in her eyes just at the thought, and this time, there was no blinking them back. She didn't want to see Nick, didn't want to see him with the beautiful, sophisticated Shelly who was so different from herself. But she couldn't very well hide out in the bathroom like a two-year-old until they left. She had to face them—just as soon as she stopped crying.

Lost in her misery, she didn't realize she had company until there was suddenly a sharp knock at the bathroom door. Even as she jumped, Nick called out, "Callie? Are you okay? Let me in."

"No!" Hurriedly, she swiped at the tears that trailed down her cheeks. "Go away!"

"Not until I see you. Did you throw up?"

She couldn't very well deny it—everyone in the diner had seen her rush to the rest room with her hand over her mouth—and she could well imagine what he was thinking. *If she was throwing up, she had to be pregnant, which meant they had to get married as soon as possible.* Yeah, right, she thought bitterly. Forget love, forget happily ever after, forget the date he'd abandoned to come chasing after her. She didn't think so.

"I picked up a stomach virus from Libby's kids," she fibbed, still stubbornly refusing to open the door. "It's just a bug. Go back to Shelly. I'm fine."

Scowling, Nick hesitated, feeling guilty. It was a feeling he didn't like, but he had no one to blame but himself. He'd done nothing but make one mistake after another lately. First, he'd seduced Callie and taken her virginity, then if that wasn't enough, he'd thrown Shelly in her face. Now he was afraid Callie was pregnant, and she wouldn't even look him in the eye. Frustrated, he eyed the door—he could bust it in with one swift kick—but even as he considered the idea, he knew he couldn't. Not when the diner was full of people and Callie wasn't feeling well. She'd never forgive him.

Still, this discussion wasn't over, not by a long shot. "All right," he growled, "have it your way— for now. I'll talk to you later." And next time there wouldn't be a bathroom door between them, he promised himself. He'd make sure of it.

Chapter 7

Shelly was still standing just inside the diner's front door when Nick rejoined her, and he wouldn't have blamed her if she'd been furious with him for leaving her high and dry while he went chasing after another woman. But worry knitted her delicately arched brows and all she said was, "Is your friend okay? If you need to take her home, I can walk back to Uncle Wayne's. It's not that far."

If he hadn't been a man of principle, Nick would have taken her up on that. He was no longer in the mood for a date—all he wanted to do was spend the rest of the evening with Callie, taking care of her. But even if she would have allowed that—

which he knew she wouldn't—he couldn't, in good
conscience, cut short an evening with one woman
so he could be with another. He'd asked Shelly out
to dinner, and he still intended to honor that com-
mitment. They wouldn't, however, eat at the diner.

"I can't let you do that—we've got a date. And
Callie's going to be okay," he assured her. "She's
just got some kind of stomach virus. I'll check on
her later. In the meantime, why don't we go someplace else? I'm not really in the mood for diner
food, and the Rooftop Café grills a great steak. It's
just down the street. We can sit outside and watch
the stars come out."

She hesitated, her sapphire blue eyes searching
his, but something in his steady gaze must have
reassured her. "Steak does sound good," she said,
then grinned ruefully as she added, "Aunt Janice
isn't a very good cook. It seems like the only thing
we've eaten since I got here is macaroni and
cheese."

"Then you're going to love the Rooftop," he
promised with a chuckle as he opened the diner
door for her and escorted her outside. "There's not
a single pasta dish on the menu."

Their steaks were delicious, the night sky spec-
tacular. Shelly was a good listener, attentive and
easygoing, and beautiful. Under different circum-

stances, Nick would have thoroughly enjoyed her company and probably asked her out again. But his thoughts had a mind of their own and kept drifting to Callie. Did she really have a virus or was she just saying that so he wouldn't guess she was pregnant? He should have insisted they sit down and talk about the situation like to two civilized adults. But Shelly had been waiting, and Callie had been so determined not to talk to him that he hadn't known what to do. Was she okay? Maybe he should call her—

"And I told him that the last blue donkey I saw had pink polka dots but that could have been a skin condition."

Lost in his thoughts, Nick blinked in confusion. "I beg your pardon?"

"It's about time," she said with a teasing smile. "What planet were you on? You haven't heard a word I said for the last ten minutes."

He had the grace to blush. "Sorry about that. I was thinking about...the festival."

They both knew he was lying, but Shelly didn't push the issue. "You've done a wonderful job," she replied. "Uncle Wayne can't believe the size of the crowds."

"We've been lucky," he said modestly. "A lot of people worked really hard to pull this off."

He told her about the town meetings, the bake

sales and garage sales that were held to raise money
for advertising and bands and Porta Potties, and
somehow, he managed to get through the rest of the
meal without his attention wandering again. But he
hadn't fooled Shelley. When he drove her home and
pulled up in front of her uncle's home, she sat back
and said quietly, "So tell me about Callie. How
long have you two been dating?"

Caught off guard, he blinked. "We're not! I
mean…her brother and I have been best friends
since grade school. I've known Callie since she was
in pigtails."

"I bet she was cute," she said with a smile.

A crooked grin pushed up the corners of his
mouth. "Yeah, she was."

"And you can't keep your eyes off her," she
guessed, and had the satisfaction of seeing his
brows snap together in a frown. "It's okay, Nick,"
she said with an understanding smile. "You don't
owe me an explanation. We're not dating—we just
went to dinner to get my uncle off our backs."

"We did not!"

"Oh, c'mon," she teased. "I saw how you and
Callie looked at each other. I definitely felt like a
third wheel. And that's okay," she quickly assured
him. "I like you, Nick. I really do, but I've been
dating this guy back in Denver I'm really crazy
about. I didn't plan to go out with anyone while I

was here, but Uncle Wayne has a hard time taking no for an answer. But I guess I don't have to tell you that. He put the same pressure on you that he did on me. And don't tell me he didn't," she added before good manners forced him to deny it. "I know my uncle."

She said it without rancor, and Nick couldn't help but grin. He worked with Wayne Barrett on a regular basis on town council business, and he knew from firsthand experience that when Wayne made up his mind to do something, he didn't let anything get in his way. Once he'd decided that Nick and his niece needed to go out, they'd never stood a chance.

Another woman might have been more than a little put out with her interfering uncle, but Shelly just accepted it with a rueful smile and didn't let it bother her. And Nick liked that about her. She was frank and understanding, and she wasn't any more interested in him than he was in her. For that alone, he could have kissed her.

Not that he would! he quickly assured himself. The only woman he wanted to really kiss was Callie. Was she all right? He should stop by and check on her on his way home....

"You're doing it again," Shelly teased.

Jerking back to attention, he grinned sheepishly. "Sorry about that."

"Don't be. It's cute. Callie is a lucky girl."

"We're just—"

"Friends," she finished for him, grinning. "I know. Good friends are hard to find. If you need someone to talk to, give me a call. I've been told I'm a good listener."

Thanking him again for dinner, she didn't let him walk her to her uncle's front door, but slipped out of the car and hurried up the walk. When she disappeared inside with a jaunty wave, Nick knew he would be wise to go home. But he was still worried about Callie. If she was really sick, he didn't want her to be alone. He'd just stop by and see if she needed anything.

He was, he acknowledged wryly, grasping at straws, using the flimsiest excuse to see her, but he didn't care. He was worried about her. There was nothing wrong with that. They were friends. She'd do the same thing for him if the situation was reversed.

But even as he tried to convince himself that he was searching her out because of their "friendship," he couldn't forget the look on her face when she'd run to the bathroom to throw up. Up until then, she'd been the picture of health. Could she really have gotten sick that quickly? Granted, a stomach virus could hit with no warning, but he couldn't shake the feeling that she was pregnant.

Needing answers and determined to get them, he arrived at her apartment and knocked firmly on her door. "Callie?" he called loudly, knocking again when she didn't answer immediately. "It's Nick. Are you all right? I need to talk to you."

For a moment, he was greeted with nothing but silence. Then, just when he thought she wasn't going to answer, he heard the dead bolt slide free, and she pulled the door open.

She was, not surprisingly, dressed in her pajamas and a summer robe that looked touchably soft. Nick took one look at her and felt his heart shift. He'd always thought she was pretty, but lately, it seemed like every time he saw her, she had this glow about her that just stole his breath. And for the life of him, he didn't know why. It wasn't as if she was trying to attract his attention. She might be dressed in her nightclothes, but her robe covered her from her neck to her knees, and the terry cloth slides she wore weren't the least bit seductive. Still, even with her face scrubbed free of makeup and her hair tied back in a simple ponytail, she'd never looked more beautiful.

"Nick, why are you here? I told you I was fine. I was just about to go to bed."

"Are you pregnant?"

He hadn't meant to hit her with that again, but the words just popped out. "I know you think you just picked up a virus," he quickly added, cursing his lack of tact, "but you got sick so quickly, I couldn't help but wonder if it might have been morning sickness instead."

"It wasn't morning."

"I don't know a lot about the subject," he acknowledged, "but I don't think morning sickness is always restricted to the morning." When she just looked at him, he said quietly, "All I'm asking is for you to be straight with me, Callie. I have a right to know. Are you pregnant?"

Sudden tears glistening in her eyes, she couldn't give him the answer he wanted. "I don't know. It's too soon."

"So when will you know?"

She shrugged and never knew how she tempted him to take her into his arms. "I don't know. I've never been in this position before. A couple of weeks, I guess."

"A couple of weeks! But that's too long!"

Confused, she frowned. "Too long for what?"

Hesitating, Nick didn't know how to explain it. She was pregnant. He knew it, though he couldn't explain how. He just knew she was carrying his baby and it was imperative that their life together start as soon as possible.

"I know this isn't something that either of us planned," he said huskily, "but everything happens for a reason, Callie. I don't want to wait two weeks to find out if you're pregnant or not. Let's get married now.''

"Now?!" she exclaimed. "But—"

"You won't regret it," he promised. "We'll buy a house, someplace with a big backyard and a family room, maybe down by the river. We can even build, if you like. I'll call Gerald Jones—he's an architect I went to college with—and he can draw up the plans. How many bedrooms do you want? Four sounds good to me, but five shouldn't be a problem if that's what you want. Do you want the master bedroom upstairs or down? You might feel better if we're upstairs with the kids—"

Listening to him make plans, Callie was amazed. He would have her entire life planned, right down to what she would wear to their fiftieth wedding anniversary party, if she didn't stop him. "Nick—"

"I don't think we should have a pool, at least not while the kids are little. It's just too dangerous—"

"Nick, stop!"

She hadn't meant to shout at him, but he had no idea what he was doing to her. For as long as she could remember, she'd dreamed of the day when he asked her to marry her and they planned their life together. But somehow, her dreams had been nothing like this. She needed him to hold her, kiss her, tell her that she was the only thing in life that mattered to him. But nothing he'd said so far came even close to that.

"What did I say?" he asked, confused.

The fact that he had to ask sent her heart plummeting. "Why do you want to marry me?" she asked for the second time in one day.

"Because you might be pregnant," he replied honestly. "If you are, I have a responsibility to you and my child."

That was an admirable sentiment…and the wrong answer…again. Disappointed, she smiled sadly. "No. I appreciate the offer, but I can't marry you."

"But you have to! Dammit, Callie, this is a small town. You know how people are. If we don't get married, everyone's going to be whispering about you, wondering who the father of your baby is. You don't deserve that."

"No, I don't," she replied, "but I'm a big girl— I can handle it."

"But the baby needs a father!"

"*If* I'm pregnant," she retorted, "the baby has a father. You. Now that we have that straightened out, I'm going to bed. It's been a long day, and I'm tired. Good night, Nick." Not giving him a chance to argue further, she shut the door firmly in his face.

Chapter 8

She was the most frustrating woman he'd ever known!

Unable to concentrate on work the next day, Nick shut down his computer with a scowl. This was all Callie's fault. He'd replayed the scene at her apartment over and over again in his head, and her answer was always the same. No. No, she wouldn't marry him. No, she wouldn't do the right thing for their baby. And for the life of him, he didn't know why. How long had they known each other? Practically all their lives. He'd always considered her a friend, but they couldn't communicate anymore. She didn't hear anything he said. If she had, she would have understood why he needed to marry her if she was pregnant.

At his wit's end, he didn't know what to do. He couldn't work, couldn't think, didn't know how to get through to her. He needed some advice, but he couldn't talk about this to just anyone, not when just the suspicion that Callie might be pregnant would spread like wildfire in a town the size of Rumor. He had to be careful what he said…and to whom.

If you need someone to talk to, give me a call. I've been told I'm a good listener.

Shelly's words echoing in his ears, he didn't doubt that she was a good listener…or that he could trust her. He didn't know her that well, but she didn't seem the type who would enjoy trashing somebody else's reputation. And she could give him a woman's point of view. God knew, he needed it. He didn't have a clue what was going on in Callie's head.

Leaving work early, he headed for Wayne Barrett's house and arrived just as Shelly came around the corner on a bicycle. "This is a nice surprise," she said with a pleased smile as he stepped from the car. "What's going on? I thought you'd be working."

"I couldn't concentrate," he replied with a grimace. "Do you have a minute? I know I should have called first, but I need some advice. About women.''

Humor twinkled in her eyes. ''You don't have to make it sound like you're talking about some kind of alien species from outer space,'' she teased. ''Generally, we're a pretty reasonable group— we're just wired differently than men. C'mon inside. I made some fresh lemonade earlier. We can have some on the back patio.''

He didn't want to put her to any trouble, but she wouldn't take no for an answer. She escorted him out to the patio, then returned a few minutes later with two glasses of ice, a pitcher of lemonade and dish of cookies. ''So you want to talk about women,'' she said dryly as she joined him at the wrought iron table by the pool. ''Any one in particular? Let me guess…Callie.''

He didn't deny it. His eyes locking with hers, he said, ''This is serious, Shelly. What I'm about to tell you can go no further.''

''Of course,'' she replied, sobering. ''I promise I won't say a word. What's wrong?''

Sitting back in his chair, he sighed. ''I wish I knew. I think she's pregnant, which is why I asked her to marry me, but she won't even consider it. Does that make sense to you? She's pregnant, for God's sake! We need to get married!''

''Because she might be pregnant?''

"You saw her at the diner," he reminded her. "She was sick just like that." Snapping his fingers, he frowned. "Doesn't that sound like morning sickness to you?"

"Since I've never been pregnant, I don't have a clue," she replied, "but I don't blame her for turning you down. I would have done the same thing."

Shocked, Nick nearly dropped his lemonade. "What?! Why?"

Shelly couldn't believe he had to ask. "How many reasons do you need? First, you show up at her diner for dinner with another woman, then you ask her to marry you because you think she might be pregnant. If I'd been in her shoes, I'd have told you to go kiss a duck."

"But she's pregnant!"

"Maybe," she agreed. "Maybe not. Either way, she needs to know that you care about her, not just the baby."

"Of course, I care about her!" he retorted, stung. "Why else do you think I asked her to marry me? I wouldn't want her to go through something like that alone."

"Did you tell her that?"

Caught off guard by the question, he blinked. "Well, yeah...sort of. If I didn't say those exact words, she still should have known...."

"And how would she know that?" she asked

reasonably. "Unless you already asked her to marry you before you thought she was pregnant."

He hadn't, of course. They'd only been friends up until a few days ago. Then they'd made love and everything had changed. And he didn't know why. "Obviously, I need some help," he said quietly. "How do I talk her into marrying me?"

"Court her," she said simply. "If you want her to marry you, you're going to have to show her that you want her and only her, Nick. Don't take me or anyone else to dinner. Make her feel special."

"She *is* special," he said promptly. "She knows that."

"Does she?" Shelly asked, lifting a delicately arched brow. "You've told her? Showed her?"

Put that way, he was forced to admit that he hadn't. "I'll send her flowers. And jewelry. I need to get her an engagement ring—"

"I wouldn't do that just yet if I were you," she warned. "Not unless you want her to stuff it down your throat. She's not ready for that, Nick. Not yet."

Scowling, he didn't like that answer at all. "Then what do you suggest I do?"

"Use your imagination. Anyone can send her flowers. Have fun with her. You two have known each other all your lives—she probably thinks she knows everything about you. Show her she doesn't.

Do something special for her. Make it impossible for her to get you out of her head.''

Nick liked to think he knew how to romance a woman, but he'd never been involved with anyone like Callie before. She was like family, but not family, a part of his past, and possibly the mother of his child. He cared about her in a way he couldn't explain.

''No woman has ever been so important before,'' he said huskily. ''I can't blow this, Shelly. There's too much at stake. I know this must be awkward for you—you don't even know Callie—but I can use all the help I can get. If you've got any suggestions…''

She grinned, pleased. ''I was just waiting for you to ask. If I were you, this is what I'd do….''

As usual, the lunchtime crowd was lined up in front of Callie's food booth, and she was in her element. Laughing and talking with her customers, she handled their orders with ease and never noticed when Nick took a place at the end of the line. Dishing up catfish, strawberry shortcake and filling dozens of glasses of iced tea, she'd just served a couple of tourists from Calgary when she looked up to find herself face-to-face with Nick. Unable to stop herself, she looked past his broad shoulders, half expecting to find Shelly standing with him in line. She was nowhere in sight.

"Hello, Nick," she said quietly. "The catfish is fresh. Can I get you an order?"

"Actually, I've got a luncheon with the mayor in a half hour," he admitted. "That's not why I stopped by. I wanted to ask a favor of you."

Her heart tripping in her breast in surprise, Callie couldn't imagine what favor he could possibly ask of her. He'd made love with her last week and was dating another woman this week. There didn't seem anything left to say. Still, she loved him and they had been friends a long time. She might be a fool, but if he needed her help with something, she couldn't deny him.

"You know you only have to ask. I'll help if I can."

"My brother and his wife haven't been to the carnival yet, so I volunteered to baby-sit Megan so Tom and Rita could go out tonight and have some fun. The only problem is I've never kept her by myself. What do I do if she starts crying for Rita? I could call her and Tom, of course, and I'm sure they'd come straight home, but I don't want to do that. I was hoping you would help me."

Surprised, she said, "You want me to baby-sit with you?"

"Well, yeah. Unless you have other plans, of

course. I realize I'm not giving you much notice, but I already called Tom and offered to baby-sit before it hit me that I probably shouldn't do this alone. If you're busy, I can handle it, but I know how much you love Megan, and I thought you might enjoy it.''

He knew her too well. She couldn't refuse him anything when it came to his ten-month-old niece, Megan. With her blond curls, twinkling blue eyes and quick smile, she was a darling. And even though a little voice in her head screamed out at her that she was only opening herself up to more hurt if she went anywhere with him, she couldn't pass up the chance to see him with Megan.

''What time?'' she asked.

''I told Tom I'd be there by seven.''

She would be leaving Martha with the dinner crowd, but she couldn't help it. She wasn't missing this. ''I'll meet you there, then,'' she said.

''I'll pick you up—''

''I can drive myself,'' she said firmly.

For a moment, she thought he was going to argue with her, but something in her tone must have warned him that she wasn't going to bend on this. Giving in, he said, ''Fine. I guess I'll see you at Tom's, then.''

With a nod of thanks, he disappeared in the crowd, leaving her staring after him, wondering what was going on. After he'd walked into her diner with Shelly Barrett, she'd sworn she'd never speak to him again. What had possessed her to agree to spend the evening with him?

Seven hours later, she was still asking herself that same question and she'd yet to come up with an answer. She just knew she had to go. So promptly at seven, she pulled up before Tom and Rita Sullivan's ranch-style house and approached their front door. Nick was already there—his truck was parked at the curb in front of her car—and her heart skipped a beat at the thought of spending time alone with him. Megan would be there, of course, but she was a baby and would no doubt fall asleep early, leaving her two baby-sitters virtually alone together.

This is crazy! Callie thought. She never should have agreed to this madness. Was there still time to back out? She could claim that she'd gotten a call on her cell phone from the diner and there was some kind of emergency only she could handle....

Suddenly, the front door opened, and before she could move, Tom greeted her with a broad grin of delight. "Callie! C'mon in. Nick was just telling us you offered to baby-sit with him tonight."

"Actually, he said he begged you to help him," Rita said with a chuckle as she stepped forward to

hug her. "The big scaredy-cat. I don't know what
he's afraid of. She's just a baby."

"Hey," Nick objected, joining them, "I don't
remember saying I was afraid—"

"You didn't have to," his brother teased. "You
haven't been able to sit still since you got here. I
was the same way before Megan was born. She was
three weeks old before I let Rita leave her alone
with me, and then I made her take both our cell
phones with her just in case."

"He was a basket case," Rita confided with a
grin. "Much worse than Nick."

"I was not!"

Laughing, she grabbed her husband's hand.
"Let's get out of here, sweetheart, while we still
can."

She didn't have to tell him twice. "You have our
cell phone numbers," he told Nick. "There are bottles in the refrigerator and diapers in the chest by
her bed. Her teddy bear's in her crib with her—she
likes to be rocked to sleep with it…"

Reeling off a list of instructions like a new
mother leaving her baby for the first time, he was
still rattling off doctor's numbers and the kind of
snacks Megan liked when Rita laughingly pulled
him out the door. Just that quickly, Callie found
herself alone with Nick.

She needn't have worried that it was for long,

however. Almost immediately, Megan let out a cry from the nursery. Grinning, Nick said, "Now the fun begins."

Another man might have expected Callie to take charge of the baby, but not Nick. Telling her to make herself at home, he hurried to the back of the house to get Megan and returned a few minutes later with the baby in his arms. Callie took one look at them together and felt her heart melt. He was so natural with her! It was clear that he'd held her many times before—with her teddy clutched close, Megan rested in his arms with complete trust—and he was just as comfortable with her. There was no awkwardness in his touch, and as Callie watched, he leaned down and nuzzled the baby's ear, making her giggle. From Megan's delighted grin, it was something he'd obviously done many times before.

"I think I've been had," Callie said dryly. "For a man who claims to be scared of a baby, you seem to be remarkably at ease."

"Oh, I always am when she's soft and cuddly like this," he replied with a grin. "Wait'll she starts crying. I'll turn her over to you quick enough then."

Callie sincerely doubted that, but then Megan greeted her with a happy gurgle and held her arms out to her, and she could no more resist her than Nick could. "Hey, sweetie," she said, reaching for

her, "When did you get to be such a big girl? The
last time I saw you, you could barely sit up. Now
look at you! Are you walking yet and driving
Mommy crazy? You're going to lead her a merry
chase, aren't you?"

His chiseled face soft with love as he gazed down
at the baby, Nick grinned. "If she's anything like
Tom was as a baby, Rita won't be able to so much
as blink without her getting into trouble. Isn't that
right, sweetheart?" he crooned, reaching out to
tickle the baby under her chin. "You're going to
give Mommy and Daddy fits. Poor old Tom will be
gray-haired before he's forty."

Megan seemed to find that immensely funny.
Giggling, she reached for Nick, but wouldn't let go
of Callie. Holding the two of them close, she dis-
solved in giggles and had no idea how she touched
Callie's heart. Suddenly, her throat was thick with
emotion and she found herself imagining that Megan was their baby. She could feel the love between
the three of them, see the home they would all have
together. It would be filled with laughter and love
as they took care of the baby together. And every
evening, after they fed and bathed her and put her
to bed in a nursery decorated with cuddly teddy
bears, they would retreat to their own room, where
they would lie in their bed and make love.

Longing rose up in her, stunning her with its

strength, and too late, Callie suddenly jerked back to reality. Dear God, what was she doing? she wondered wildly. She couldn't let herself fall into the fantasy of playing house with Nick. Even if she was pregnant with his baby, he didn't love her. If he had, he would have never gone out with another woman so quickly after he'd made love with her. So there would be no happily ever after for the two of them. Not now, not ever. The sooner she accepted that, the better.

Chapter 9

Shaken, her heart breaking, Callie didn't know how she got through the rest of the evening. Megan was so sweet, and every time her little arms encircled Callie's neck, she found herself fighting tears. If Nick noticed, he made no comment, but more than once, she caught him studying her reflectively. Then, just when she was sure she was going to make a fool of herself, Rita and Tom came sweeping through the frown door, laughing and talking like teenagers in love.

Flushed and happy, Rita launched herself at her brother-in-law and gave him a big hug. "Thank you *so* much! We had a great time!"

Laughing, he hugged her back. "I guess I don't have to ask if you worried about the baby all night. You didn't call once. She's fine, by the way," he assured her with a grin. "We put her to bed about a half hour ago."

"She was a little angel," Callie told Rita as she turned from Nick to envelope her in a hug, too. "We didn't have a bit of trouble with her."

"That's my baby girl," Tom said proudly. "Hey, you're not going to run off so soon, are you?" he asked with a frown when Callie grabbed her purse. "The night's still young. Why don't you stay for a nightcap? And some of Rita's Mississippi mud cake? You and Rita can visit while Nick and I watch TV. There's bound to be a baseball game on."

Tempted, Callie regretfully shook her head. "I'd love to, but I've got to be at work in the morning at six. Maybe another time."

Understanding completely, Rita told her, "You've got to be exhausted. The festival's turned out to be much bigger than anyone expected, and you're running not only the diner, but two food booths. I don't know how you do it and have any time left over for yourself."

Callie smiled ruefully. "It's been pretty wild, but it's been a lot of fun. I do have to go to bed at a decent hour, though, or I'll be wiped out."

"You should have let me pick you up," Nick said quietly. "Then you wouldn't have had to drive home."

"It's not that far," she assured him. "I'll be fine."

He wanted to argue—Callie could see it in his eyes—but there was little else he could say. It wasn't as if she was driving halfway across the state. Her apartment was only a couple of blocks away. So quietly wishing them all good-night, she slipped out the front door before Nick could offer to walk her to her car.

Later, she couldn't have said when she started crying. Suddenly, her eyes were swimming in tears. She felt like she was driving away from every dream she'd ever had about Nick.

Don't! a voice cried out in her head. Don't give up on him. Not yet. Just give him a chance. He loves you—he just doesn't realize it yet.

She desperately wanted to believe that, but she couldn't take the chance. What if she was wrong? She'd loved him for years already and it hadn't gotten her anywhere. If she held out hope and he let her down, she didn't think she would be able to bear the pain. She had to let him go, had to let go of the fantasy that she would share her life with him. And she had to do it now.

Numb with the loss, she didn't remember how

she made it home. Stumbling into her apartment, she went straight to bed, but not to sleep. Instead, she lay there for hours, staring at the ceiling, aching for what she had lost. She'd never felt so empty in her life.

The next morning, she was exhausted as she dragged herself into work, but all she could think of was Nick. She told herself she didn't want to see him, but as the breakfast crowd began to stream in and the tables and booths filled up, she couldn't stop herself from looking for him. He never came in.

At first, she told herself he must have overslept. After all, he had, on rare occasions in the past, slept through his alarm. He always, however, came in later, if for nothing else than a quick cup of coffee and a doughnut. But not today. The bell over the front door rang time and time again, the breakfast crowd came and went and there was still no sign of him.

Worried, she wondered if he was sick, then toyed with the idea of calling him. But he wasn't her concern any longer, she reminded herself. And he'd been fine last night. If he was sick, he could call Shelly. She'd probably jump at the chance to rush over to his place and nurse him back to health.

So she turned away from the front door and tried to focus on work. And for a while, at least, she succeeded. Customers distracted her and when she was able to grab a few minutes of downtime, she had to consult with Ben about next week's menu. The lunch crowd began to arrive at eleven, and that, thankfully, kept her busy until well after two. Before she knew it, the day was half over.

Chatting easily with her customers, she smiled and laughed and had never been so depressed in her life. She'd never expected to miss him so much.

"Hey, are you all right?" Marisa asked, her green eyes dark with concern as she joined her behind the counter. "You look sad. What's wrong?"

Hesitating, Callie almost told her. But if Marisa showed her the least bit of sympathy, she was afraid she'd dissolve in tears. "Nothing," she said with a shrug. "I'm just tired. I'll get my second wind by the time the dinner crowd arrives."

"Why don't you take the evening off," she suggested. "You have been working awfully hard. You should go home, put your feet up and just do nothing for the rest of the night."

"And leave you to handle all this?" Callie retorted with a crooked smile. "I can just hear what Jordan would have to say about that. You're the one who's pregnant. You need to be taking the night off, not me. I had last night off."

"But you didn't rest—you were baby-sitting. And I'm fine," she assured her. "Don't worry about Jordan. I'll explain everything to him. You go home and rest.''

"But—''

"I mean it, Callie,'' she cut in firmly. "I'm worried about you. You need to take the night off.''

Surprised by her insistence, Callie frowned suspiciously. "All right, what's going on? Why are you trying to get me away from the diner tonight? Has something happened that I don't know about? Ben didn't order shrimp from that fish market in Billings again, did he? It was fantastic, but it cost me a fortune, and he swore he'd never do that again. Please tell me we don't have a truckload of shrimp coming in tonight.''

For a minute, she thought she caught a flicker of an emotion she couldn't put a name to in Marisa's eyes, but then she laughed gaily. "No, there's no shrimp coming in tonight—or any other shipments that I know of,'' she said, her green eyes twinkling. "There's no conspiracy, Ms. Suspicion. I was just trying to help. You look tired. You're always sending me home to put my feet up when I'm tired, so I thought I'd return the favor. You never take any time for yourself. But if you want to work, hey, who am I to complain? Maybe I'll go home early!''

Put that way, Callie had to laugh. "Whoa, I don't think so. Now that you mention it, some time off does sound good. There's a new horror book I've been wanting to read, and I never can seem to find the time.''

''Then tonight's your night,'' her friend said promptly. ''Go. Escape while you still can. Take a bubble bath, curl up in bed and scare yourself to death. I'll take care of everything here.''

She practically pushed her out the door, and before Callie quite knew how it happened, she found herself heading home with a free evening on her hands. She couldn't remember the last time she'd been off two nights in a row. It was a heady feeling.

Impulsively, she stopped by the grocery store and bought a frozen pizza and a quart of rocky road ice cream. This was her night, she thought with a grin. She wasn't going to spend it in the kitchen, cooking something that was good for her. Tonight was a night for comfort foods and eating in bed. Before the night was over with, she just might eat not only the entire pizza, but a whole quart of ice cream, too. Just because she could.

Laughing at herself, knowing she would do neither, she pulled up in front of her apartment and sent up a silent prayer of thanks for Marisa. How had she known she needed this when she hadn't known herself? She'd have to return the favor for her after the baby came, when she and Jordan would need some time to themselves.

Smiling as her thoughts jumped ahead to baby-sitting Marisa's baby, she unlocked her front door and stepped inside without even noticing that she wasn't alone in the apartment. Then she caught the scent of spaghetti sauce drifting from her own kitchen. Her heart suddenly pounding, she stopped dead in her tracks just as Nick stepped through the kitchen door into her living room. "What are you doing here?"

"Marisa loaned me your spare key," he said simply. Crossing to her, he took the bag of groceries from her and peeked inside. "Pizza and rocky road," he said with a grin. "I should have known. They always were your favorites, weren't they?"

She didn't deny it. Instead, she nodded toward the kitchen, where she could clearly see a pot of spaghetti sauce simmering on the stove. "Let me guess. Something is wrong with your stove, so you decided to cook dinner here."

"Actually, my stove's just fine," he replied with a grin. "I thought I'd surprise you and cook dinner for you since you eat your own cooking all the time. I hope you don't mind."

Caught off guard, Callie couldn't have been more surprised if he'd presented her with a diamond the size of a rock. "You cooked for me?"

"Well, it's not pizza," he said wryly, "but if that's what you really want, we can have that instead. I haven't cooked the spaghetti yet and you can save the marinara sauce for tomorrow. Or I'll freeze it for you and you can have it whenever you want.''

Touched, Callie almost cried, *Don't! Don't be so sweet, so thoughtful. Don't give me a reason to love you anymore than I already do.*

But it was too late for that. Lately, every time she saw him, she seemed to fall more in love with him. How could she deny herself the opportunity to spend more time with him? After all, what could it hurt? It was just dinner.

''I can have frozen pizza any time,'' she said with a slow smile. ''Spaghetti sounds great. What can I do to help?''

''Absolutely nothing,'' he replied promptly. ''This is your evening to be pampered. All you have to do is enjoy.''

He was a man who knew how to show a woman a good time, and with an easy smile, he showed her into the kitchen, seated her at the table, and proceeded to entertain her with funny stories as he prepared the rest of the meal. Delighted, Callie couldn't have said later if the food was any good or not. She just knew she didn't want the evening to ever end.

It couldn't, however, last forever, and before she quite knew where the time had gone, Nick had put the leftovers away in the refrigerator, cleared off the table and put the dirty dishes in the dishwasher. It was nearly ten o'clock, and he had to leave.

"We'll have to do this again sometime," he said as she followed him to her front door to say good-night. "I had a great time."

"So did I," she said softly. "No one's ever done anything like this for me before. It was wonderful."

Giving into impulse, she raised up on tiptoe to brush his cheek with a kiss. "Thank you."

Her heart aching with need, she would have given anything if he'd taken her in his arms and kissed her the way she longed for him to. But he only smiled, took one of her hands and gave it a squeeze, then quietly wished her good-night. A heartbeat later, he was gone.

Wandering into the quiet stillness of her apartment, Callie missed him almost immediately. That's when she knew she was in trouble. When had he taken over her thoughts so completely? How? It wasn't as if he was dating her or anything. Granted, he'd surprised her by making dinner for her, but she wouldn't fool herself into thinking there'd been anything the least romantic about the meal. There'd been no candles, no music—he hadn't even touched her! And when she'd clearly given him an opening to kiss her, he'd turned and walked away. Obviously, he didn't want anything more from her than friendship.

That hurt. Because she couldn't stop herself from loving him any more than she could change the color of her eyes. She dreamed of him... again...and ached for something she couldn't have. By the time her alarm went off at five-thirty the next morning, she just wanted to cry herself back to sleep. She couldn't, of course. She had a business to run and customers who looked forward to greeting her every morning for breakfast. With a groan of defeat, she pushed herself from bed and headed for the shower.

If she'd secretly hoped that he would show up at the diner for breakfast or any other meal, she was doomed to disappointment. He didn't come by all day. Confused, hurt, not sure where she stood with him anymore, she couldn't help but wonder where he was and who he was with. And that thoroughly irritated her. Sternly lecturing herself, she reminded herself that just because they'd made love one time didn't mean he had to account to her for his whereabouts. After all, it wasn't as if they were engaged or anything.

You had your chance, the voice in her head pointed out bluntly as she closed up the diner for the night. *You're the one who turned him down when he proposed, so you have to live with the consequences. That doesn't mean you have to sit around the house and mope over the man. Get out* and have some fun. Clear your head. Maybe you'll feel better.

From down the street, the music and laughter of the carnival called to her on the night air as she locked the back door of the diner and headed for her car. Hesitating, she considered going, then almost rejected the idea. She was tired, and Marisa was handling the food booth tonight and didn't need her help. It had been a lousy, lonely day, and going to the carnival by herself would only make her feel more lonely. But the thought of going home to her empty apartment, where Nick's scent still lingered from last night, twisted her heart. With a will of their own, her feet headed for the carnival.

Chapter 10

Nick saw her the minute she stepped on the midway.

Stopping in his tracks, he laughed wryly at the ironies of Fate. He hadn't planned to come to the carnival tonight, but he'd been there since sundown, hoping the distraction of the gathering crowds would be enough to keep his mind off Callie. It hadn't worked. She was all he could think of. The minute he'd walked out her front door last night, he'd wanted to turn around and go back to her. But he couldn't rush her, not now that he was finally making some progress with her. So he'd deliberately stayed away all day, hoping that absence would make the heart grow fonder.

It was the hardest thing he'd ever done. He'd lost track of the number of times he'd picked up the phone to call her. And he must have driven by the diner at least a half-dozen times, hoping to catch a glimpse of her. And now, here she was, walking straight toward him.

After his talk with Shelly the other day, he'd worked out a strategy to court Callie, and that plan hadn't included seeing her tonight. But, damn, she looked good! And he wanted to be with her. What was wrong with that?

Giving in to impulse, he approached her with a grin. "Just the woman I was looking for!"

"Really?" she said, arching a brow in amusement. "Then maybe you should have dropped by the diner. I was there all day."

So she had missed him, he thought, pleased. Encouraged, he said, "I know, but I was tied up in meetings and couldn't get away. But I'm free now. How about you?"

"That depends," she hedged with twinkling eyes. "What'd you have in mind?"

"A ride on the Ferris wheel with the prettiest girl in town," he said promptly. "What do you say? Are you game?"

She shouldn't have. But how could she resist him when he held out his hand to her and smiled at her like she was the only woman in the world? Giving in to temptation, she gave him her hand and loved the feel of his fingers closing around hers. ''I thought you'd never ask,'' she said softly.

It was a beautiful night, and half the crowd seemed to be in line to ride the Ferris wheel. Her eyes sparkling with excitement, Callie didn't voice a single word of complaint. Nick was at his most charming and she could have stood there all evening and just listened to him talk. Time, however, flew, and before she knew it, they were at the front of the line and the attendant was holding a gently swinging gondola still directly in front of them.

His fingers tightening around hers, Nick stepped into the gondola first, then steadied her as she followed him inside. The safety bar clanged into place, locking them inside, and a split second later, the huge wheel started to turn.

Callie had ridden a Ferris wheel dozens of times before, but never with Nick. With the upward sweep of the wheel, her breath caught, her eyes met his, and suddenly, they were both grinning like kids, and she couldn't have said why. She just knew she'd never felt the way she did at that moment…happy, lighter than air.

Sitting side by side, they swung their feet, making the gondola swing, and a few seconds later, they reached the top. Just that quickly, the whole world was spread out before them. Awash with lights, it was beautiful. Her hand still in his, Callie didn't know if she wanted to laugh or cry. The day that had been so long and lonely just turned magical.

She didn't make a sound, but she didn't have to. Nick squeezed her hand, then, before she could suspect his intentions, he released her, but only to slip his arm around her shoulders and pull her close. A heartbeat later, his mouth covered hers.

Her heart sighed—there was no other way to describe it.

She knew it had only been days since he'd kissed her, but it seemed like weeks, months. Did he know how she'd longed to be in his arms again? How much she ached to lose herself in the taste and feel and wonder of him? She loved him with all her heart. He had to know it—she couldn't hide it anymore. But how did he feel about her? Did he love her? Or just want her?

Too late, she realized she'd given him the power to break her heart without knowing if he cared anything about her at all. And that scared the hell out of her. What if this was all just sex to him and all he really wanted was to get her back into bed?

Shaken, her heart pounding, she pulled back just as the Ferris wheel began its gentle descent toward the ground. She would have given anything if the ride had been over then, but they made three more rounds before it was finally their turn to unload.

Beside her, Nick seemed to be content just to hold her. He didn't say a word, and neither did she. In fact, he seemed to deliberately avoid her gaze, and she had to wonder if he was already regretting the kiss they'd just shared.

In desperate need of some time to herself to think, she turned to him the second they'd both stepped free of the gondola and were once again firmly on the ground. "Thanks for the ride," she said huskily. "I wish I could stick around, but I've got some paperwork at home that I promised myself I'd do tonight. I guess I'll see you around."

She was gone before Nick could even think to stop her, disappearing into the crowd like she couldn't get away from him fast enough, and it hurt. It hurt a lot, dammit! Did she know what she'd done to him with just a kiss? She'd taken him apart and put him back together again, and he had a feeling that he would never be the same again. And he didn't have a clue how she'd done it.

"Nick? Are you okay? What's wrong?"

Blindsided by emotions he hadn't expected, he looked up from his thoughts to find Shelly standing in front of him, frowning in concern. "I don't know," he said roughly. "Callie and I just rode the Ferris wheel, and I feel like I just got flattened by a Mack truck."

Far from concerned, Shelly only grinned. "No

kidding? I've heard that's what it feels like. Have you told Callie yet?''

Surprised, he frowned. ''Told her what? What are you talking about?''

''Love,'' she replied, chuckling. ''You're in love with her, Nick. Didn't you know? Why do you think you've been so upset that she wouldn't marry you? It isn't because of the baby—you don't even know if there *is* a baby.''

For a moment, he just stood there, stunned as the truth plowed into him, staggering him. She was right, he thought, dazed. All this time, he'd told himself he had to do the right thing because of the baby, but it was really because of Callie. It was Callie he wanted, Callie he loved, Callie he wanted to spend the rest of his life with. And he'd never realized it until now.

Elated, scared, he impulsively reached for Shelly and snatched her into a bear hug. ''I don't know what I would have done if you hadn't been here to walk me through this,'' he said when she laughed in surprise. ''Help me. What do I do next? How do I convince her I really love her when she thinks I'm just doing the responsible thing? She's going to think this is just a trick to convince her to marry me.''

''Tell her what's in your heart,'' she said gently. ''Show her. If she cares about you at all—and I

truly believe she does—she just needs to know you
feel the same way."

"But how?"

"You'll figure out a way," she assured him,
smiling. "When you do, send me an invitation to
the wedding."

When she slipped away into the crowd, he almost
panicked. She made it sound so easy. Didn't she
realize that this was his life, his future happiness,
they were talking about? When he told Callie he
loved her for the first time, he had to do it just right
or he could lose her forever. The question was how?

The idea that popped full blown in his head was
so simple, he couldn't believe he hadn't thought of
it earlier. This, he thought with a grin, could work.
It was just a question of getting everyone together....

Restless, unable to think of anything but Nick,
Callie hardly slept that night. By the time her alarm
went off the next morning, she would have liked
nothing more than to pull the covers over her head
and just lie there for the rest of the day. But even
though it was Marisa's day to open early, she'd
called late last night and asked if she could have
the day off. She hadn't been feeling well all day
yesterday, and Jordan wanted her to spend the day

resting. Concerned for her and the baby, Callie had ordered her to stay in bed all day.

Which meant she had to open this morning. Groaning at the thought, she rolled out of bed and stumbled to the bathroom. Maybe a cold shower would help clear her head. Then she wanted coffee, lots and lots of coffee.

Thirty minutes later, she was ready for work, but just barely. Her head was throbbing, her stomach queasy and as she headed for the diner and drove through the deserted predawn streets of Rumor, she tried to convince herself her stomach was upset from lack of sleep. But she'd missed sleep in the past and never felt this way. It had to be something else.

Maybe you really are pregnant.

The thought slipped into her head without warning…and shook her to the core. Stunned, she pulled over to the side of the road because if she hadn't, she would have hit something. No, she thought, dazed. She couldn't be. It wasn't possible. She couldn't be pregnant. Not after just one time.

But even as she tried to convince herself otherwise, she knew it was true. She knew her body, knew its rhythms and cycles, and over the course of the past few days, it hadn't been the same. Because she was pregnant.

Later, she couldn't have said how long she sat

there, reeling. Tears flooded her eyes, but suddenly she was laughing with joy. She was pregnant! She didn't have a clue where she stood with Nick and that should have worried her, but it didn't. She was having a baby and she was thrilled. Nothing else mattered.

On any other morning, she would have noticed there were more cars than usual parked along the street near the diner, but all she could think of was the baby…and Nick. She had to tell him. After seeing him with Megan the other night, she knew she didn't have to worry about his reaction. He loved children and would be as happy as she was.

Lost in her thoughts, she pulled into her usual parking spot in the diner's empty parking lot and unlocked the front door without ever noticing that the lights were already on inside. Then she stepped across the threshold and stopped in surprise.

"Mom! Dad! What are you doing here?"

"We thought we'd handle the breakfast shift for you this morning," her mother said with a smile.

"Just in case you don't feel like working," her father added with a grin, kissing her on the cheek.

Confused, she frowned. "Why wouldn't I feel like working? What's going on?"

Before he could answer, the bell over the front door rang, and she whirled to see what looked like half the population of Rumor walking into the diner. Her brother was at the front of the line, and behind him trailed a grinning Libby, Marisa and Jordan and all her other employees.

Stunned, she couldn't have been more surprised if the Wizard of Oz had suddenly appeared before her. Then Nick stepped into the diner. She took one look at his face and the light shining in his eyes and felt her heart turn over in her breast. Over the course of all the years she'd known him, he'd never looked at her that way before. If she hadn't known better, she would have sworn his eyes were alight with love.

An expectant hush fell over the crowd of friends and family, and before she could guess his intentions, he stepped in front of her and took her hand. With a will of their own, her fingers clung to his as her eyes searched his. "Nick...what..."

"I hope you don't mind," he said huskily, "but I called everyone here to celebrate."

Her heart sank with disappointment. He was going to ask her to marry him again because he thought she was pregnant—which she was! But she couldn't marry him because of that. "Don't," she whispered hoarsely. "We need to talk."

She might as well have saved her breath. His hand tightened around hers, and before she could begin to guess his intentions, he went down on one knee in front of her. "I wanted all your friends and family to be here to witness the most important day of our lives. Will you marry me, Callie?''

He'd asked her before, but never like this. Her hand trembling in his, she stared down at him and caught her breath as her eyes met his. He *did* love her! He didn't say the words, but she hadn't mistaken the love she saw shining in his eyes. Suddenly, her heart was pounding with hope. Was this for real? Did he really love her? Was it possible?

Desperate to hear the words, determined that there would be no misunderstandings between them, she only had one question for him. It was the same one she'd asked every time he'd proposed. ''Why?''

''Because I love you with all my heart,'' he said honestly.

That was the only answer she'd ever wanted to hear. Smiling through the tears that streamed down her face, she tightened her fingers around his and pulled him to his feet. ''Yes, I will. Because I love you, too.''

Her family and friends were crying and clapping, but she had eyes only for Nick. ''There's something else you need to know,'' she said in a quiet voice that carried only to his ears. ''You were right.''

She didn't have to say what he was right about— he knew. She saw joy flare in his eyes and knew that later, they would lie in each other's arms and talk about the future and their baby. For now, though, he grinned and opened his arms. Everything that needed to be said had been said. Without another word, she stepped into his arms.

* * * * *

DADDY TAKES
THE CAKE
Allison Leigh

To my dear friend, Lanci,
whose personal strength has long been an
inspiration to me.

Chapter 1

"Hi, Libby. Did you bring us more treats?"

Libby Adler glanced up at the man who'd just spoken and smiled, her hands never stopping as she arranged still-warm brownies on a wide platter that would soon be covered again by a crystal-clear dome. "Brownies and lemon bars," she assured absently.

The man grinned and rubbed his hands. "I'll go scare up my wife and we'll be back. Don't know why that woman doesn't trust me with the wallet," he mumbled as he headed into the milling crowds.

Callie Griffin, standing with Libby in the booth that the Calico Diner had at Rumor's Crazy Moon

Festival, chuckled. "I'm not sure what we sell more of. Your pastries, or my grilled burgers." Callie owned the popular diner located on Main Street in downtown Rumor.

Libby wasn't really listening, though. She covered the brownies with the dome and glanced again at her watch. "I gave those kids ten minutes," she murmured.

"What trouble can two six-year-old twins get into in ten minutes?" Callie snitched a lemon bar and pinched off a corner, popping it into her mouth. She closed her eyes in exaggerated pleasure as the confection melted on her tongue.

What trouble, indeed? Libby pulled off the thin plastic gloves she'd worn to handle the baked goods. "You'd be surprised," she said wryly. Bundling up the gloves, she dropped them in the big trash bin behind the booth. "Ten minutes of silence in the house, for instance, usually means total mischief."

"Unless they're asleep," Callie countered.

Libby couldn't help smiling. "Spoken like a woman who has yet to have her baby."

Her friend's cheeks colored prettily. Callie had just recently accepted Nick Sullivan's marriage proposal and the two of them were already adding to their family with Callie's unexpected pregnancy.

"Mark my words, Callie," Libby went on, teasing her friend. "Just because you *think* they're sleeping doesn't mean anything. One night last week, I checked the twins, and they were sound asleep. I went back downstairs to finish up a batch of cinnamon rolls for the next morning, then went to bed myself. I woke up two hours later for some reason. Went out to the porch, and found my little darlings had built a tent out there, and were watching for shooting stars to wish upon."

"That's sweet," Callie grinned. "What were they wishing for?"

Libby rolled her eyes and sighed a little. "Same thing they always wish for. A dad, what else? They used my best lace tablecloth for their tent, Callie. And a staple gun to attach it to the wood rails. They also pinched the neighbor's telescope from their backyard."

"No! That old crab?"

"He's not an old crab," Libby defended.

"Maybe not to you, since you seem able to tame every beast. In fact, I believe Old Man Mel has run off every other person who's lived in that house within months. But you've been there since right after the twins were born. You probably bribed the man with your peach tarts or strawberry shortcake or something."

"It was Death by Chocolate, actually." She smiled. "In any case, *Mr.* Melville was understand-

ing about the whole incident. Bobby already knows
more about telescopes than kids twice his age, but
still. I can't even imagine how they lugged the huge
thing from his yard to ours." She shook her head,
smiling despite herself. "Ten minutes can be a
veddy, veddy *dangerous*," she drew out the word
humorously, "thing."

"Well, I'm sure Bobby and Patty will be back
any minute. I heard you telling them to come back
on time, and they're both wearing watches, right?"

Libby nodded. And they were able to read them.
She watched the people passing by the booth, expecting to see her kids any minute. They'd been so
excited to come to the carnival. She could make
allowances for a few minutes tardiness. Even if it
was growing darker by the minute.

As she watched the crowd, one man in particular
caught her eye and she felt her cheeks warm just a
little at the way he looked right back at her. Reminding her that she wasn't *just* a mother to two
rambunctious twins. She was also a woman. One
who could feel her stomach go as soft and gooey
as melting chocolate from a single, long look from
a man. There were other, taller men around, but
something about the turn of his dark-haired head,
the carriage of his broad shoulders caught her attention. And held it.

Much longer than was decent.

She finally blinked and looked down at her watch again. She was no more interested in men ''that'' way than she was interested in appearing stark naked in the town park on a crowded Sunday afternoon, she reminded herself silently. And when she looked back up again, the man had moved off.

She blew out a little breath. How silly of her.

Callie was busy filling an order for lemonade and Libby stacked together the containers she'd used to transport the pastries from her kitchen to the carnival inside a wide, mesh carrying bag. When she was finished, she left the booth and looked up and down the row for any sign of her children.

She was long used to her children's mischief. Not that Bobby and Patty ever did anything mean-spirited. They were just so enthusiastic about everything they did in their lives. And since the Crazy Moon Festival had opened that week, they'd been anticipating this night when she could bring them to enjoy all the appropriate rides and games.

They'd jabbered a mile a minute begging to scope out things while she'd taken care of delivering her pastries to the Calico Diner booth, and she simply hadn't seen any harm in letting them go exploring for a few minutes. Nothing bad ever happened in Rumor, Montana, after all.

But as the second hand of her watch swept around and around and around, Libby focused more on the faces passing by the booth. Faces she didn't recognize. Faces of strangers who'd come from out of town to participate in the widely publicized festival.

And now, it really *was* dark.

"Callie, I know I promised to help you until Nick comes by, but—"

"Go," Callie shooed, not needing Libby to explain. "As soon as Nick gets here, I'll have him go look for them, too. Check back here when you find them, okay?"

So Libby went. It shouldn't take her long to find them, she thought. After all, there was an entire town's worth of people present at the festival, and everyone knew everyone.

Not everyone.

She stopped at booth after booth after booth. "Have you seen the twins?" Only to receive a shake of the head, or a comment that they had, but it had been a good five or ten minutes ago, and nobody seemed to know in which direction her pair had been headed.

Libby stopped dead center in the festival, looking about her. Lights twinkled. Music blared from speakers. Kids laughed and yelled at each other. Smoke from the food booths whispered up into the increasingly dark sky, looking ghostly amid the floodlights that illuminated the grounds.

Her heart felt like it would burst from her chest, just then. ''Bobby! Patty!'' She called their names.

But nobody answered.

Where were her children?

Marcus Jessup wasn't used to crowds. Not anymore, anyway. As he walked through the milling throng of people standing in line for rides or food or games, he wondered what strangeness had gotten into him.

He lived a quiet, secluded life. He didn't long for the company of people. Mostly because he didn't like the stares he usually received. But tonight, instead of working on the refinishing of the crown moulding for his dining room as he'd expected to be doing, he'd come down off his hill and into town to the Crazy Moon Festival.

It was probably that the memories were just too vivid in his mind tonight, he reasoned darkly. Better to brave some stares than dwell too much on the ghosts that haunted him.

This time last year, he'd been in Europe. Scaling a treacherous mountain in his vain attempt to outclimb the memories. The year before that…Marcus realized he couldn't remember what he'd been doing the year before that. Probably risking his life in some other activity he'd thrown himself into. Either that, or trying to drown in a bottle. Anything that helped to keep the ghosts at bay.

He'd been wandering through the lanes of the festival, and stopped short, narrowly missing a small cluster of teenagers who'd stopped in front of a pie-tossing booth. One girl absently looked at him. Despite the shadows that the floodlights couldn't completely eclipse, he saw the way her eyes widened and the way she stepped closer to her boyfriend.

Marcus ignored the girl, and headed toward the final lane where it seemed less congested, not quite as well lit. The enormous Ferris wheel was situated there, illuminated by its own garland of tiny white lights. He watched it for a moment as it lazily halted, and two little kids clambered into a car before it began moving once again.

Sam would have been about that age now.

The thought accosted Marcus before he could stop it, and he braced against the dull pain that washed over him, focusing on anything and everything as a defense against it.

From where he stood, he couldn't see anyone else in the Ferris wheel cars. It was just too dark. And as it *was* dark, he imagined it was a pretty popular ride. Not just for two little dark-haired children, but for couples wanting to sneak a kiss while looking out over the pretty town of Rumor, as well.

He would walk by the Ferris wheel, he decided, and then head on home. If he couldn't tire himself out enough with the moulding to fall into a dreamless sleep, then he'd stay up all damn night if he had to. Anything to avoid the nightmares.

Coming out, being among people, tonight of all nights, was only so much folly. He passed the last game booth before the huge Ferris wheel. Lined with narrow mirrors around the center, it reflected everything from the crystal dishes stacked up for people to toss their coins into, to the people crowding around the edges.

He even caught a glimpse of himself in one of the mirrors—in need of a shave, his hair too long, dressed in black only because it was the easiest way to match his clothes together. No wonder that teenager had looked scared of him, he thought grimly. Seeing his splintered reflection now reminded him why he avoided mirrors at home.

He didn't much like the man who looked back at him.

His gaze slid from his own reflection to the people moving around behind him. He noticed the pretty, dark-haired woman who'd caught his eye earlier. She'd been up to her elbows in brownies that were as rich a chocolate-brown as her shoulder-length hair.

She was obviously looking for someone. A husband, undoubtedly.

She looked the marrying type.

For a half a second, an all-too-brief moment, her gaze collided with his in one of those narrow mirrored reflections. And held. But then someone jostled him and when he looked back, she was gone.

He turned around to look where she went, but there was no sign of her. Even if she hadn't been looking for a husband, or a fiancé or a date or whatever, she'd never look twice at a man like him.

To remind himself why, he took a long look back toward the mirrors. He was nobody's hero. And where he'd once had emotions inside of him, now he had nothing. Nothing at all.

He was heading down the lane again when the festival lights suddenly blinked once, then went out. His footsteps didn't pause, even though all around him people were stopping and staring around them, wondering what had occurred.

Somewhere nearby, a girl gave a short, scared scream.

Not everyone was as at ease in the dark as he was. And he couldn't help but aware of how ironic it was that—when he finally did go out into the town—the darkness followed him.

The lights didn't flicker back on. They were well and truly out. One portion of his mind was aware of the escalating voices around him. Excited. Agitated. He heard snippets of conversations, speculations over the cause of the blackout.

The moon was out, giving some measure of light. Just enough for him to avoid bumping into the huddled groups of teenagers as he continued past the Ferris wheel. One girl gave a high-pitched, nervous giggle before being folded securely against her brawny young boyfriend.

Marcus wondered if he'd ever been that young.

He doubted it.

The Ferris wheel was dead silent, dead still as he walked right by it. He figured he'd cut across the field and save some steps on his way home, as he'd come on foot. But the soft sob that whispered through the dark made his feet slow. Then stop completely. He tilted his head, listening more closely.

"I want Mom."

"Well, she's not here, is she."

"I *told* you we shouldn't have done this."

This wasn't a teenager huddling with her boyfriend. It was younger than that. *They* were younger than that, he thought, tuning out all the other noise so he could hear the faint words. He was good at focusing. Once upon a time, that ability had earned him millions in the computer industry. It had also cost him everything that mattered in the world.

In that moment, Marcus knew who belonged to those whispered, fearful little voices. The two kids he'd earlier seen scramble into one of the Ferris wheel cars.

He looked around. The young man who'd been operating the ride was nowhere in sight. When Marcus went over to the controls, rapidly taking in the fairly simple operation that should have allowed for some means of lowering the cars even without power, he muttered an oath at the slipshod way the equipment had been maintained. The generator wouldn't even kick on.

He stepped back, craning his head back to try and see which car the children were in. But it was too damned dark. He had no idea how far up the kids were, but he suspected it was pretty high.

''We're never gonna get down.''

''No, we won't. And I want Mom.'' The voice was thick with tears, repeating the demand. And it cut right through the ice encasing Marcus's soul as surely as thoughts of Sam always did.

''We could prob'ly climb down.''

Marcus's blood ran cold as he stared up at the enormous wheel. Before thinking twice, he moved to the base of the ride, and hooked hands and feet over metal and pipe, climbing steadily toward those children. His movements were steady and sure. He wouldn't fail these kids. Not the way he'd failed four years ago.

He passed empty car after empty car, never slowing because he could hear the childish voices debating the merits of climbing down from their perch. And finally, at the uppermost car, he found them.

"I guess you guys want to climb down, huh?"

Two little mouths dropped, staring at him. In the moonlight, he could see their worried expressions, the way one held tight to the other's hand. Twins, he thought. As alike as two peas in a pod, except for one being a boy and one being a girl.

The little girl's lips trembled and great fat tears collected in her wide eyes. He figured he'd probably scared the daylights out of her. But the words that came out of her mouth had nothing whatsoever to do with his appearance.

"Mommy's gonna ground us for the rest of our *lives*," she whispered thickly.

He absorbed that for a moment. "You weren't supposed to go on the ride," he concluded.

They both reluctantly shook their heads. And Marcus felt a completely unexpected spurt of amusement. Which was stupid, considering he was perched like a damn idiot on the frame of a Ferris wheel. "Guess it's too bad the ride stopped, leaving you stuck up here, then."

"We're gonna be up here for*ever*," the boy said, looking glum. A reminder that made his sister start crying in earnest. Particularly when a gust of wind made the car sway gently.

"Come on," Marcus said. "You ever watch monkeys in a zoo?" At their nods, he inched his feet along the crossbar, getting as close to the car as he could. "Have you seen the way the little monkeys ride on the big monkey's back?"

The little girl wiped away her tears with a fierce motion. "*You're* gonna get us down? Aren't we s'posed t' wait for the fire department or somethin'? When Bobby got stuck on the roof at home, Mommy called the fire department and they brought a big ladder."

Marcus knew the fire department ladder wouldn't extend this high, but he didn't want to scare the child any more than she already was. "I guess if you want to wait," he said easily. "But, I didn't climb up here because I wanted a piece of cheese from the moon."

The boy rolled his eyes. "The moon's not made of cheese," he scoffed.

Marcus frowned. "You sure?"

"Yeah, I'm sure. I look at it in the telescope all the time."

The girl nodded. "He does. Bobby sneaks over to Mr. Melville's—"

"Patty!"

Marcus felt a grin tug at his lips. He couldn't remember the last time he'd smiled. "Well, I'll take your word for it about the cheese thing, but for now, which one of you is gonna get off this thing with me first? I have to go back down anyway to call the fire department, so one of you might as well come with me."

All the ease that had come into their expressions fled. "We gotta go together," Patty said flatly. "*I'm* not staying up here by myself."

Her brother nodded. "My mom'll kill me if I leave Patty behind."

If the woman had any sense, she'd be going out of her gourd worrying about where her kids were in the darkened carnival grounds, Marcus thought. "Okay. One on my back, one in the front. Which one is which?"

The boy nearly scoffed again. There was no way he was going to be rescued off the Ferris wheel in some man's arms. "I call piggyback," he said quickly.

Marcus winked at the little girl and she smiled shyly, her tears once again forgotten. He helped the boy onto his back. Judging by the tight grip of the kid's arms, Marcus knew the boy wasn't going anywhere. Then he lifted the little girl out and she ducked her head trustingly against his chest. He took the squishy stuffed rabbit she was holding and stuffed it in his pocket so that she would concentrate on holding on to him instead of the toy.

Surrounded by clinging hands and entwined legs, Marcus slowly backed his way down the Ferris wheel until he came to the crossbars. Then he slid inch by inch to the center of the wheel where a series of bars formed a sort of ladder. He hadn't come up that way, but with the additional load of the children, he figured it'd be safer.

"You're not ascared of falling?" Patty's voice was muffled against his neck.

"No."

"How come?" That came from the vicinity of his shoulder blade.

"Because I used to do a lot of mountain climbing."

"Big mountains?" Patty asked. "As big as the Ferris wheel?"

"Yup. And some a lot bigger." Another twenty feet and they'd be on the ground, he figured.

"With all the ropes and stuff?"

"Nope."

Bobby was silent for a minute. "Kewell," he finally breathed, awestruck.

The closer they got to the ground, the more Marcus realized that a crowd had formed at the base of the ride. He hadn't expected that.

"Hey, mister, you like kids?"

Marcus's boot hesitated for just a moment before it found the next rung. "Yes."

The twins fell silent then, until Marcus's feet hit the ground. He set down Patty, and reaching around, swung Bobby, who giggled at the action, to his feet.

"Thank you," the two stared up at him. Then suddenly, Patty wrapped her arms around his waist and hugged him exuberantly.

A cheer went up, and Marcus jerked around, realizing the crowd was much larger than he'd thought. Someone had brought in a heavy-duty flashlight and the beam was focused on the kids. And one petite woman—the dark-haired one he'd noticed more than once that evening—dashed forward, falling to her knees, grabbing the kids against her. The absolute relief on her pretty face was plain to see.

He faded back from the cluster of people surrounding the trio. Feeling the coldness inside him settle right back into its familiar place.

Everyone was safe, he thought, dragging his attention from the woman and her twins.

This time, at least, he hadn't failed.

Chapter 2

"She's crying again."

"Sshh."

Bobby sat up in his bed, looking at his sister. "That guy tonight was pretty cool, huh."

"Bobby," Patty urged, "be quiet or Mommy is going to hear you. She told us to go to sleep."

"She can't hear us," Bobby retorted in a hot whisper. "She's *crying* again. Besides, I ain't sleepy."

Patty sighed heavily and sat up, too, facing her brother from her bed on the opposite side of the room. "I bet she's lonely," she said sagely. "She doesn't got anybody like Callie's got Nick and Marisa's got Mr. Rush."

"She doesn't even got a Mr. Bunny Rags," Bobby said morosely. "How come you didn't remember to get it back from the man? *That's* why I'm not sleepy."

Patty felt like crying, herself. She'd been badly scared, on top of that ride. And now, the only thing they had from their dad was lost. He'd died before they were born, and while their mom had given them a little book of photos of their dad, it was the stuffed rabbit he'd bought before they'd been born that she and Bobby slept with. Bobby on one night. Patty on the other.

"I forgot," she whispered. After they'd gotten down from the ride, and their mom had grabbed her and Bobby hard enough to squeeze them to death, everything had gotten even more crazy. The man had disappeared, and not long after that everyone had been told to go back home "'cause the 'lectricity wasn't gonna be fixed any time soon."

Bobby was quiet for a minute. But Patty knew he wasn't done talking. For a boy he talked an awful lot, sometimes. "Who d'ya think he is?"

"I dunno. I think," her whisper dropped even lower, "maybe he's the guy on the hill."

The admission made both children fall silent for a while. Until Patty finally pushed back her covers and padded across to Bobby's bed, dragging her favorite pillow with her. She climbed up and sat on the foot of the bed, hugging the pillow to her. It wasn't much of a substitute for Mr. Bunny Rags, though.

''I don't care if he is,'' Bobby whispered defiantly. They both knew the rumors the other kids whispered about the creepy guy who lived in the old haunted mansion on the hill. ''He was cool. I wasn't ascared of him. He climbs *mountains*. And you know, he was just foolin' about the moon.''

Patty nodded, rubbing her cheek absently against the cool pillowcase. The man had held her in his arms all the way down the Ferris wheel, and she'd liked it. A lot. He'd smelled good and she hadn't been scared, then. It had felt almost as safe as it had when their mom had hugged them to her on the ground.

''I bet Mommy would like a hug like that, too,'' she said.

Bobby nodded and Patty knew he understood exactly what she'd been thinking. They were twins. And sometimes it seemed like they could read each other's minds.

They both smiled slowly.

And then, they began to plan.

The stream of men began about 10:00 a.m.

One after another, strange men, familiar men, young men, old men. They all began appearing at

Libby's door. Sometimes just one at a time. At one point, after she'd returned from downtown, there were *four* waiting for her on her doorstep.

The only thing they had in common, Libby realized quickly enough, was the variety of stuffed animals each one carried with him.

She chalked up her slowness in realizing what was going on to the fact that it was a Monday, following an otherwise restless weekend. The kids had seemed subdued after their ''adventure'' at the carnival, and hadn't even argued when she'd decided their punishment would be to *not* return to the carnival at all that weekend.

But not until Libby got the call from a laughing Callie shortly after noon, did she fully understand just what her darling children had done.

''Well, take it down!'' Libby had gasped immediately when Callie admitted that the children had begged to hang a poster in the window of the Calico Diner. It wasn't so bad that, apparently with the help of the other kids at their day camp, they'd fashioned a number of ''Pet Lost'' posters to see if someone would come forward with the stuffed toy they'd lost the other night at the carnival. She knew how attached they were to it. They believed their father had bought it for them before his death. And though Libby had gone back to the carnival grounds the next morning as soon as it was light, and looked

over every inch of the place, she hadn't been able
to find it.

So, no, it didn't surprise her terribly that the kids
had made up a lost pet poster. It was what the rest
of the poster proclaimed that made her want to tear
out her hair by the roots. She hadn't even quite
believed how bad it would be until she'd run down
to Main Street.

There, in the windows of nearly every establish-
ment, had been one of the handmade posters. The
top of each and every one had contained a remark-
able likeness of Mr. Bunny Rags, the ragtag stuffed
rabbit, with the Lost Pet headline. Below that, in
careful letters, was Libby's name and home address. Below *that* in bright scarlet letters, was the
proclamation that made Libby want to hide her
head under the covers for a month of Sundays.

Help Wanted: Daddy, they all proclaimed.

At the bottom of each poster were drawings of
two dark-haired children, obviously meant to be
Bobby and Patty, a stick figure with long dark
hair—Libby, she presumed, and finally, a taller figure, also with dark hair. And all four stick figures
were holding each other's stick-hands.

In between delivering her pastries, Libby had
gathered up the posters, as many as she could find.
But Callie had nearly barred Libby from the window to protect her copy. ''I promised the kids that

they could hang it here, and I meant it. Besides,''
Callie had looked at Marisa Stewart, then, who was
not only one of Callie's waitresses but her friend,
to boot. "Maybe the daddy thing is taking it a bit
far even for your rambunctious two, but it wouldn't
hurt if their efforts netted you a date. And before
you start protesting, I know you've said over and
over again that you don't date. But, for heaven's
sake, Libby. You're twenty-seven years old. You
can't continue focusing your entire existence
around Bobby and Patty. They'll eventually grow
up!''

There'd been no point in arguing with her two
friends. Both Callie and Marisa had found the loves
of their lives. Men who had chosen them for the
person they were, rather than the family from which
they came. They seemed determined to have the
rest of the world be just as lucky and happy as they
were.

Now, Libby closed the door on another prospec-
tive suitor bearing a stuffed animal that was so obviously not Mr. Bunny Rags—considering it was a
giraffe with the price tag still on it—and eyed her
children where they sat like meek little mice on the
third step of the staircase leading to their room.

"How many posters did you make," she asked
patiently.

"Seventy-two," Bobby answered promptly. "We got all the kids at day camp to help."

Seventy-two. She rubbed her temples. She'd collected about fifteen. "And just *how* did they get all over town?"

"It's Monday," Patty offered. "Swim day. Everyone walks together from day camp to the park pool."

"And all of you kids just happened to be carrying your posters with you to drop off at every business along the way. It must have been quite a busy morning."

Patty nodded, her mother's facetiousness completely escaping her. "Even the teachers helped us. We hanged them everywhere. Even on some of the trees in the park."

"Lovely," Libby muttered. "Did it occur to *any*one that putting our home address on a poster might not be the safest thing to do? It's sort of like talking to strangers, my sweets. You don't just go around giving out personal information like where we live to people you don't know."

Twin expressions of concern came over their faces. "Oh."

"Yes," Libby said. *"Oh."* She blew out a breath and went over to sit by her children. "Listen, you two. I know how much you love that rabbit."

"Daddy gave it to us," Patty said.

Bobby nodded. "We don't sleep good without it."

Libby sighed, well aware of the sleep that none of them had gotten that weekend as a result of the missing rabbit. "I know. And trying to get him back was fine—except for the address thing. You might have used the phone number instead. And you might have gotten my permission first. But the rest of what you put—"

The ringing of the doorbell interrupted her. Libby felt like leaving it unanswered, but she knew that whoever stood on the other side of the door could probably see her sitting on the steps through the faceted windows on the top section of the door.

She pushed to her feet. "We're not finished," she warned the two imps, as she walked over to the door and pulled it open. "So don't run off to your room, thinking we are."

She turned and greeted the man on the step, aware of the furtive whispers from behind her. Her gaze went first to the stuffed animal the balding man was clutching in his hand. A cat. A pretty, pink and white cat. But definitely not Mr. Bunny Rags.

For a second, Libby felt an urge to laugh. Were men in Rumor so desperate for female companionship? Couldn't they even get the right breed of stuffed animal? "Thank you for coming," she told the stranger, "but I'm sorry, that's not my children's toy."

The man blinked rapidly, his eyes running over Libby, making her wish she wore sackcloth instead of cutoffs and a T-shirt. "Well, are you sure?" He placed a foot on the threshold, and Libby felt a curl of unease.

Bobby and Patty had come to stand beside her, their heads resting on her hips. She rested her hands on their shoulders for a moment. "Quite sure," she said flatly and began to close the door.

But the children suddenly darted forward, startling her as they ran past the stranger on her step, heading pell-mell down her long driveway. "You came, you came!" they were yelling.

Libby looked beyond the cat-man and went still. Sitting on top of her bricked-in mailbox sat Mr. Bunny Rags. And walking away was the same dark-haired man who'd rescued her children from the Ferris wheel.

She hurriedly stepped out onto the porch and closed the door firmly behind her. "I'm sorry," she said to the cat-man as she darted, barefoot, after her children. "You'll have to excuse us."

"Well, I never," she heard him mutter behind her.

And you never will, she thought, her humor spiking. Not with this lady.

She jogged the rest of the way to the mailbox. Which was the only thing that accounted for the breathless sensation in her chest, she reasoned. Bobby and Patty were staring up at the man with delight. Neither one seemed all that interested in the stuffed toy, either. She plucked it off the mailbox and moistened her lips, feeling foolish standing there in her bare feet. "You brought Mr. Bunny Rags back?"

The man nodded. His thick, dark hair skimmed his shoulders and his lean cheeks were bristled. But it was his eyes that held her attention. The same eyes that she'd noticed at the festival. Thickly lashed, so dark a brown they looked nearly black. Her fingertips curled into the squishy rabbit. "Then I owe you my thanks, again. You, um, you left so quickly the other night. I didn't get a chance to thank you for what you did."

He lifted one shoulder, barely looking at her. When he looked at the children, however, his solemn expression seemed to lighten. "I forgot all about the toy in my pocket," he told them. "And I didn't know your last names, or I'd have gotten it back to you, earlier."

"You saw our poster though, huh," Bobby stated emphatically. "I *knew* you would." Her son looked up at her. "He's the mountain-climber man, mom. The one who rescued us."

"I know he is, sweetheart." Libby brushed her son's tumbled hair away from his excited face. The children had recounted their adventure so many times over the weekend that Libby almost felt as if he'd carried *her* down the center of the Ferris wheel, too. An entire cloud of butterflies had taken up residence in her tummy and she felt silly because of it.

"Did you read the rest of the poster?" Patty asked softly.

Libby's butterflies fled in a flurry of mortification. *How* could she have forgotten about her kids' advertisement? She quickly stuck out her hand, hoping to distract him from having to answer *that* particular question. "Libby Adler," she said hurriedly.

"Marcus." His lips twisted a little and then he slowly shook her hand. "Jessup."

She curled her fingertips against her tingling palm when their hands parted. "After you left Friday evening, the deputy sheriff and Nick Sullivan sent everyone home. Apparently, a truck hit a transformer, and that's why the electricity went out."

"I heard."

"Even the fire department had been tied up."

He nodded, clearly unsurprised.

If he read the local newspaper, then of course he'd know all about the electrical outage. "Anyway," she trained her gaze on her children, trying to ignore Callie's statement about being overdue for a date that was circling in her head. "Who knows how long they'd have been stuck up there, if not for you. Nick…oh, he's the president of the Chamber of Commerce, you know…he made sure the safety features on the Ferris wheel were repaired before anyone could use it again this weekend." Now, she was babbling, she thought, even more embarrassed.

"Mr. Jessup, did you read the rest of our poster?" Patty's little voice piped up. She was clearly not going to be distracted from getting an answer.

"Patty, honey, I think I might have left the water running in the sink. Would you go check?"

Patty's soft brown eyebrows drew together. "Mommy—"

Libby tilted her head, pointedly.

Her daughter heaved a sigh. She grabbed her brother's hand. "Come on."

"No, wait. Mr. Jessup can stay and have supper with us," Bobby announced brightly. "Right, Mom?"

"I…uh—" She didn't think she'd ever seen a man with such long eyelashes, she thought stupidly. "What? Oh. Dinner. Right." She brushed her palms down her cutoffs. "Of course. It's the least

I can do," she managed to say. "It's not much—pasta salad…" Her voice trailed off. She could already read the refusal on his face.

But then Patty slid her hand into his, staring up at him with hope written all over her sweet face. "Please stay?"

Libby's heart stuttered for her daughter. Neither Patty nor Bobby knew what rejection felt like. And she hoped to keep it that way for a good long while. "Honey, Mr. Jessup probably already has plans," she said smoothly. "And I already asked you to check the water, remember?"

"Actually, I don't." Marcus heard the words come out of his lips and wondered for a moment where the hell they'd come from. He gave Patty's little starfish hand a gentle squeeze. "Thank you for the invitation."

The smiles on the children's faces could have powered the carnival, he thought, as they ran off toward the house and the supposedly running water.

Which left Marcus looking at the pretty woman who was their mother. She didn't even come up to his shoulder, he thought. And she looked more like a teenager than a woman raising two children on her own.

At least, he assumed she was on her own, thanks to the "Daddy wanted" portion of the poster he'd seen in the window at the gas station.

"Listen," Libby said, looking distinctly awkward. "You are very welcome to stay for dinner. But if you have plans, don't worry about my children. They'll understand."

Marcus doubted that. "How old are they?"

"Six. They'll be seven on Christmas Day."

Sam would have been seven, he thought. "Quite a Christmas present."

She grinned, and a sexy little dimple peeped at him from her right cheek. He kept waiting for her eyes to focus on his scars, the way everyone's eyes always did, but she hardly seemed to notice. "Particularly since they weren't due until late January." She sucked in one corner of her soft lips. "Well, come on in, then. I was just finishing up things except the doorbell kept ringing."

Marcus could only imagine. Libby Adler was petite, pretty and sexy as hell. Every available man— maybe even some that weren't—in Rumor who'd seen one of those posters had probably hoofed right to her door.

Suddenly, Libby looked up at him, her eyes wide. Embarrassed. "You know, they, um, they did all that without my permission."

"I gathered."

She brushed her shining brown hair behind one ear and waited for him to walk into her house. "You probably think I'm a terrible mother," she said. "First you get them off that Ferris wheel, and then they plaster their artwork all over town—"

"I think," Marcus interrupted, "you have two bright, enthusiastic children on your hands."

She pressed her lips together for a moment, seeming to study him. Then she blinked, and turned into the living room, waving at the arrangement of sofa and chairs upholstered in a cheerful green-and-blue plaid. "Have a seat," she invited. "Can I get you a glass of iced tea or something before dinner?"

"No." Now that he was inside her home, he realized he should have gotten out of the meal when she'd given him a chance. Everywhere he turned there were signs of family.

Things he'd hardly been able to bear thinking about even after four years.

Libby didn't seem to notice anything amiss, however, and just smiled as she disappeared along a short hallway. Then he could see her again through the breakfast bar opening that separated the dining room from the kitchen. The early evening sunlight shafted through the window over the sink, causing red highlights to spring to life in her thick, wavy hair.

As he watched, she tucked it behind her ear again, then opened up a cupboard. He could see the neat arrangement of plates inside it in the second before she closed it again.

Then opened it.

And closed it.

The core of ice inside him seemed a little less cold. And it was almost addictive. "Anything I can help with?"

She jerked and whirled around, smiling brightly at him through the opening. "Nope. No, you just, um, have a seat."

So, he did. But he sat on the couch where he could still watch her through that opening.

He liked watching Libby Adler, he thought. She was a pint-size woman, moving capably about in her kitchen, and he liked that, too. She'd opened that same cupboard door once more, and snatched out a handful of plates, then came around into the dining room and began setting the gleaming table.

So gleaming, he had a feeling that they didn't usually eat there. Not unless she polished it within an inch of its life after the kids had sat at it and left an assortment of their fingerprints.

She went back into the kitchen again, then reappeared, casually setting a bottle of beer on the coffee table in front of him before going to the staircase and calling the kids.

They fairly tumbled down the stairs, almost immediately, and Marcus saw the way Libby's eyebrows shot halfway up her forehead. Bobby's hair was wet and slicked back from his face, and he wore a button-down shirt. Patty had two gold barrettes in her long hair, and she was wearing a ruffled dress.

"Well," Libby murmured. "Dressing for dinner, I see. You both look very nice."

The kids preened. It didn't matter that Bobby's shirt buttons were mismatched, or that Patty wore muddy tennis shoes with her dress.

And Marcus liked Libby even more.

Which meant that staying for dinner had *really* been a bad idea.

"You should change too, Mommy," he heard Patty whisper. "'Cause you look like a, a... urchin," she finally settled on.

Libby's muffled laughter whispered through him. "I guess I'd better, then," she agreed softly. She turned and focused her warm brown eyes on him. "Mr. Jessup, if you'll excuse me for just a moment?"

"Marcus," he said.

She hesitated, one foot on the first tread, as she looked back at him. "Marcus." Her lips curved over his name, making it sound almost like a caress. Then her cheeks colored again in a way he found entirely too enchanting. "The beer's for you, by the way. Nick sometimes has one when he's here for dinner.''

The pleasure that had been building inside of Marcus fizzled like a spent balloon. Fortunately, Libby was already darting up the staircase, so she didn't witness his deflation. He picked up the long-neck and popped off the top. It was icy cold against his tongue when he drank. But it tasted bitter as hell. And not because there was something wrong with the brew.

''Wanna play checkers?''

He looked down at two hopeful faces. Well, why not, he thought wryly. It *was* because of the kids that he'd agreed to dinner, wasn't it? The mental assurance fizzled, too. He sat down on the couch. ''Sure,'' he told them. ''But who goes first?''

''I do,'' Patty said promptly. ''Then Bobby.''

''Uh-uh,'' Bobby protested. ''You *always* go first.''

''That's 'cause I'm a girl.''

Bobby rolled his eyes. ''So?''

''So, girls always gotta go first. Right?'' She looked at Marcus.

''Sometimes,'' he allowed. ''What about a game we can all play at the same time?''

Bobby perked right up at that. He scrambled over to the wooden bookshelf against one wall, next to a computer that was powered off. The shelves were stuffed to the gills with paperback novels, children's books and a wide assortment of games. Board games. Computer games.

Even in the game room they'd had, Julia had kept everything in pristine order, behind closed doors.

He nodded absently when Bobby held up a box. The twins began setting out the game on the coffee table and Marcus sat back on the sofa, balancing the beer on his knee. He glanced around the living room.

It was spotlessly clean and smelled vaguely like lemon blossoms and ripe peaches. Wood surfaces shined, and multipaned windows fairly twinkled against the deepening sunlight. But there were still obvious signs of children. Like the bookcase, for one. And the paintings—obviously done in a child's hand—that were hung along the staircase as if they were priceless oils.

Feeling odd inside, Marcus lifted the bottle for another drink before sitting forward to select a game piece from the box when Patty instructed him to do so. He wondered, as he set aside his beer, why the kids were advertising for a dad when there was *Nick* around.

In any case, he figured the other man was a lucky guy. He hoped Nick was smart enough to realize it.

Just as Marcus was smart enough to realize that no matter how appealing he found Libby Adler and her twin munchkins, she'd never go for someone like him. No woman with two eyes in her head would ever go for someone like him.

And just as well. Because he'd already failed one family.

Fatally.

He couldn't take a chance with another.

Chapter 3

"Do you got any kids of your own?"

At Bobby's question, Libby's hand trembled as she poured the piping hot coffee into two fat white mugs. Standing in the kitchen, she felt herself going tense as she waited for Marcus to answer. Of course he'd probably have a family somewhere. Maybe even a wife, for all she knew. Just because he'd accepted their invitation to dinner didn't mean anything. He'd obviously accepted just to please Bobby and Patty.

He still hadn't answered, and Libby hurriedly mopped up the little spill she'd made before carrying the tray out to the living room.

Dinner was over, and Marcus was again sitting on the couch, flanked by her children who eyed him as if he were Santa Claus and Superman all rolled into one. They'd badgered him with questions throughout dinner, despite Libby's attempts to maintain some control, but Marcus had patiently answered them. Carrying on a conversation with her children with ease.

Oh yeah, this man had kids, she thought as she sat the tray, loaded with servings of fresh custard peach pie and coffee for her and Marcus.

She smoothly handed Bobby and Patty their plates, letting them sit at the coffee table just this once, rather than at the dinner table or the smaller one in the kitchen's breakfast nook. She was grateful that the treat seemed to distract them from Bobby's latest query.

"Marcus?" She held a plate out for him.

He was sort of staring at the wedge of pie that she'd garnished with tiny curls of minted chocolate and wafer thin wedges of fresh peaches. "I thought it smelled like peaches in here," he said.

Whether or not he was married with an entire passel of offspring, didn't matter in the least, she told herself firmly. She was only repaying his kindness to her children with a meal. Nothing more.

She smiled at him, wishing that she'd thought to invite his wife—if he did have one—earlier, when it would have seemed more natural. "Is that good or bad? Smelling like peaches."

He slowly took the plate, his long fingers unintentionally brushing hers. He glanced up at her, the emotion in his dark eyes so raw that she suddenly felt her eyes sting. "It's good," he said.

Oh, she really was being ridiculous. Libby sat down in the armchair and picked up her coffee, sipping gingerly. He liked peaches. So did she. So what?

"Aren't you going to eat yours?"

Libby smiled faintly. "If I ate everything I ever baked, you'd have to roll me out the door in the mornings. Most of what I make goes to the Calico Diner, and I try to keep what *I* eat down to just a bite or two so I don't end up as wide as I am tall."

"You don't look in danger of that." For just a moment, an impossibly long, impossibly brief, ridiculously intense moment, he looked at her and she saw the frank appreciation there.

It made her heart climb right into her throat. She'd given up on love and picket fences when she'd learned that Terry had not married her because he'd been as head over heels in love with her as she was with him, but because she came with a well-financed Bostonian pedigree that served his activist needs in ways she'd been too blind to see.

The coffee was still too hot to drink, so she set

it aside and picked up her plate just to keep herself from fidgeting. "How long have you lived in Rumor?" She managed a natural smile. "We're not so big that sooner or later the residents don't at least recognize the other residents."

"A few years. I don't go down to Main Street much." His eyes, those eyes which held so much that wasn't revealed in his impassive expression, met hers and she knew the reason for him staying away from the central area of the small town had a great deal to do with the ridge of silvered scars that rose from the unbuttoned collar of his navy blue shirt on one side of his strong neck. They fanned along his jaw, disappearing beneath the bristle of his beard that wasn't quite a beard, but wasn't exactly a five o'clock shadow.

She wondered for a moment about the hint of challenge in his gaze. As if he expected her to turn her gaze away from his disfigurement. Undoubtedly, he'd had more than his share of people who did look away from his scarred visage. But, she wouldn't be one of them. Frankly, she could hardly look at him without nearly swallowing her tongue. He was just so…intense. Utterly male. And his gentleness every time he interacted with her children was uncomfortably moving.

Oblivious to Marcus's tension, Bobby said, "He

lives in the house on the hill.'' He spoke around a mouthful of pie.

As there was more than one hill, and definitely more than one house, that didn't say much to Libby as she handed her son a napkin.

"Is it really haunted?" Patty asked. "The kids at day camp all say it is."

Clearly, her children had more of a clue about Marcus Jessup than she did.

"No, it's not haunted." He didn't look at Libby. "You can see the place from your backyard, probably. I'm at the top of Hill Street, practically right behind you."

"The Victorian? That's where you live? Oh, Marcus, that's a lovely house. You're the one who has been refurbishing it, then." She *was* able to see the stately home high on the hill from her backyard, though it was only via the sharply curving Hill Street that one could reach it. There had been many times when she'd been gardening that she'd found herself looking up at that house and wondering about the people who dwelled there. "Have you always been interested in that period?"

"Not exactly," he said, an odd twist to his lips. "My wife always wanted a Victorian."

Disappointment buffeted her. She didn't feel badly in the least about opening her home to him after what he'd done, but the man had no business looking at her the way he had with a wife at home. She knew what it was like to be *that* wife. "She must be very pleased now, then. I'm sorry that I didn't think to have you call her and join us."

He set his empty plate carefully on the coffee table. "She died several years ago."

As surely as the disappointment had hit, shock swept through her like wildfire. "Marcus, I'm…I'm so sorry." She barely kept herself from reaching forward and folding her hand around his. She knew what it was like to be the wife left at home by a husband more interested in company other than hers. She also knew what it was like to bury a spouse. And no matter how badly things had turned between her and Terry, she'd truly grieved when he'd been killed.

"Our daddy died, too," Patty said, innocently breaking the tension that had once again filled the room. "Before we was born."

"And now you've got Nick." Marcus said, his hooded gaze drifting over Libby's face.

"I…what?"

"Nick." He reached over and lifted the long neck that still sat on the end table.

"Nick *Sullivan?*" Libby felt jumbled inside. She shouldn't be so glad that this man didn't have a wife at home, she just shouldn't. Not when his expression clearly said the loss was still painful.

"He's engaged to my best friend Callie Griffin. I thought I mentioned that."

Marcus didn't much care for feeling like an idiot. But he did now. Big time. The man he'd once been, wealthy, smooth, powerful, seemed like a dream. Now he just felt like what he'd always been even under the trappings of success—a street kid with a knack for computers who'd gotten lucky. The kid who'd never felt quite at home in his own skin, only now his skin had the scars of his sins to add to the discomfort.

He had no business being around Libby Adler and her twins, no business soaking up the balm of their presence when he was so far from deserving it. "You mentioned he was president of the Chamber of Commerce."

Libby just looked back at him with a vaguely confused expression. "Well, I guess I wasn't much thinking about them," she said after a moment. Then her cheeks colored as if she'd said too much. "How about another piece of pie?"

She was too kind for her own good, Marcus thought. She didn't know what she'd invited into her home. He made himself turn her down, even though his mouth pretty much watered at the notion of more. More of her, more of that peach dessert. "No, thanks."

She'd started to reach for his plate, had half risen

from her chair, and she immediately sat back, her hands folding together in her lap. Her expression didn't change a whit, but he still felt as if he'd slighted her.

"I really like peaches," he found himself admitting. An understatement. But now was not the time to admit that he was figuring her soft pink lips probably tasted of peaches, figuring that the satiny skin covering the rest of her body probably tasted even sweeter.

There'd never be a time to admit *that.*

And suddenly, her eyes seemed to grow even more soft—which should've been impossible considering they looked as warm and rich as velvet. He had the sensation that she had somehow read his thoughts.

"If you like the custard pie, you'd love my peach tarts."

Just like that, the collar of his shirt felt way too tight. "I'm sure I would," he said, abruptly pushing to his feet. "Thank you for dinner. It really wasn't necessary, though."

Libby rose, also. Looking a little bewildered, he thought. He'd never known a woman whose thoughts were so clearly mirrored on her face. "We were glad to have you," she said smoothly. "Weren't we, kids?"

Bobby and Patty were staring up at him, still

kneeling beside the coffee table. "You're leaving already?"

"Bobby," Libby reminded gently, "We wouldn't want to monopolize Mr. Jessup's entire evening."

The boy looked Marcus squarely in the eye. "Why not? Unless you got kids of your own waiting for you."

He should have known the boy wasn't going to be sidetracked from his question forever. And it was an odd sensation to get a man-to-man look from a squirt of a kid who had a front tooth missing, a stuffed rabbit clutched in one hand and a fork oozing with custard pie in the other hand.

"I did have a son," he heard himself admit. "Sam. But he died with his mom."

"That's sad," Patty whispered after a moment.

Marcus caught the liquid sheen in Libby's eyes when she reached out and gently smoothed her hand over her daughter's head.

"It was a long time ago." Why he felt the need to soothe this family, he didn't know. But he did know that he had to get out of there. Now.

So, while Libby was still standing there with her slender hand lovingly resting on her daughter's brown hair, while the children were still occupied with the desserts they were systematically demolishing, he swiftly told them good-night, and walked right out the door.

"D'ya think she likes him?" Bobby's whisper reached Patty's ears that night in their bedroom. It was nearly dark, except for the light from the Mickey Mouse-shaped night-light. He'd let Patty have Mr. Bunny Rags to sleep with even though it was *his* night. It'd just seemed like the right thing to do, he'd thought. Something that Marcus Jessup would probably approve of. Because it seemed like girls needed stuff like that sometimes more than men.

"Yeah," Patty whispered back. "I think she does."

"And he likes her."

"How can you tell?"

Bobby snorted. "I can tell."

Patty rolled her eyes. "How?"

"Because he looked at Mom the same way he looked at that last piece of pie."

Patty fell silent, thinking about that. "He left like he was upset, though. D'ya think he left 'cause of us? 'Cause his son died? I think Mommy wanted to cry when he told."

Bobby chewed the ragged edge of his favorite blanket. "I don't know. I still like him, though."

"Me, too."

"So what are we gonna do next?"

"Bobby! Patty!" Their mom's voice floated up from downstairs. "If I have to come up there *again* to tell you to stop talking, I'm going to clean out the sewing room and give you separate rooms!"

Bobby and Patty looked at each other and giggled. Their mom's threats were a lot better to hear than her soft sniffles.

"You mean you actually got the man to stay for dinner? Marcus *Jessup?*"

Libby carefully arranged new paper doilies on the glass shelves inside the chilled pastry display. She didn't look up at Callie who was standing behind her, cleaning the coffeemaker. "I didn't *get* him to do anything. I offered him dinner. He accepted. It was the least I could do, you know. The man *did* climb up a Ferris wheel for my children." She'd justified her reasoning so many times to herself that it was beginning to sound old.

"Of course you did," Marisa—sitting at the counter refilling salt and pepper shakers—agreed, soothingly. "You'd welcome anybody into your home very nearly. I think Callie's point—which you are deliberately ignoring—is that Mr. Jessup *agreed.*"

Libby's cheeks felt as if they'd become permanently hot. "I should've never told you two in the first place," she muttered.

Callie chuckled. "Oh, like you'd be able to keep that a secret? When was the last time you had an eligible man in your house? It's a wonder the printing presses didn't stop."

"The last time was two weeks ago, Thursday. When you and Nick came to dinner."

Callie snorted softly. "He doesn't count."

"What? Nick isn't eligible?"

"Nick isn't available," Callie said sweetly. "Smart aleck."

"So what was he like?"

Libby glanced at Marisa as she reached for the container of éclairs and began arranging them atop the lacy-looking doily. "Intelligent and—" attractive, compelling and far too heartbreakingly dangerous for her peace of mind "—good with the kids," she finished.

"Are you going to see him again?"

"Why would I?" Her voice was a little sharper than she intended and she made herself lift a casual shoulder. "You know me. The only things I have time to concentrate on in my life are Bobby and Patty." If she occasionally let her worries get the best of her like they had the night of the blackout when she'd cried into her pillow until she'd fallen asleep, she chose to ignore it. "Did I tell you they

decided we needed a goldfish pond in our backyard? This morning before I could take them to day
camp they'd already begun digging the hole. Right
by the back step. I nearly cracked my ankle in half
when I stepped right in it.''

''Stop changing the subject.''

Libby eyed Callie, all innocence.

It was midmorning and the Calico Diner only had
a few patrons sitting at the red vinyl booths. Harriet
Martel, the tart-tongued librarian who often came
in from the library down the block for a cup of tea
at this time of day, sat alone, her sharp nose stuck
in a book. Everyone knew not to bug Harriet once
she'd gotten her cup of tea. She wasn't mean. But
she wasn't exactly friendly, either. Nobody would
slide into her booth and strike up a chat. Not like
they did at one of the other booths where Dee Dee
Reingard sat, chattering with her group of friends.
Dee Dee was married to the sheriff and was always
involved in one event—like the PTA bake sale, or
some such thing.

There were a few other folks there, too. But the
real lunch rush wouldn't begin for another hour or
so. Libby would be long gone by then.

''You know, he never comes into town,'' one of
the ladies sitting with Dee Dee suddenly piped up.
''I hear he's got some secret laboratory up in that

house of his and he's busy killing off mice and monkeys with his experiments.''

Dee Dee had the presence of mind to shush her friend. "He's a businessman," she said emphatically.

"That face 'a his is prob'ly on some wanted poster somewhere," someone else countered.

Libby stood at that. She pressed her hands to the top of the pastry case. "Why would he *want* to browse Main Street," she said sharply. "When the only thing that might greet him is that kind of ridiculous speculation!" Her voice rang out through the dining room, and everyone was staring at her. Lord, she hated being the center of attention.

Harriet stood, slamming her book shut. "Crazy moon is coming. It's making everyone *act* crazy," she said balefully, and strode out the door, making it jingle furiously.

Libby shook her head, impatient with them as well as herself, and ducked back down behind the case to continue arranging her baked goods. Maybe Harriet was right. Maybe it was the coming crazy moon that was messing with everyone's emotions.

"So. You liked him, then," Callie leaned over, keeping her voice low.

Libby sighed, remembering the way Marcus had left her home, so abruptly, two nights earlier. She studiously wiped a smudge of chocolate from her thumb. "He...confuses me," she admitted softly.

"That's a start," Marisa commented.

A reluctant chuckle escaped Libby's lips and she looked up at them. "How many times do I have to tell you two? I am *not* interested in having a man in my life."

"Not even a *little* interested?" Marisa wheedled gently. Her pregnant tummy would allow her to lean over the countertop only so far. "You're not interested in having a man's arms around you? In having someone to share the joys and burdens of life with?"

Libby opened her mouth to deny it, but how could she? Yes, there were times when she felt very alone in the world, raising her two children by herself. But she'd chosen that path after Terry's betrayal, and until lately she'd been just fine with that decision.

Until lately.

Until she'd looked into the black-brown eyes of a man whose very soul seemed to speak to hers. Since that first moment she'd noticed him at the festival, even before he'd carried her children from danger, she'd been stopped in her tracks by the chance meeting of their gazes. Just that one fleeing connection and her heart had climbed into her throat in a way that had had nothing to do with her worry over Bobby and Patty.

Since last night at dinner, she hadn't been able to get thoughts of him out of her mind. At the pain he'd endured in losing his wife and son. She knew instinctively that their loss had something to do with his scars. Just as she knew, instinctively, that he'd felt some of that same *confusion* when he'd looked at her.

None of which explained the way he'd practically bolted from her living room last night.

"Maybe there are times when it would be nice to have someone," Libby allowed, finally. "But, trust me." She managed a smile as she carefully lifted two oversized, painfully rich brownies from their box onto one of the shelves. "It is a fleeting thought on my part."

The bell over the diner door jingled just as she finished speaking, seeming to punctuate her thought. Considering the topic of her lack of a love life complete, Libby pushed one empty container out of her way and, still kneeling on the floor, leaned over to reach the last container. She heard Callie greet the newcomer just as she usually did, but Libby simply froze when she heard the voice that responded.

Marcus.

"Pick any seat you like," Callie invited.

"No, thanks. I…heard you sometimes have peach tarts. Thought I'd stop in and pick up a few."

Hunched way over behind the counter to reach the container, Libby closed her eyes, catching her breath at his low husky voice. He sounded even better than she remembered.

"Libby's peach tarts?" Callie's voice lifted and she stepped back until Libby could see her. "I'm so sorry. I wish I did. But…she didn't bring any in today. Is there, um, something else you'd be interested in?"

Libby didn't need Callie's pointed nudge with her shoe to tell her she should stand up. She *knew* it. But she simply couldn't make her legs straighten, make her hands push her up until her head, at least, would be visible above the countertop over which Marisa was giving her an arch look.

"No," Marcus said after a moment. "Thanks, anyway." He left with another jingle from the bell over the door.

The diner was silent.

Libby covered her face with her hands. She could feel Callie and Marisa looking at her.

"In the six years I have known you," Callie said tartly, "I have never seen you act so outrageously. And you want us to *believe* that there's nothing going on between you and Marcus Jessup. The man has never, ever, not once, stepped foot into this diner. Yet he came here today for *your* peach tarts. I can't believe you just hid there!''

Libby covered her face with her hands, emotions tangling inside her. ''I can't believe it, either,'' she mumbled.

Was the coming crazy moon also turning her into a coward?

Chapter 4

She'd made far too many peach tarts.

There was no way they'd all sell. Not even *with* the extra business provided by Calico's food booth at the Crazy Moon Festival. So, she was merely doing the logical thing, Libby told herself as she carefully steered her little car up the twists and turns of Hill Street so as not to send the plastic container on the seat behind her careening onto the floor.

And the fact that you just *happened* to make too many peach tarts is merely a coincidence?

She ignored the skeptical little voice that poked at her and made the final turn up to where the Victorian stood.

From her backyard, she could only see the back of the stately house with the scallops and curlicues. She wasn't sure she'd ever seen the front, she realized as she sat in her car and stared out at Marcus's home. It wasn't painted yet, and there were portions of the house that were obviously new repairs alongside the scraped original sections. But she could see it would be beautiful when the refurbishing was completed.

It was beautiful now.

Surrounding the house was a very green yard. Tidy. Well-groomed even though the rosebushes clustered along one side of the house were in desperate need of pruning.

She slowly shut off the engine, and climbed from her car, smoothing down the front of her off-white slacks.

Another thing that made no sense. Instead of wearing her usual cutoffs or jeans to make her delivery into town, today she'd chosen to wear linen slacks and a lightweight, sleeveless sweater. She pressed her lips together, feeling the unfamiliar slick of lipstick. Most days, she was so busy she forgot to fiddle with cosmetics.

Her heart was thundering inside her chest and she sternly ordered it to settle right back down. She'd only come to deliver the extra tarts. That was all.

She even nodded to confirm the thought. Then,

moving briskly, she retrieved the sealed plastic container from her back seat and with it in hand, turned resolutely to face the house.

Swallowing past the knot in her throat, she headed up the concrete walkway, the half-dozen steps of the porch, and pushed her finger against the bell. She chose not to notice the trembling of her finger, but she couldn't help but notice that she didn't hear even the faintest of door chimes from within. So, she rapped her knuckles on the paneled door, nearly jumping back a foot when the door creaked open a few inches.

She chewed the inside of her lip and gingerly knocked again. "Marcus?"

Her only answer was the door. Which creaked open two more inches.

Maybe she'd misunderstood him at dinner that night when he'd shared that he worked at home. The place was almost deathly quiet and she suddenly felt very much aware that his house *was* set somewhat apart from the neighbors.

When she realized that some of the ludicrous speculations from the diner yesterday were now going around inside her head, she huffed out a breath.

Marcus Jessup was a kind, decent, albeit reclusive, man. That did *not* make him a lunatic, or an ex-criminal, or a social misfit.

She called out his name a little louder, but still heard no response.

He *was* gone.

There was no pretending she wasn't disappointed. Turning away with a sigh, her fingers tightened on the container. She supposed she could leave the tarts on the porch, but the shade was rapidly dwindling under the June sun.

Nibbling her lip again, she looked at the opened door. She *could* set the container inside, then close the door and be out of there. She still had more deliveries to make, after all. And she couldn't leave the door open like that anyway. Nothing bad ever happened in Rumor, but still it would be foolish to invite an intruder. Actually, he shouldn't leave the door unlocked at all. Not while he was gone. Or maybe he just had a faulty catch. It was an old house, after all. And he *had* said he was in the process of refurbishing it.

Heart knocking against the wall of her chest, she nudged the door open a little more. "Marcus?" When there was still no response, she slipped into the shadowy interior.

Inside, it was cool and dim.

And empty.

Her jaw dropped a little at the sheer emptiness of the place. He'd said he'd lived there a few years, but there was not one single stick of furniture in the front rooms!

Unaware of the way she was clutching the container tightly to her midriff, she tentatively called out his name yet again. Her voice seemed to echo through the emptiness. And when she slowly crossed the gleaming, wood floor, her strappy little sandals sounded impossibly loud.

But then she was through a doorway and in his kitchen, and her nerves calmed just a bit. She'd just leave the tarts right there on that glorious stretch of granite countertop, and get out of there.

She slid the container on the counter, unable to resist smoothing her palm over the pristine, nearly-silken surface. The kitchen would be a dream to cook and bake in, she thought faintly.

Marcus would know who'd brought him the tarts. There was no reason for her to linger in the hopes of running into him. She hadn't come specifically to *see* him, after all. Because she wasn't interested in pursuing anything with the man. She only had those extra tarts and after knowing that he'd gone to town to get some, she'd thought he might appreciate them.

Satisfied with her shaky justification, but still feeling very much as if she'd invaded his privacy, she turned to go.

Marcus stood behind her.

Her startled gasp sounded loud and she pressed her palm to her heart. "Hi." Her voice trembled, embarrassingly. "I, uh, didn't hear you."

Marcus's eyes narrowed. Libby looked as enticing as a scoop of vanilla with chocolate topping on a hot summer afternoon.

She also looked positively dismayed that he'd caught her inside his house. Dismayed and more than a little guilty, if the flood of color in her cheeks was any indication.

"I was out back," he said after a moment. He wondered what she was doing there. Particularly after the way she'd hidden from him at the diner. If he'd ever needed to reinforce his knowledge that a woman like her wouldn't be interested in a man like him, *that* had provided it.

And then it dawned on him.

He usually wasn't so slow.

Just because he didn't mix much with the people of Rumor didn't mean he was unaware of the gossip surrounding him. Nor would it be the first time an overly curious woman poked and prodded her way into his home, nudging her way into his life as if he were a thing to be studied. Or worse, a thing to be pitied. Still, he hadn't thought that Libby Adler was that type.

"Why do you look so startled?" His voice was cold, masking the disappointment he didn't even

like to admit to. He specially didn't want to think
about the way she'd consumed his thoughts all
week. He didn't want to acknowledge that when he
did think about her, he'd felt a little more human.
A little less alone.

She sucked in her lower lip for a half a second,
leaving it slick and way too inviting. "I'm sorry,
Marcus, I shouldn't have—"

He *was* alone, he reminded himself harshly.
Through no one's fault but his own. "Shouldn't
have come to see me? Is it more frightening than
you'd expected?" He stepped closer to her, feeling
a frustrated satisfaction at the way her eyes widened
and her foot slid back a half step until the counter
at her back stopped her.

"Frightening?"

"Your curiosity wasn't satisfied that night at
dinner?"

Her smooth brown eyebrows drew together.
"Marcus, I don't—"

His voice dropped a notch. "You want to know
if the stories are true?"

Libby frowned, confused more than ever by his
cold tone.

He was an intimidating presence. His thick hair
was pulled back in a ponytail as thick as her wrist
and, unlike the other times she'd seen him when
he'd worn button-down shirts with only the very

top button unfastened, he now wore a completely
ragged black shirt with the sleeves and collar torn
out.

His shoulders were hard with muscle and darkly
tanned from the sun. And his neck was corded with
sinew. She knew men who were slightly taller than
Marcus. Nick Sullivan, for one. But she didn't
know a single one who was so powerfully built.

He looked tough, and dark, and with the ridge of
scar tissue rising on his throat, he looked, well,
menacing.

*He's the man who played Chutes 'n' Ladders
with your kids for an hour.* Not menacing, she
amended. But definitely fierce. "What stories?"

His lips twisted. She'd never seen such emptiness
in a man's eyes before. And she almost wished she
hadn't asked.

Marcus didn't look away from her. "The stories
about whether or not I killed my family."

She blinked once, her mind going blank. "Did
you?" The words came without thought.

His eyes went even colder. And her heart
plunged straight to her toes when he nodded.

Just once.

Only once.

But it *was* a nod.

Then he turned away from her, walking out

of the room as silently as he'd walked in and found her.

Her knees weakened and she pressed her hand on the countertop, brushing against the plastic container. What kind of agony had Marcus endured? Was still enduring, that he'd be able to state so flatly, so unemotionally, that he'd been responsible for the deaths of his wife and son?

There was no logic for it, no reasonable explanation, but Libby knew with unquestioning certainty that Marcus Jessup would never have caused harm to his family any more than she would harm her own children.

Realizing it, her mortification over being caught invading his home faded. She followed him.

There was a drawing room off the living room. One day she figured it would probably hold lovely wing chairs and a settee, perhaps centered around the fireplace. But now, the floor was covered with canvas and heavy plastic, while sawhorses, ladders and an assortment of tools and supplies provided decoration.

Marcus was bent over a section of long, narrow wood. He was obviously painstakingly sanding away the dull tan paint that was caked into the intricate pattern.

She didn't know what to say. Only that she had to say something. "I never thought that." The words came out, blunt, and awkward and completely without her usual tact. ''And I don't believe you, anyway. I don't know why you're trying to scare me, Marcus. Why you are so determined to hold everyone at bay for that matter.'' She moistened her lips, her hands clenching over the plastic container that she hadn't even realized she'd picked up again from the kitchen counter.

''I don't want pity,'' he didn't look up as he said it. He didn't even sound particularly emphatic about it. He just…said it. And her heart seemed to break a little inside.

''Most people don't.'' She hadn't. She'd loathed the looks of pity she'd received after Terry's death. After his associates had tried to use her to further their cause. ''And I don't pity you, Marcus. I don't understand you. I hardly know you.''

At that, his dark gaze lifted. Met hers.

Her stomach dipped. Swayed unsteadily. She looked down. Anywhere but at him, because she just couldn't seem to think straight when she was looking at him. ''I'm sorry I invaded your privacy. I owe you my children's safety, and if I've offended you, I am very sorry.''

She didn't really expect him to respond and when he didn't, she turned and left. But at the front door, still ajar, she paused.

Extra tarts?

She'd made tarts in the first place because of what he'd done—gone into the Calico and asked for them.

She set the container on the floor near the door, and quietly let herself out of the house, closing the door behind her.

The latch clicked, securely into place.

It felt as if she'd just closed the door on something special.

Chapter 5

Bobby and Patty were playing in their front yard.

Marcus slowed his truck to a crawl, and gave up the notion that he'd drive on past the Adler home on his way home from a trip into Whitehorn. Instead, he parked at the side of the road, diagonally across from her house.

The note that he'd found tucked inside the container of tarts was now folded inside his pocket. A tiny little slip of paper, penned in her pretty hand, with pretty words.

She'd left the tarts and the note, even after what he'd said at his house yesterday.

His common sense told that other nonsensical

part of him—the part that kept drawing him back to Libby Adler and her kids like a magnet heading north—that there was no way in hell she still meant what she'd written on the note. She'd probably left the tarts because she was sick of them, and sick of him, only she was too polite and gentle to say so.

In the yard, Bobby and Patty were crouching down, playing leapfrog in the thick, green grass. It needed mowing.

He shoved his fingers through his hair, then propped his elbow on the opened window. What the hell was wrong with him? Noticing that some woman's yard was a little overgrown?

Was this just his latest brand of insanity, then?

Every year about this time he sort of lost his sanity. Ever since the fire. Instead of chancing life and limb on some mountaintop or some treacherous river run, he was now sticking his head out with something even more dangerous? Like an entrancing woman and her two kids.

He snorted impatiently and reached for the key, but didn't turn it. Instead, he looked at the plastic container that Libby had used for the peach tarts. The container was empty now. He'd absently tossed it in the truck when he headed out to Whitehorn that morning, thinking that sooner or later, he'd get it back to her.

The easiest thing would be to walk across the

road, hand it to the kids and tell them to give it to their mom.

Cowardly? Maybe. Smart? Hell, yeah.

He closed his keys in his fist and reached for the container and the door in one motion.

But he hadn't factored in the twins' typical enthusiasm, and as soon as he closed his truck door, they'd noticed him. He could feel the smile forming on his face as they yelled his name and practically fell over their feet waving. But his smile died when they barreled down the drive and with complete disregard for the road, charged across it.

His heart climbed into his throat and he grabbed them both by the collars yanking them from the middle of the road. It didn't matter to him that there'd been no traffic. He crouched down in front of them, staring hard into their faces. "*What* was that about? You never cross that street like that again, you hear me? Never."

Two pairs of dark brown eyes blinked owlishly. Then Patty's eyes flooded and Bobby scuffed his shoe on the pavement. "We're sorry, Marcus. We were, you know, just glad to see you. We didn't think."

Hell. Who could be mad at these two?

He exhaled a short, sharp breath and thumbed away Patty's tear. "Next time, think," he suggested. Before he could straighten and walk them home, though, he heard Libby's voice, sharp and breathless as she charged across the road.

"What do you think you're doing?" Her chocolate gaze was anything but melting and warm as she glared at him. "How dare you encourage my children to cross the street like that! Have you no sense?"

He straightened, bemused, ready to explain.

But her children beat him to the punch. "We was the ones who did it," Bobby said, almost defiantly. "Marcus already told us we was wrong."

"Don't be mad at Marcus, Mommy." Patty caught her hand, squeezing it tightly. "Please."

"You two crossed the street without my permission."

Their heads hung. Nodded.

Libby blew out a breath, glancing at him from the corner of her eye. "I owe you an apology, it seems."

He shrugged. "You don't owe me anything. You never did." But he'd pay a fortune to see her eyes soften up again.

A little line appeared between her brows. "What are you doing here, anyway?"

"I was in Whitehorn today. On business." Avoiding business, if he were really going to be accurate. "I was on my way home."

"On my street." She looked skeptical. As well

she might. There was a much more direct route for him to get to his place from the highway than via her street.

"I wanted to get this back to you." He grabbed the container that he'd dropped on the ground when the kids made their mad dash.

Her lashes swept down, hiding her expression. She slowly took it from him. "You didn't have to bother."

"It's a good container."

Her eyebrows rose slightly.

"A lifetime guarantee."

At that, her lips twitched. "Marcus?"

"Yeah."

"Are we—" she sucked at her lower lip in that way that made him nuts, "—are we actually discussing Tupperware?"

"One of my foster moms used to drool over the catalogs that patients left in the dentist office where she worked."

Libby absorbed that. *One* of his foster moms. Plural. She didn't look at him. Nor could she look at her children because she was painfully aware of their breathless, silent fascination. She knew she should not encourage Marcus in any way, because her children were already thoroughly infatuated with the man. She toyed with the seal on the con-

tainer and turned utterly away from common sense.
"Stay for dinner?"

"I didn't think you'd still mean what you said in
the note. Not after the other day."

"I didn't think you'd bother to open the container and even see the note," she admitted. She
knew good and well what she'd written on that
note. That he was welcome for dinner at her home,
any time. *Any time.* She'd barely kept herself from
underlining the words. She finally looked up at him.
"Not after the other day when I barged in the way
I did."

"Mommy?"

Libby dragged her attention from Marcus and
looked at Patty. "Hmm?"

"Aren't we not supposed to stand in the street?"

She laughed suddenly. "Absolutely we are *not*
supposed to stand in the street." She held out her
hands for the children. And nearly cried with relief
when Marcus, oh so slowly, tucked Bobby's trustingly outstretched little hand in his darkly tanned
one.

At the faint smile on Marcus's face as they
crossed the street, though, Libby's eyes *did* sting.

Dinner—that ubiquitous standby of macaroni and
cheese that seemed to please her children no matter
what—couldn't have tasted more delicious. Mostly
because Libby had never seen her kids so thor-

oughly happy. And while her knowledge of Marcus was admittedly limited, she felt, down inside, that he was happy, too.

But the evening wore on much longer than Libby expected. By the time she'd cleaned up the kitchen after dinner—insisting that Marcus needn't help when he'd offered because she would have been positively fumble-fingered—Bobby and Patty simply begged for Marcus to stay long enough to read them a story after they took their baths.

Libby thought that was going a bit far. She didn't know how long ago Marcus's son had died, but whether it was recent or in the distant past, she still suspected that being invited into her children's nighttime ritual was hard for him. Not from anything he said. It was more the way he went utterly still when the twins—who'd been perched one on each of his knees for a good hour while they played a computer game—posed their question.

She popped up to her feet. They'd had a lovely evening and she didn't want Marcus feeling like he had to race off again like he had the last time. "Nope. Bedtime stories are mine." She rubbed her hands together, fiendishly. "Alllll miiiine, my dahlinks."

Marcus smiled faintly as the twins giggled wildly and slid off him. Bobby turned and stuck out his hand, manfully. "Good night, Marcus."

"Good night, Bobby." He shook his hand.

Then Patty clambered up on the couch beside him and wound her arms around his neck, kissing his cheek with a loud smack. "G'night, Marcus," she giggled. And beamed when he gently tugged her ponytail.

"Good night, Patty."

Then Libby was smoothly scurrying them along, up the steps, promising to be right behind them. She stopped, her hand curled over the shining wood banister as she looked back at him. "Stay. Finish your coffee."

He figured he surprised them both, by doing just that.

Libby's cooking and baking were out of this world. But her coffee, well, her coffee left something to be desired. Maybe he'd spent too many years in Seattle, home of the world's best cup of coffee as far as he was concerned. Nevertheless, he drank it. He popped a couple grapes in his mouth from the tray of fruit and cheese she'd quickly tossed together for dessert—much to the kids' dismay. They'd wanted a slice of the cheesecake that was destined for the Calico's food booth at the festival.

Marcus had found it interesting to watch Libby. Well, watching her was sure in hell no hardship.

She was beautiful. But with the kids, she was amazing. She really enjoyed them.

Not everyone did. He knew that from personal experience.

His wife had loved their son, unquestionably. But Julia had never seemed to simply enjoy Sam for who he'd been. She'd been too busy making sure he didn't leave any marks on their white carpet, any smudgy little-boy fingerprints on the glass-and-chrome furnishings.

His head fell back against the couch, memories washing over him. When they were in college, Julia had dreamed about having a romantic old Victorian. Yet, she'd been the one to choose the thoroughly modern house in Seattle; the thoroughly modern furnishings that fairly shouted financial success. Marcus hadn't cared where they'd lived, as long as the drive into his office building didn't take up too much of the precious business day.

From upstairs, he could hear sounds that were familiar, but alien. Running footsteps overhead. Rushing water. Childish giggles. The low, musical tone of a woman's voice.

He waited for the inevitable wave of pain and guilt.

But it didn't come.

Instead, he just felt…felt…

He went still. He just *felt*.

After a while, he heard the water again. More running footsteps.

Maybe it *was* his latest bout with insanity, but Marcus didn't care. He rose, and climbed the stairs. It wasn't hard to find their room. He just followed the sounds. Past the hall bathroom where a mound of wet towels half tumbled from the edge of the ivory tub to the caramel-colored tile. Past an open doorway through which he could see the dim outline of an ironing board and a sewing machine.

At the end of the hall was a set of opened double doors. A small light from inside illuminated the corner of a quilt-covered bed.

Libby's.

Hunger hit him, low and tight, and his feet dragged to a halt before he could walk into the opened doorway of the twins' bedroom.

Instead, he stood there, back pressed against the wall, listening to Libby read *Green Eggs and Ham* to her children while he tortured himself with that view of her bed.

Then she finished reading. And before Marcus knew it, she'd stepped out into the hallway, pulling the door nearly closed.

"I thought I heard you. I think you accomplished the impossible. They fell right to sleep tonight." Her voice was soft. As soft as the touch of the hand she laid on his arm. "Are you all right?"

He was too damned aware of her bedroom five steps away. Too damned aware of her children, sleeping or not, on the other side of a thin door. Too damned aware that her eyes were deep and warm.

"I need to go."

Her lashes swept her cheeks for a moment then she looked at him again with those drowning eyes of hers. "Need? Or want to?"

His jaw felt tight. He closed his hand around hers, intending only to move it away from his arm. Instead, he held on. Brushed his thumb slowly over her satin-soft skin. Slowly rolled his palm around to meet hers. And felt the strength in those tender, soft hands as her palm pressed against his. "I don't *want* to," he admitted roughly.

Fire burned from her palm, streaking greedily, addictively through Libby's bloodstream. It ought to have been odd feeling so connected to this man. This virtual stranger.

Why didn't it feel odd?

Her mind wanted an answer. Her heart didn't care.

She looked into his eyes, so shadowed, so wary. "What are you afraid of, Marcus?"

His jaw cocked. "Maybe the same thing that made you hide from me in the diner," he finally said.

He touched her jaw and she would have swayed if not for locking her knees. Then he smoothed his thumb over her cheek and she realized he'd wiped away a tear she hadn't known was there.

"I need to go."

She nodded. Stepped aside and watched him silently descend the stairs and let himself out the front door.

Only then did Libby's knees give.

She slid her back down the wall and sat there on the floor in her upstairs hallway, and trembled.

"Any dinner guests last night?"

Libby loved Callie and Marisa. But just then, she really wished they weren't so curious. Or that orders for her desserts weren't so brisk that she had to make a daily delivery to the Calico. "Yes." She caught the wide smile on Marisa's face. "Don't look so pleased," she warned. "I don't know anything about Marcus Jessup."

"Except you know you like him," Callie said. Mirroring Marisa, she slid onto one of the red leather stools and propped her elbows on the gleaming counter. "Am I right?"

Libby knew her friends meant well. She just wasn't feeling up to sharing the tangle of emotions inside her. "I don't think I should see him again."

Marisa's eyebrows shot up. "Why ever not?"

Libby finished arranging a trio of swan-shaped cream puffs on the top display shelf of the pastry case. "Bobby and Patty are already attached to him. You know how they are about, well, about having a dad. I don't want them hurt." She slowly fit the lid back on the container she'd used for the cream puffs. "Marcus is—"

"Getting out of his truck," Callie cut in.

"What?"

"Striding across the sidewalk," she continued. Then, the bell jingled and she greeted Marcus with her usual smile and welcome.

There was no way Libby would hide behind the pastry case again. She straightened and carefully stacked her containers on the counter, ordering her nerves to just settle back down.

Marcus didn't so much as spare anyone else a glance. He walked right over to face Libby. "Bobby and Patty are at day camp?"

Libby nodded warily.

"Will you come with me?"

"Where?" Why?

"Lunch."

"We're standing in a diner already."

"I had something else in mind."

Libby was aware of the avid expressions of her friends, as well as the few other people scattered about the booths. "Marcus, I—" The words

wouldn't come that would tell him she'd reconsid-
ered their friendship. If you could even classify
their odd encounters as that. "All right."

The corner of his lips lifted a little. He plucked
the empty containers off the counter and carried
them out to Libby's car where she stowed them in
the trunk. "What did you have in mind?"

"You'll see." He took her arm and started back
around to the street in front of the 50s-style diner.

Libby dug in her heels, though. "Wait."

He let go of her arm. "You can trust me, Libby."

"Can I?"

"About a picnic lunch? Yeah." His words were
easy, but the expression in his eyes was not. "I
figure I ought to feed *you* for once."

A picnic. Longing nearly choked her. "What's
the real reason you've invited me to lunch?"

His dark eyes narrowed. "What are you talking
about?"

She folded her arms around her waist. "Marcus,
I was married to a man whose interest in me wasn't
what it seemed. I don't want to head back that direction." Her cheeks felt hot. "Not that I think you
want to marry me, or anything," she corrected hastily. "I just mean that if we're going to spend an
hour or two together seeming to enjoy each other's
company only for you to tear off in a hurry again
without explanation, I'd rather know ahead of time.

If there's something about me that keeps pushing you away, then just tell me. I'd rather have honesty. Friends should have honesty.''

She meant it. Marcus studied her and knew if he didn't say something now, she would walk back into the diner or back to her car and their ''friendship'' would be finished. She looked like a puff of cotton candy in her pale pink shorts and white T-shirt, her hair pulled into a bouncy ponytail at the back of her head. But she wasn't a puff at all. She was stronger than that. Stronger than he was, because—clearly—he couldn't manage to keep his distance from her. ''Is that what we are? Friends?''

She lifted her shoulder diffidently. ''I don't know. I'd like to think we could be.''

''I don't have friends.''

''Only because you close yourself off from everyone.''

''Are you always so blunt?'' He knew she wasn't. She was everything graceful and elegant. She was completely out of his class.

And he couldn't stay away from her. He'd tried.

''With you?'' She was blushing again. ''Apparently.''

''My interest, Libby Adler, is very much in *you*. Does that answer your question?''

She colored even more. ''I'm not very good at this.''

"*This* being…what? Friendship?" He suddenly felt like smiling when she made a face. "I'll agree to not 'tear off' as you put it, if you'll agree not to hide behind pastry cases."

Her cheeks flushed prettily. But it looked as if she was fighting a smile, too. "Just where did you have in mind for this picnic of yours?"

"Out past The Getaway."

Her eyebrows rose, but she began walking again toward his truck. "That's kind of far. Wouldn't the town park be closer?"

Closer and a lot more public than he preferred. "There are all the craft booths and stuff there for the festival."

Yes, Libby thought faintly. A built-in plethora of people to keep her from forgetting her common sense altogether. "As long as we're back in time for me to pick up Bobby and Patty from day camp."

"Two-thirty."

She ought to have been surprised that he knew what time the kids were through for the day. It seemed strangely right, though, that he'd known. At his truck, he opened the passenger side and helped her up. She watched him through the windshield as he rounded the hood, moving with his smooth, silent stride and had the insane thought that she could watch him walk, forever.

He climbed in and started the engine. Then looked at her. ''What?''

She smiled faintly and shook her head. ''Nothing.''

He didn't smile back. But his eyes crinkled at the corners and Libby sank back into the soft leather seat, very much afraid she was losing control of her heart.

Chapter 6

"No, no, please. No more." Libby fell back against the red-and-black-checkered blanket spread across the billowing grass and laughed, avoiding the sliver of grilled chicken that Marcus was pushing toward her. "If I eat anymore, I'll pop, I swear."

He chuckled and stuck the bite into his own mouth.

Libby lay there, replete with good food and delicate wine and squinted into the sunlight, looking at him. He was sitting, one blue-jeaned knee up, his other leg extended. The breeze kept his hair drifting around his beard-shadowed face, and the bright sunlight shafting across his face made golden glints appear in his dark eyes.

He was beautiful.

"How long ago did you lose your husband?"

Libby propped her head on her hand. "Now see," she pointed out, "if you ever mingled with Rumor's citizens, you'd have already heard all the details about my life."

"But you're not from Rumor."

"How do you know?"

The corner of his lips curled. "*East* is in your voice."

"Still?" She shook her head regretfully. "And here I've tried so hard to get rid of that in the six years I've lived here. Does it count that my children are born and bred Rumor natives?" She was far too relaxed to let unpleasant memories bother her. Maybe it was the wine. Maybe it was Marcus. "I left Boston where I was born and raised, shortly after my husband died."

"Do you still love him?"

Of all the questions she might have expected, that wasn't one of them. She sighed a little. "I met Terry when we were college students. He was everything my parents hated."

"And that was the appeal?"

"Partly," she said honestly. "Not that I realized it at the time. Terry was idealistic. An activist."

Marcus's eyebrows shot up, but he refrained from any other comment.

"He had absolutely no interest in my pedigree."

"Money?"

"Old name. Old money. When they learned *who* I was socializing with, my parents forbade me from seeing him. Of course, I didn't listen. My grandmother entered her protests, as well, and nobody in my family had the nerve to flout her decrees."

"Except you."

She smiled sadly. "I was in love. And he loved me. *Me*. He cared more about the world around us than my privileged background. We eloped, which caused my parents considerable consternation. I quit school in order to help him with his various causes, which horrified them even more, I think. Then I learned I was pregnant with the twins. Terry and I hadn't planned it so soon, but I was thrilled."

"Yet you ended up in Rumor before those babies were born?"

"Mmm. After I learned I was pregnant, I also learned that Terry *had* married me specifically because of my pedigree. Because of my family name, my family money." She closed her eyes, vividly remembering the day her dreams of creating the loving family she'd always wanted had died. "I learned that Terry was still involved with an old girlfriend—had never broken it off with her, in fact.''

"He was an idiot. Did you go back to your folks?''

She made a face and laughed softly. Surprised that she *could* laugh about it at all. "My pride kept me from doing that. Oh, they'd have taken me in, I don't doubt that. But their doing so would have been attached to too many conditions that I knew I couldn't tolerate. So, I stayed with Terry.''

"He didn't deserve you.''

"His methods were no less manipulative than my parents', and I had my babies to consider.''

So she'd stayed with a husband who'd betrayed her. Marcus toyed with the handle of the woven picnic basket. "How'd he die?''

"In a demonstration that got way out of hand.''

"And you don't like talking about it.''

"Not much," she admitted. "Not usually." Her gaze danced shyly away from his. "I didn't leave Boston, though, until Terry's associates tried to use me to further their cause." Her expression didn't change. "Terry's death provided them with an honest-to-goodness martyr. One who'd left behind a grieving, noticeably pregnant, widow. As soon as the media got wind of it—which was quickly thanks to the savvy of Terry's group—they were relentless. So I left Boston. And got as far as Rumor

before going into labor. I was having lunch at the
Calico Diner, in fact.''

"And you've been here ever since.''

"It's the first place I've ever really felt at home.
Callie and Marisa are all the family the twins and
I need.''

"Do you still communicate with your parents?''

"Distantly.'' She smiled wryly. "My parents
never understood me. They just didn't get it that I
wasn't happy being their little princess with everything provided for me, with all my decisions made
for me. They send very proper cards on my birthday, though, and we speak on Christmas. When the
twins were three, they came out to visit me. My
mother nearly had a nervous breakdown at the notion that I was playing at being a baker to support
myself and my children. My father wanted to buy
out one of the businesses in town to give to me.''
She shook her head, rolling her eyes. "I love them.
I know they love me. But we're all happier keeping
our lives fairly separate. I'm okay with that.''

"Never want to get married again?''

Her lips curved. "You don't really expect me to
answer that, do you? If I say no, you'll think I'm
still bitter about it all, and if I say yes, you'll think
I'm hinting.''

He laughed softly.

And she smiled, nearly shivering with delight

that he'd actually laughed. "So, if we're playing show and tell, as it were, I believe it's your turn. The only thing I know about you, Marcus Jessup, is that you were apparently in a foster home or two."

"That's all you know?"

Libby knew a good deal more, but she had no intention of saying so. She knew he was a decent man. An honorable man. One who enjoyed children, who was intelligent and humorous, and one who went out of his way to hide that fact from nearly everyone. She also knew that, no matter what she'd told Callie and Marisa, she was getting in over her head with this man. And fast. "I know you don't come from Rumor, either."

"Not even Montana," he confirmed, slowly. "It's not very interesting."

"Everything about you is interesting to me, Marcus. Don't you know that, yet?" She sat up, hugging her knees, embarrassed at having revealed so much and very aware that the aura of relaxation around him had suddenly tightened up. "Tell me about the woman who taught you to appreciate Tupperware."

"Junie McNamara." He picked up his wineglass and stared into it. "She and her husband Ford were my last foster parents before I graduated from high school."

"How long were you with them?"

"Two years." He tilted the glass and drank. "I started a business in college. It did fairly well. When I signed my first contract, I bought Junie the entire Tupperware catalog."

Libby smiled. "What was your business?"

He shrugged. "I lived in Seattle. Computers. What else?" He shook his head, obviously lost in memories. "Junie didn't even have room for all the stuff I bought her."

She realized she was rather avidly watching his strong throat and plucked a fat blade of grass from beside the checkered blanket.

"Julia was their niece."

Her fingers paused for a moment before she continued shredding the grass blade. "Julia, being your wife," she surmised.

"We married after college."

"What did you study?"

"Underwater basket weaving."

Her eyebrows rose. "What a coincidence. That was *my* major. Are you still in love with her?"

"Thought you'd just slide that in there? Like I wouldn't notice?"

If it weren't for the humor in his eyes, Libby would never have asked the question. "Turnabout is fair play, Marcus."

''I don't feel unfaithful to her memory being here with you.''

It wasn't as much of an answer as she'd have liked, but she wasn't about to probe and possibly chase the ease from his expression. ''Of course you don't. We're just friends, Marcus. Or trying to be, anyway.''

I don't feel very friendly toward you. Marcus kept the words inside. She'd take them the wrong way, be offended. If he went around announcing to her that he wanted her more than his next breath, that he couldn't see her face without wanting to taste her lips, that he couldn't hear her speak without wanting to hear her voice, soft and breathless with want, he'd scare her off for certain. She'd just said it. Friendship was all she wanted.

It was just as well, he reminded himself. Libby Adler and her cute kids were too precious to risk hurting.

Being with her was a double-edged sword. But the balm of her company was more than he wanted to give up.

So, friendship it would remain.

Libby sat on her couch and stared at the cordless phone resting innocuously on the coffee table in front of her.

Just pick it up and call him.

She blew out a breath, impatient with herself. Since the day of their picnic two weeks ago, hardly a single day had passed without seeing Marcus. He'd dropped by their house many times. He'd mowed her lawn, hung a tire swing for the children in the backyard, sat with them all at the kitchen table for dinner and fallen asleep sprawled on the living room floor with her twins during a video. Just yesterday, he'd herded them into his extended cab truck and driven up to his house where the kids explored the cavernous space and she'd helped him choose furniture from a fancy magazine before pushing him outside where she trimmed his overgrown roses.

She'd learned more about his childhood. About his life before he'd married Julia. She'd told him how she'd ended up going into business for herself as a baker and he'd shared that there was a young man in Whitehorn who wanted to go into a software design business with him.

He'd alternately delighted her and tormented her with his company—his very courteous, humorous, intelligent and frustratingly platonic company.

But she'd never called Marcus on the telephone. She'd had to look him up in the directory, in fact, to find the number.

Just call the man.

She snatched up the telephone. Just as quickly, she set it back down.

It was a good thing Bobby and Patty were sound asleep and she had no witnesses to her silly indecisiveness.

She snatched up the phone again, but before she could punch out the numbers, it rang. Startled, she dropped the phone and it clattered against the coffee table, making a huge racket as the back piece popped off and the battery, still connected to its host of little wires, dangled.

And still it rang.

Muttering under her breath, she gathered up the phone parts and pushed the button to answer it.

"Libby?"

It was Marcus. She very nearly dropped the phone again. "I was just going to call you," she blurted.

The silence seemed as if it had a life of its own. "What about?"

Now that she had him on the phone, she was stricken with a tied tongue. "You called me. You first." *Oh, Libby. Juvenile.* Her face burned.

"Did the telescope get delivered?"

Of course. Her heart settled back down in her chest. "This morning. It's far too generous, though, Marcus. I was going to get Bobby a small one for his birthday."

"Well, now you won't need to. And it's nonreturnable, so you might as well accept it."

Libby sighed. She'd figured out that Marcus was very well set, financially. "They're both going to be thrilled with it."

"Good. That was the plan. And now they can stop sneaking over to your neighbor's. Think of the lives of crime we're preventing."

She chuckled. As he'd meant her to.

"Do you have plans for Saturday?"

"I, well, sort of. What'd you have in mind?" If Callie or Nick had gone around Libby's back and just invited Marcus outright to their engagement party because she'd been dragging her feet on it, she'd strangle her friends.

"Patty was telling me how your smoke alarm went off the other day."

"Oh, great. My daughter is blabbing that I burned a batch of cookies and set off the alarm. That'll get me a lot of business."

"She said you beat the tar out of the thing with a broom to get it to shut up."

"Did she also tell you that I had to stand on the kitchen table to reach it?" Libby closed her eyes, laughter in her voice. "I can just imagine the picture I created for my kids with such dignified behavior."

He chuckled, and her blood warmed. "Well, I

know how busy you are and I thought I'd make sure all the alarms in your house are working.''

There was still a smile on her face, but her eyes suddenly blurred. Oh, Marcus. He hadn't had to tell her that his scars were from being burned. She'd been able to figure that out for herself.

She had to swallow past the lump in her throat and was grateful that her voice, when it did come, sounded natural. ''Actually, I already bought a new one to replace the broom-battered one. And the two upstairs have new batteries from last month.''

''Are you sure? Because—''

''I'm sure. Though if you wouldn't mind rehanging the new one for the kitchen, that'd be great. Then I won't have to drag out my ladder. Right now, it's sitting on top of the refrigerator.'' It was entirely too comfortable discussing such mundane matters. If she weren't careful, the next thing she knew, she'd be asking him to pick up a carton of milk on his way home from work.

''The ladder is on top of your refrigerator?''

She smiled. ''Isn't that where everyone keeps them? Listen, about Saturday, though. Callie and Nick are having a barbecue at noon to celebrate their engagement and—'' she had to swallow past that annoying lump again, ''—I wondered if you'd like to go along with me.''

He didn't answer immediately, and it seemed as

if the sound of her heartbeat filled her ears. He was going to decline. She knew it even before he finally told her he was busy.

Confused and far too disappointed for a woman who'd eschewed relationships with men since her marriage, Libby's fingers tightened on the telephone. "I see." But she didn't. He was too busy to go with her to a barbecue, but not too busy for checking her smoke alarms? "Well, that's too bad. They've got most of the town coming and it's sure to be a lot of fun."

Marcus, sitting on the counter in his empty kitchen heard Libby's smooth words, but he also heard the wealth of disappointment beneath them. And along with that disappointment, he heard something he'd never expected to hear from her. The definite edge of feminine pique. "Libby—"

"Marcus, my other line is buzzing in. I'd better grab it in case it's the kids. They went to a friend's house after day camp today."

"Sure, I—"

The buzz of the dial tone sounded in his ear. She hadn't just switched over to the other line. She'd hung up on him.

He absorbed that for a moment. Then he hopped off the counter, grinning as he went back to finish the varnish on the banister. He had a truck full of furniture arriving the next day and he needed to get the last touches done beforehand.

He replayed their conversation in his mind. Definitely feminine pique. Maybe Libby wasn't so dead set on being "just friends" after all.

He was whistling by the time he stuck the paintbrush into the varnish.

By Saturday evening, however, Marcus was all whistled out. Sitting on a woman's front porch while the sun went down, picturing Libby among "most of the town"—a good portion who were men, her smile lightening the souls of anyone lucky enough to come into contact with her, tended to kill the whistle in a man.

But he figured Libby should've been home some time ago. How long could a barbecue last?

Too damn long as far as Marcus was concerned.

She'd probably been cornered by every eligible man in Rumor. Considering Nick's high profile in town, he'd probably had friends coming from Whitehorn. Maybe even as far as Billings. Male friends. Sociable, unscarred, friendly men. Wolves, who'd take advantage of Libby's kind, gentle nature.

"Marcus?"

His boots crashed down from where he'd propped them up on the porch rail and he stood as Libby came up the steps to peer at him.

"What are you doing here sitting in the dark?"

"The switch for the porch light is inside the house."

"It's on a photocell," she murmured faintly. "Supposed to come on automatically when it gets dark. Maybe the bulb is burned out."

"I'll replace it."

She moved past him to unlock the door and the flowing folds of her pale colored sundress grazed his jeans. She smelled like sunshine and green grass and pure, heady summertime. "I can replace my own lightbulbs, Marcus." She pushed open the door, but didn't enter. She merely set her purse inside and turned around to face him in the doorway, bare arms folded. The soft light from a lamp inside glowed behind her. "I can replace my own smoke alarm batteries and hang the darned thing back on the wall. I can mow my own grass, and, though it would be a pure horror to my relatives should they ever learn of it, I can *even* unclog my own sinks. What I cannot do, however, is figure you out."

"Where are Bobby and Patty?" He was used to their company, their innocent roles as chaperones.

"They are both at overnighters. Why? Are *they* the real appeal, Marcus?"

He wished she'd back up. Into the light. So he could see her eyes. "You know what the appeal is," he said evenly.

"I know what you said before. But how?" She stepped onto the porch, looking up at him. "How would I really know, Marcus? You come here, you play with my children, are wonderful with them. You've sat at our table, you've even loaded my dishwasher after dinner. But you won't share an afternoon with me and my friends. What else am I supposed to think? Look at you." She waved her hand at him. "I told you the children were gone, and you stepped off the porch, all ready to take your leave. I think *they* are the appeal, Marcus, because you miss your son so desperately!"

Her words rang out, hanging there between them.

Libby sucked in a horrified breath, covering her mouth with her hand. What on earth had come over her? Just because she'd spent the entire afternoon awkwardly fielding well-meaning questions about her friendship with Marcus was no excuse to say such a cruel thing. "I'm sorry," she said thickly, reaching for him. Closing her hands over his arm for fear that he'd walk away. And never come back. "I didn't mean that, Marcus. Please, *please* don't think I really meant that."

His dark eyes were intense as he pulled her onto her toes. "Well, I do mean this."

Then he ducked his head, and pressed his lips against hers.

Chapter 7

Shock stiffened her.

Pleasure destroyed her.

His lips were softer than she'd imagined. And his chest even harder.

Libby's knees went weak, but it didn't matter, for Marcus's arms were secure bands about her back, her waist, easily taking her weight. She pushed her fingers through his hair, a low moan rising when his head lifted from hers.

"Open your mouth."

"Marcus—"

His mouth covered hers. Seduced. Devoured. And left her swaying when he deliberately pulled her hands from his neck, and set her from him. "Make no mistake, Libby. You are the appeal. But we both know that I'm not the man for you."

"We?" Her voice sounded choked. *"We* both know? What is it *we* both know, Marcus?"

His arms akimbo, he looked away for a long moment. Then back again. "My scars. You've never asked about them. You know they're there. I don't fit in with others anymore. You accepted me because I helped your kids. The rest of this town—no."

Libby reached out and nearly cried when he almost flinched away from her. But she didn't lower her hand. She pressed her palm to his bristled jaw, her fingertips curving gently down over the pale ridges that rode upward from his collar. "Everyone has wounds, Marcus. Scars. Some are visible. Some aren't. But part of the healing is in letting the scars breathe. Letting them see the light of day."

"And have children run crying to their mothers because the monster who lives on the hill has come down to mingle among the normal."

"What is normal? My children haven't run crying from you. Nor has anyone else in this town, none that I have witnessed. I spent the entire afternoon today answering questions about you."

"Curiosity, nothing more."

"Yes, they're curious! You've held everyone at

bay. They are also my friends, and they know you're my friend. They know I'm—" *more than half in love with you.*

"Know you're what?"

She moistened her lips. Hurting for them both. "You've made your home in Rumor the same as I have, Marcus. The people here would be just as healing to you as they've been to me. Terry broke my heart. But I loved him and I was devastated when he died. The people here were the ones that helped me live again. All you have to do is give a little. Open up a little, and the rest will take care of itself. I know how much you value your privacy. But even private men need people in their life."

"I need you in my life."

Her lips parted. Tears blurred her vision.

"But I don't think I should see you again."

She absorbed that like a physical blow. "You didn't hear a word I said, did you."

"I heard everything you said. But you need a man who can take care of you. I didn't take care of Julia and Sam. And they died because I didn't protect them. Because I was too damned busy with my business to make sure the smoke alarms were working in that high-tech house I bought as a symbol of our success. I can't take a chance with you and the twins and fail."

"Fail to protect us?" Her emotions were in a

tailspin. "What on earth makes you think I need *anyone* to protect us? I walked away from all the *protectiveness* my family had to offer. I've made a home for myself. For my children. And I've done it on my own. I want a partner in life, Marcus, a man whom I can take care of just as much as he takes care of me. Friendship or love, it doesn't matter. It's all a two-way street. So if you want to stop *seeing* me, then you just go right on ahead! It's just fine with me!"

Furious with him, she turned on her heel and stormed into the house, slamming the door shut behind her.

Then she fell back against the wood, the tears scalding her cheeks.

She hadn't meant the angry words. Not really. But how could she admit to him that his refusal to move on with his life was breaking her heart?

Patty slipped out of her bed and padded over to her brother's bed, nimbly stepping around the toys scattered on the floor. She shoved at Bobby's shoulder until he flopped over on his back, sighing mightily. "D'ya hear her?"

"Yeah, I hear her. D'ya think I'm deaf or something?"

"Marcus hasn't come over for *days*."

Bobby didn't like thinking about it. 'Cause it

made him feel like crying, too. And crying wasn't what men did. "I know."

"What're we gonna do?"

"Mom told us we wasn't supposed t' do nothing."

"That didn't stop us before," Patty whispered. "Did we do something wrong, you think? To make him not like us no more?"

Bobby sat up, knuckling away a hot tear. "I dunno. I hate him," he blurted. "I thought he was nice, but he's not. He made Mommy cry and I *hate* him."

The squeak of the bedroom door startled them both and they stared, dismayed as their mother appeared in the light from the hallway.

Libby watched her children for a moment, well aware of their hushed conversation. And she wanted to throttle Marcus. For hurting them. But she also wanted to hug the man. For she knew in her heart that he was the one hurting most of all. She tightened the belt on her robe and walked over to Bobby's bed, pulling Patty up beside her, too. "Don't hate Marcus," she said quietly. "It would break his heart if he knew you felt like that."

"So?" Bobby buried his face against her shoulder. "I don't care."

Libby rested her cheek on his tousled head. Patty rested sweetly against her other side. She had her children and if for no other reason in life, they were blessing enough. "I care," she murmured. "And Marcus cares."

"Then why'd he go 'way?"

How could she explain something she didn't understand herself? Hadn't she just that night broken down after a week of no contact from him whatsoever, and dialed his phone number, only to hear it endlessly ring? Unanswered. He'd really meant it about not seeing her. Which broke her heart. But knowing that he'd hurt her children infuriated her. The only problem was, she wasn't sure if she was angrier with him or with herself for letting it occur in the first place.

"I think Marcus is still hurting from losing his wife and little boy," she told her children.

"So can't he hurt *with* us?" Patty asked tearfully.

Libby sighed and cuddled her children close to her. She didn't have an answer for that, and she couldn't pretend that she did.

She stayed with the twins until they'd both fallen asleep. And then she went back downstairs. She gave the telephone a wide berth and went into the kitchen. Kneading bread dough was what she wanted to do. The act had never failed to soothe her in the past. But she didn't have any dough ready for kneading. So she made do with mixing up a plain old chocolate cake.

While it was baking, she sat at the kitchen table, staring at the bowl of fruit in the center. All the peaches were gone.

After a long while, she pulled the cake from the oven. Tidied up the kitchen. And went to bed. She'd gotten through another night without calling Marcus.

She'd do it again tomorrow. And again and again and again.

One of these days, it would get easier.

The silent assurance didn't comfort her in the least.

Marcus pulled his truck into his driveway and killed the lights. He leaned his head back against the seat and let out a long breath. The 30-mile drive to and from Whitehorn wasn't in the least tiring. But the negotiations he'd engaged in for the past three days had been more than tiring. They'd been exhausting.

And long overdue.

He grabbed his briefcase and the garment bag from the seat beside him and got out of the truck. He was all the way up the veranda steps when he noticed them.

Bobby and Patty.

Huddled together on a plastic-sheeted stack of lumber, staring at him with wide eyes as if they expected him to suddenly bare his teeth and chew them up. And why not, he thought, disgusted. They'd done nothing but be themselves, and he'd rewarded them by shutting them out.

"Kinda late for you two to be out, isn't it?" He unlocked the front door and pushed it wide. From the corner of his eye, he could see Patty nudging Bobby with her elbow, and Bobby's throat working with a great, huge swallow. "Is your mom here, too?"

"Uh-uh. Can we spend the night?"

It was then that Marcus noticed the dark lump near their feet. Sleeping bags, presumably.

"You said we could," Patty reminded.

"So I did," he agreed. He wasn't sure if he was disappointed that Libby wasn't there, or relieved. He did know it was odd, though. "Does your mom know you're here?"

Both their heads nodded furiously.

Marcus, however, decided to reserve judgment as neither child could quite meet his gaze. "How long have you been sitting out here?"

"Not long," Patty said hurriedly. "Can I use your bathroom, though?"

He hid a smile and nodded. She scampered inside, obviously remembering the way. "How 'bout

you, sport?'' He looked at Bobby who shook his
head. ''All right. You'd better come in.''

The boy's face was set in angry lines that Marcus
recognized easily enough. But Bobby preceded him
inside, giving Marcus's leather garment bag a long
look. ''Where you been?''

''Whitehorn.''

''How come?''

''I had business there.''

''You're wearing a suit.''

''Yup.''

''Are you gonna move away?''

''Nope.''

''You made my mom cry.''

Marcus carefully set his briefcase on the hall table. He closed his eyes for a moment. ''I'm sorry.''
He was. He'd never wanted to hurt Libby. That's
why he was keeping his distance.

''You made Patty cry, too.''

''But not you.''

Bobby's sturdy chest puffed out. ''Men don't
cry.''

''You'd be surprised about that, pal.''

The boy looked skeptical. But Patty returned, and
somehow—later he'd be damned if he could figure
out what the sweet little girl had said or done—he
ended up in the kitchen with them, fixing them
sandwiches. Followed by cookies and milk.

Store-bought cookies. The kind with the frosting in the middle. Patty's eyes had lit up at that, making Marcus want to grin. Bobby surreptitiously took two more after eating the first two.

Marcus wondered how long it would take for them to realize that it was their mother's home-baked ones that were the real treat.

"Okay," he finally said. "I'm gonna call your mom."

"She's out," Patty said. She licked a chocolate crumb from her finger.

"On a date," Bobby added, not looking at Marcus.

He wasn't gonna be played by two six-year-old munchkins. "Yeah? With who?"

"The deputy sheriff." Bobby started to reach for the half-eaten sleeve of cookies, but yanked his hand back. "He wears a gun."

Marcus knew Holt Tanner. The man definitely did not carry a gun. Marcus also knew that Holt was nearly as bad at opening up to people as he was.

But maybe Libby was working her magic on Holt, too. Still, he didn't believe for a minute that she'd let her kids just mosey on up to his place for a sleepover. Particularly after the way he'd ended things with her. Nor did he believe she'd leave them unattended while she went out.

"Maybe she's back already," he suggested blandly and reached for his telephone. "It's nearly ten."

"Way past our bedtime," Patty said. "She'll be mad if we're not asleep. We'll prob'ly get grounded."

Bobby nodded morosely.

Marcus set down the phone. Truth was, he wasn't all that anxious to hear Libby's voice. Because, truth was, he was keeping away from her by the skin of his teeth. If he heard her voice, he wasn't sure he'd have the strength to walk away. Not again.

"Then I guess you'd better find a room and bunk down."

It was all the encouragement the twins needed. They scrambled from the high barstools and grabbed their sleeping bags, darting from the room without a second look his way.

He heard their footsteps pounding on the stairs. Giggles. A door slam shut.

Staring at the bread crusts, cookie crumbs and nearly empty glasses of milk, Marcus slowly reached for the telephone and punched out Libby's telephone number.

"Yeah?" The voice that answered was low. And male.

Marcus's knuckles went white on the phone.

Maybe the kids hadn't been so full of stories as he'd thought.

In her house down the hill, Libby stared at the deputy sheriff as he picked up her ringing phone. Her stomach was in knots. She'd called the sheriff's office as soon as she'd realized that the twins were missing.

Then she'd called Callie. Her friend and Nick had arrived moments behind Holt Tanner. Using her cell phone, Callie had helped Libby call every parent in town. Holt had been taking down a description of what the twins had been wearing when she'd taken them to day camp.

She hugged her hands around her waist. It seemed so many hours ago.

"Libby."

She looked up, realizing that Holt had been saying her name, more than once. He was holding out the phone toward her. "It's Marcus Jessup."

She was barely holding it together. She snatched the phone. "Marcus, are you—"

"They told me you were on a date, but I didn't believe them."

—finally home, were the words she'd been going to say. "*They?* Oh my God, Marcus, are they there?" Her knees gave way and she was hardly aware of Holt hastily shoving a dining room chair under her. "My babies, are they with *you?*"

"Upstairs. They decided to take me up on that invitation to spend the night."

She dropped the phone, running blindly for the door. "It's okay. They're safe," she cried thickly. "They're safe with Marcus."

Chapter 8

He was waiting in the opened doorway when she got there. But while she would have charged up the steps, he caught her round the waist and halted her.

He'd heard about things first from Holt Tanner who'd told him that he'd call off the missing persons report, then Callie, who'd told him that if he ever expected to show his face in town, he'd better not hurt Libby any more than he already had.

"They're already asleep," he told Libby when he caught her mad flight.

She struggled against him. "I don't care."

"Are you going to wake them up and drag them home? Because they're pretty sure they're going to be grounded for being up past their bedtime."

"They're going to be grounded for scaring the life out of me," she snapped. Then all the strength, the adrenaline that had been fueling her since she'd acknowledged the worst of all possible fears, oozed out of her and she just collapsed against Marcus. "I was so scared," she cried. "How could they do this to me? Don't they know they're my life?"

Marcus gathered Libby against him, pressing his lips against her temple as she cried out her worry. He carried her to the leather chair that she'd helped him choose from a catalog. It was more comfortable than he'd ever expected. And it had plenty of room to hold her slight body against his as he sat there.

She was trembling. Tears wet the front of his shirt. He didn't care. He only wanted her to stop shaking. To stop bearing the weight of her world, alone.

He smoothed back her tumbled hair, tilting her tear-stained face. "I'm sorry."

"For not loving us?" She pressed her lips together. "You don't choose who you love, Marcus. I learned that long ago."

Did she even know what she'd admitted? "There's always a choice," he murmured.

She dashed her hand across her cheeks, shifting. He loosened his hold, and felt cold when she slid off his lap. "I need to see them."

"Upstairs." She would go up there and wake her kids, and then they'd walk out of his life, for good.

It was what he'd wanted, wasn't it? Because she, they, were safer on their own than with him?

But when she came back downstairs a long while later, she was alone. She eyed his squat glass of whiskey. "Is there another one of those?"

He got up and poured her a drink. She took it, being careful not to brush her fingers against his. Then she cradled the glass with both hands. But she didn't drink.

Instead, she looked around at the house. "It looks good. Furnished, I mean."

"It's still just a house." She and the twins, they had a home.

She sat on the edge of the couch. Just sort of plopped down as if her legs had given out. Maybe they had. "How old was Sam when he died?"

Marcus sipped his whiskey. "Three. He'd have been seven, now. The night of the carnival, when I got the kids down. That was the anniversary of Sam and Jule's death."

Her long, lovely throat worked. And still she didn't drink from the glass.

"Your children are fine, Libby. Nothing has happened to them. Nothing is *going* to happen to them."

"There are no guarantees, though, are there?"

Her gaze skidded nervously around the interior. "You didn't know something would happen to take your family from you. Or you'd have done something to prevent it."

He frowned into his drink. "I told you before. I could have prevented it if I hadn't been so consumed with my business."

"I should go."

He shoved his glass onto the end table, half rising. What did he think he could do? Pin her to the couch? Make her stay? He sat back down. "Relax a while. Let them sleep." *She* should sleep, he thought. She was beautiful. But now she looked particularly delicate in her pretty dress and there were dark smudges beneath her eyes, as if she hadn't been sleeping well.

God knows he hadn't been sleeping much.

She nibbled at her lip, then slid back on the couch, pulling her legs up beside her, arranging the full, gauzy skirt of her peach-colored dress over them.

Her gaze danced over him, then away. "I called." She picked up her glass again, but only seemed to want to trace her slender fingertip over the etched pattern. "You, I mean. I called you. I couldn't find them and I picked up the phone and my fingers just sort of automatically dialed your number."

"I wish I'd been here, Libby. Then you'd have known right away where they were. You wouldn't have worried."

"It didn't occur to me that they'd actually come up here. On their own. I should have realized."

"I was in Whitehorn." It didn't matter that she hadn't asked him where he'd been. "Taking care of some details with my business."

"MJ Innerworks is rather more than a *business*." Her lips twisted when he couldn't hide his surprise. "Come on, Marcus, did you think I lived under a rock? Your name is rather distinctive. My own computer has a little sticker on the back of it that has your logo. My parents' portfolio contains *your* stock, for heaven's sake." She shook her head, pressing her fingertips to the bridge of her nose as if she had a headache. "Holt told me you'd donated all the equipment down at the sheriff's station. That they'd have never been able to afford such high-end equipment on their budget."

"Are you dating him?"

Her hand dropped. "Who?"

"Holt Tanner."

Her lips twisted. "Would it matter to you if I were?"

"Yes."

"Well, I'm not. As far as I know, he doesn't date anyone."

"I don't want you dating him. Or anyone else for that matter."

"Well, gee, Marcus, how romantic of you." She suddenly reached for her drink and tossed it back, barely blinking at the shock it had to give to her system. "Yet you don't want to date me, either. You're so good for my ego." She rose, suddenly. "I'll pick up the children in the morning. And I'll be more careful in the future to keep them from bothering you."

"Dammit, Libby, they're not a bother." He caught her arms. "And you shouldn't be driving. Not when you're still upset."

"I can't stay here, Marcus. I can't sit there on the couch and carry on a civilized conversation as if we're just friendly acquaintances." She twisted her arms from his hold. "I can't pretend like that."

"I don't want you to leave."

"But you don't want to be in our lives."

"It's not you!" He shoveled his hands through his hair. "It's not the kids. It's me, okay? Me. If I lost you, it'd kill me. Julia...she was my college sweetheart, and God help me, I never felt for her what I feel for you. But after they died, I wanted to die, too. I couldn't go through that again."

"Who says you will? Marcus, their deaths were an accident. You can't predict accidents, you were just talking about that very thing when it came to Bobby and Patty!''

''I should have prevented it. Dammit, don't you get it? It was a preventable accident! I didn't check the batteries, like Julia had been bugging me to do. And one night, I came home late from work and the house was in flames. She was using a space heater, 'cause she was always cold. And she fell asleep. It sparked.''

''And you've blamed yourself ever since, because you didn't change the batteries. Marcus, I'm sorry, but it does not take a rocket scientist to change a battery! It's tragic and it's awful. But it happened. It could have happened to anyone. Whether the smoke alarm worked or not, the space heater might still have sparked!'' Her arms spread. Slowly fell back to her sides. ''I have to go.''

''Don't.'' He stepped in front of her, barring the way to the door.

''Marcus, please. I want—'' Her throat worked and she shook her head.

''You want what?''

She closed her eyes for a long moment. When she looked at him, they were full of pain. ''You. My children are upstairs sleeping in one of your bedrooms, and I want to be upstairs sleeping with you. Is that what you want to know? I want you to put your arms around me, go to sleep with them around me, because there is no safer feeling in the world. Are you happy now? Is there another pound of flesh you'd like to strip from me before you'll stand aside and let me get to the bloody door?''

He ripped the lapels of his shirt apart so roughly the buttons flew, pinging against the hardwood floor like little bullets. "You want to lie against this?" he asked harshly, as he tossed the ruined shirt away. "You want to feel *this* against you?"

His voice rang out, almost echoing.

Libby suddenly felt calm. Maybe it was the heat of the whiskey that had slipped stealthily into her bloodstream. Maybe it was simply that it was finally out in the open.

She stepped over to him, laying her palm against his chest. Feeling the charged, unsteady beat of his heart beneath the mottled flesh that covered nearly a third of his chest. She lay her other hand on his chest, too. Smooth, perfect, hard flesh. Both parts of one whole. A man who'd tried to save his family, but hadn't been able to. A man who'd burned himself in the process and had endured the unbearable. "Yes," she said softly. Surely. "That's what I want."

She pressed her lips against his chest. Scarred. Unscarred. It was all him. And she loved him. Whether she'd planned to or not, she'd fallen in love with this man. "Take me upstairs, Marcus. To your room." She slid her palms up his arms, curving over the rounded, muscular thrust of his shoulders. "I don't want to be alone," she whispered.

"Libby."

"Please, Marcus. Don't turn away from me. Not again."

"I've never turned away from you, Libby." His admission was low. Rough. "Only myself."

She caught his neck in her hands, her fingers tangling in his thick, silky hair. "Then don't turn away from this. From us," she breathed. "Marcus—"

Her words dried when he turned his lips toward her palm. Kissing her. Then curling his hands around her wrists and inexorably pulling them from him.

He was going to walk away. Leave her.

Her heart felt like it was cracking in two.

But he swept her up in his arms, and she caught her breath. Up the stairs, he carried her. And into his room where he pushed the door shut with his foot before settling her in the center of his wide bed.

She reached for him again, but he caught her wrists and pressed them gently to the pillow above her head. "I don't want to hurt you."

Her fingers curled. "You're only hurting me if you leave. Don't you understand that, Marcus? Can't you feel it? What's between us? Just...lie with me, Marcus. I don't want to be alone. Not tonight.''

She was a woman who should never be alone. She deserved so much more than that. So much more than a man like him could give her.

He ran his hands down her arms, curving around her shoulders. He pressed his forehead against hers, willing himself to move away. But her arms slid sweetly around his neck and the gentle weight was more than he could tear away from.

He pressed his knee against the mattress. ''Libby—''

She arched against him, pressing her mouth to his. Fitting her curves against him. She tasted faintly of the whiskey. Mostly, she tasted of Libby.

Headier than moonshine, sweeter than summer-ripe peaches. More addictive than any drug the doctors had pumped into his system after the fire.

''I can't.'' He sucked in a hard breath when her fingers flitted down his chest, slid delicately under his belt. ''I can't lie here with you and not want more.''

''Then want it,'' she whispered. ''Want me. Want *me*, Marcus.''

He understood what the words meant. ''Only you.'' He gathered her against him. She was so small. Petite. But when her arms twined around his shoulders, her legs tangling with his, he felt her strength. The power she possessed. Over him. For him.

He wanted to take his time, savor every moment. But her hands were racing over him, fumbling with the buckle of his belt.

He twisted, rolling onto his back, setting her above him. Want settled, a hard tight fist in his gut, as he looked at her.

Lips soft and full from his kisses, parted as she drew in rapid breaths that made her breasts rise tauntingly against the scoop neck of her dress. Her knees fell to either side of him, the gauzy folds of fabric swirling around them. The pearly edge of her teeth sank into her lower lip as she looked at him. His hands cupped her hips, fingers flexing against her taut body. Her eyes fluttered closed, her head falling back as she rocked against him. It didn't matter that there were layers of fabric between them. He could feel her heat, wanted to drown in it. In her.

He rolled upward, cradling her in his lap, and pushed the straps of her dress off her arms. He filled his hands with the warm, lush weight of her breasts, bent over and caught one tight peak in his mouth.

She cried out, softly, urgently. Her hands slid up his stomach, burning over his chest, up to his neck, flexing, releasing, needful.

He fumbled with her zipper. A moment later, the dress pooled about her slender waist.

Then, there. Skin to skin. Curves to angles. His hands gathered up her skirt, sliding along her knees. Her thighs, upward over the flare of her hips, tangling with the scrap of satin that guarded the very center of her. "Hurry," she breathed. She pushed at his shoulders and he fell back against the pillows, clenching his jaw when her fingers finally conquered his belt and began struggling with his fly.

He shuddered, nearly coming unglued by her efforts. "Lift up," he growled, barely waiting for her to do so before he dealt with his trousers. And then the only thing separating them was that narrow slip of satin and the yards of gauzy peach skirt bunched at the top of her thighs.

Her head fell forward weakly, her fingers curling into his shoulders. "Hurry," she whispered again. "Hurry, Marcus. I need you." She trembled wildly and his fingers tangled in the narrow satin band over her hip, too impatient to wait. The satin tore away, and with a little twist, she sank over him.

Absorbed him.

Accepted him.

"I need you, too," he admitted roughly.

Then her mouth parted on a soundless cry, and Marcus caught her to him as they shot into oblivion.

He'd never be able to let her go.

Chapter 9

He'd fixed pancakes.

Libby couldn't keep the smile from her face as she entered the kitchen the next morning. Bobby and Patty were sitting at high barstools at that glorious granite counter, and they looked up at her as if it were a totally natural thing for them all to be in Marcus Jessup's kitchen at such an early hour.

She started to head for Marcus, but he stuck a plate in her hand as she neared him. She looked down, stupidly, at the pancake, then back up at him. He'd turned around to face the stove.

Unease shot through her.

They'd made love. All night long.

And now, he wouldn't look at her.

She carefully set the plate on the counter and moved around to kiss the children's cheeks. "Hurry up, my sweets," she urged. "We've got stuff to do this morning."

Patty frowned. "Like what?"

"Shopping," Libby said the first thing that came to her mind. She just wanted out of there. Before she made more of a fool of herself than she already had.

"For what?"

"Groceries." She bussed Bobby's cheek. "And you need new tennis shoes. Maybe we'll drive into Whitehorn."

"Can Marcus go, too?"

Libby looked at him. His eyes were guarded. His hair was damp, his chambray shirt buttoned to the hollow at his throat. It was as if the hours they'd spent in each other's arms had never occurred. "Not this time," she said. And was grateful that her voice sounded fairly normal. "Finish up," she urged. "I'll put your sleeping bags in the car while you do."

She dashed out of the room, hurrying up the stairs. She had to keep moving. Had to. Because if she stopped, she wasn't sure if she'd ever start again.

* * *

"Mommy looks mad." Patty's fork clattered against the plate.

"She's gonna ground us," Bobby hissed. "She always looks mad before she gots to ground us."

Marcus listened with half an ear to the kids. The rest of his mind was on Libby. And the things he'd have to do if he really was going to keep her in his life. Things he wasn't sure he'd even be able to do after all these years.

Patty slid off the barstool and hugged him before the kids hurried after their mother.

Keep *them* in his life, Marcus corrected.

Libby carried the ladder to the kitchen, stepping over the shopping bags that she'd dumped on the floor when they'd come in that afternoon from Whitehorn.

She'd spent far too much money. And it hadn't made her feel better one whit. But the children had had fun. Even when she'd sat them down and told them how terribly they'd scared her with their disappearing act, they'd had fun.

It was the one bright spot in an otherwise impossibly miserable afternoon.

She positioned the ladder and grabbed the smoke alarm off the top of the refrigerator. When the doorbell rang, she had absolutely no desire to answer it. The children were in the backyard, using their new shovel to continue digging on the pond that she'd relocated from just behind the back step to the rear corner near the fence.

Marcus had helped her fill in what had already been dug up. He'd helped soften up the grass near the fence, so the twins would have an easier time with their shovels.

She pushed her hand through her hair, wishing she could push away thoughts of Marcus so easily.

The doorbell rang again. Long and insistent.

She sighed and headed to the door. She'd told Callie on the phone earlier that she didn't want company. But it would be just like her friend to ignore that.

Only the person standing on the other side of the door wasn't her leggy, blond-haired friend.

It was Marcus.

A Marcus she'd never before seen.

The Marcus she knew had tumbled shoulder-length hair and bristled cheeks. He either wore black shirts and jeans or chambray shirts and jeans and heavy work boots.

"Well." Her eyes drifted over him. From his short, perfectly cut hair. Over the lean, clean-shaven face that—despite the scars that were slightly more visible—seemed younger. And his clothes. She recognized silk when she saw it. And the tan crewneck pullover that draped his broad shoulders and hugged his hard, flat stomach before disappearing in the waist of excruciatingly well-cut black pants was definitely a silk weave.

This wasn't *her* Marcus.

This was Marcus Jessup. Brilliant businessman, progressive computer programmer, who'd amassed a fortune with his upstart MJ Innerworks. "Have we met?"

He smiled faintly. But it died when he noticed that she was holding her smoke alarm in her hand. And when his eyes softened, Libby knew that no matter what exterior Marcus presented—and goodness knew there was nothing wrong with this spiffed-up version—it was still *her* Marcus inside.

"What are you doing here?"

"I sold off the rest of Innerworks," he said.

She blinked. "Oh. I see." But she didn't.

"After Julia and Sam died in the fire, after I was finally released from the hospital, I walked away from the company. It kept on running even without me, though. Didn't matter where I went. Europe. South America. Innerworks kept right on trucking. I'd set it up that well. I'd focused too much on the business and not enough on what mattered."

"Why are you telling me this, Marcus? Why are you here at all?"

"The guy in Whitehorn, the one who's been after

me to start up a new business—a non-profit actually. I've taken him up on it.''

"Congratulations."

"I won't make the same mistake as I did before." His voice was low. Intense. "I've set it up so that my personal involvement is limited."

"Marcus, I—"

"Marry me."

She dropped the smoke alarm. Neither one of them reached for it as it rolled off her porch. "What?"

He stepped closer, pulling a small square box from his pocket. He flipped it open with his thumb and the ring inside glittered in the afternoon sunlight. "I'm a better man with you, Libby Adler. Marry me."

Her legs felt weak. "Why? So you won't accidentally slide back into being a workaholic?"

"Because I love you. I love your kids. And I think you all love me. Or what happened last night would never have occurred."

"But this morning you acted as if nothing had happened."

"What would you have had me do? Bobby and Patty were there, all eyes and ears. I didn't know how you'd feel about them knowing you'd spent the night with me. And I needed to make sure you knew I was serious about this. That I'm not just asking you to come into my life. But that I'm asking you to let me come into yours.''

He looked over his shoulder and Libby's jaw loosened as her friends walked up her drive. Callie and Nick. Marisa and Jordan.

Libby's throat was tight. "What have you done?"

''I told them I was in love with you. I'm showing you that your friends will be part of our life. I'm doing what you said, Libby. Letting the scars breathe.'' He pulled the ring from the box. ''But you're the one who's thawed my heart, Libby. I love you. I want to spend my life with you. With your children. With our children,'' he said huskily. ''Be my partner. Take care of me. And I'll take care of you.''

She pressed her fingertips to her lips. Vaguely aware that Bobby and Patty had joined her.

''All you have to do is say yes, and the rest will take care of itself.''

''Oh, Marcus.'' She laid her palm along his hard jaw and stepped up to him. Looking into his face. His beautiful, solemn face with the crinkles beside his eyes that told her he was smiling inside.

Her lips slowly curved and tears slid from the corners of her eyes. She'd spend the rest of their lives together cherishing that smile, she thought.

This was the man with whom she'd finally have what she'd always wanted. A family. A home.

A man who loved her just for her.

She held out her left hand and he slid the beautiful ring in place.

And she said yes.

Epilogue

"Some kind of nonsense," Harriet Martel muttered to her assistant librarian, Molly, as they joined the other guests assembling on the wide grassy field in front of the schools across the street from the Calico Diner. "Getting married practically right on Main Street. I never heard of such nonsense."

"I don't know," Molly murmured softly. "I think it's kind of romantic."

"Romantic? It's lunacy. The crazy moon, you know. It is making everyone act oddly." Harriet crossed her thin arms and sank down onto one of the few remaining empty white folding chairs. "Everyone," she repeated.

"I understand that Callie and Libby both felt their relationships with Nick and Marcus were woven in with the Crazy Moon Festival and they felt it fitting to marry tonight."

"Well," Harriet looked at the moon, rising fat and brilliant from the darkened horizon. "It is a beautiful sight," she admitted brusquely. Then she sat back in her chair since the music had begun to play.

Well behind the chairs, next to a stand of trees that not long ago had sported a tacked-up Daddy Wanted poster designed by her twins, Libby pressed a nervous hand against her stomach when the quartet—situated off to one side of the rows and rows of chairs—began to play. She shifted and the hem of her peach-tinted watered silk sheath brushed her ankles.

"Who'd have thought high school kids would sound so fabulous?" Beside her, Callie was smoothing her hand down her own dress. Then she took her bouquet from her father and quickly hugged Libby. "This is so perfect," she said. "Having a double wedding."

"Stop," Libby smiled, rapidly blinking back tears. "Or we're going to ruin our makeup and look like sin when we walk up the aisle."

"It wouldn't matter to them," Callie whispered. "They'd love us, anyway."

"I know." Libby nodded, her gaze moving toward the head of the aisle where the minister and the grooms had taken their place in front of the guests. Her heart clutched when she looked at Marcus.

His dark hair gleamed beneath the bright moonlight and the soft lights that had been placed around the field to help illuminate the ceremony. He wore the classically tailored tuxedo as if he'd been born to it.

"Callie? Do you think all this is just because of the crazy moon?"

Callie's smile was slow. "All this is because of crazy love." Then she turned and faced the aisle. The notes of the processional dripped with crystal clear purity from the string quartet. With her hand on her father's arm, she headed slowly, confidently, her long white gown trailing beautifully behind her, along the aisle to meet her future with Nick. A man she'd loved for so long. Who'd finally figured out that he'd loved her, too.

"Mom? Is my tie straight? Marcus said I had t' make sure my tie was straight before we got married."

"Your tie is perfect," Libby assured Bobby. "And the flowers in your hair are perfect, too," she added for Patty.

Callie had joined Nick before the minister.

It was Libby's turn.

Her heart racing madly, she moved into place. Bobby on one side of her. Patty on the other. Marcus had wanted her children to be part of their wedding ceremony, and so had Libby. They were *all* getting married, just like Bobby had said.

But still, she felt positively weak with nervousness. Her parents had flown in from Boston to attend the wedding, and they were sitting in the front row. Even her father hadn't been able to look down his nose at Marcus, because Marcus had, quite simply, been himself when they'd all met the previous day at the airport in Billings. And Marcus just being Marcus was a pretty impressive person.

Looking up the aisle, Libby watched Marcus move toward the center. Waiting for her. For them.

Her nervousness subsided. Peace flooded through her. She stepped forward, her children beside her.

But they were impatient. Anxious to get on with the marrying. Their pace sped up. Until they were practically running up the aisle, to Marcus. The guests murmured, chuckling indulgently.

Though she did have a moment there when she felt just as impatient as her children, Libby followed behind rather more sedately.

Marcus held out his hand when she neared, and she took it, loving the feel of his warm fingers closing about hers. The twins, fairly wriggling with excitement, stood on the other side of her, and the whole lot of them faced the minister who began speaking with a welcome for all the guests.

"You didn't run up the aisle like the twins," Marcus murmured for her ears alone.

"I wanted to," she admitted. "Only I was afraid I'd trip because of my high heels. And my parents would probably die of mortification if I married you with grass stains marring my dress."

His eyes crinkled. A deep, sexy slash appeared along his cheek when he smiled. Libby's heart simply turned over. "I love you, Marcus Jessup," she said softly.

"I love you, too." His fingers tangled with hers and whether or not it was untimely, he lifted their linked hands and kissed her knuckles.

When the minister eventually turned to them and it was their turn to exchange their vows, Marcus's voice was steady and sure. Libby's voice trembled with conviction.

The guests, to a one, sighed with happiness when the bridal couples shared their first kisses as husbands and wives.

Libby and Marcus, so thoroughly wrapped in each other's arms at that moment, never saw the look the twins gave each other.

They never heard what the guests in the front rows heard, as Patty and Bobby leaned toward each other, exchanging a high five. ''D'ya think a poster would work to get us a baby brother or a sister, too?''

* * * * *

A
mysterious
Woman